The Slow Constellations Wheeled On

The Slow Constellations Wheeled On

a novel

by David Wayne Hampton

Maul & Froe Press 2012

Published by Maul & Froe Press

Morganton, NC 28655

maulandfroepress@yahoo.com

Second Edition, Revised 2019

Cover Art by Kathryn B. Smith

This is a work of fiction. While, as in all fiction, the literary perceptions and insights are based upon experience, all names, characters, places, and incidents are either products of the author's imagination or are used in a fictitious manner. No reference to any real person is intended or should be inferred.

ISBN   978-0-9829973-3-8

For

Dad, Mom, and Steve

Who did their best to raise me right

And did a pretty good job of it, I think

– Thank you

I can't say I saw it coming, as I lay in my bed, staring up at the textured ceiling patterns around the light fixture, dusty cobwebs filling the spaces in between. It was raining outside again, thunder rumbling off the bluffs along the river. All I could do was think about him. The dirt was still fresh on his grave. The topsoil of everything I hoped for was beginning to dissolve, my parents hastening the erosion by their inaction, their apathy. I wasn't a selfish person, but I was tired of other people being selfish and screwing with my life. I hardly knew why at the time, but I had packed a trunk and a suitcase of extra clothes, and it was already in my car. But I needed to see Cathy first. I wanted to start a new life with her. We had talked about it, at least.

I jumped out of bed, slipped my shoes on, and grabbed my car keys, as if one more second of inaction would trap me there forever. I didn't even tell my mother where I was going. I walked right past her out the front door as if I was just going for a drive. She sat quietly on the couch. The ice clinked in her glass as it melted. She didn't say anything. She didn't even look at me.

1 _____

"Thank you for calling Papa's Pizza Place. We deliver. Can I take your order?"

"Hey! Yeah, I want your three toppings for $9.99 special. You still have that one, don't ya?"

"Yes, sir. We do."

"Okay. Make it double anchovies with extra cheese."

"Um, would that be delivery or...?"

"I'm going to come by and pick it up directly. Appreciate it."

"The total's going to be $10.59, but I...."

Click.

It was a busy night. I finished mixing a tub of sauce in the back while watching the choreographed assembly line. Two guys with huge white aprons slapped dough between their hands, pounded the elastic gobs down on a stainless steel counter, and then spread them out with their palms and a light dusting of corn meal. The flattened dough was stretched onto a metal screen and passed to someone else who ladled it with sauce in a circular motion, dipping from a five-gallon tub recessed into the counter. The pizzas were then passed to two lanky boys who looked like they should be twins. They reached gracefully to spread toppings and cheese before sending them onto the oven's conveyor belt. No sooner had it been done than two more sauced pies sat waiting for them. A computer screen blinked with orders that had not yet cleared. I slowed the mixer to a stop and sealed the lid.

Everyone wore green shirts and ball caps, except for the manager whose shirt was a burgundy red and not as faded as the others were. He flitted between answering phones, pulling pizzas from the oven, and giving orders. With his head tilted to one side, he stopped to check the labeled boxes sitting on end, orders waiting to be filled.

"Ham and pineapple; one half sausage, one half green peppers; sun-dried tomatoes and portabella, light sauce. Dammit." He snapped. A sharp, yet familiar smell wafting from the convection oven confirmed his suspicion. "Who took the order for the anchovies?!" He turned his head around slowly. His mustache bristled and his eyes were wide behind black-rimmed spectacles.

"Don't look at me, I just made what the computer told me to," said one of the topping boys. The other nodded. The rest of the crew who had looked up at his question turned back to what they were doing.

"I did, sir," I quietly replied from the back as I stepped out from where the drivers dropped their money into lock boxes. "I just came in from a delivery and no one was near the phones but me. I was just about ready to clock out with another run." I knew I was about to catch hell.

"Geez, Randall. How many times have I told everyone that we need a phone number to call back so we can halfway confirm it's not a prank call? The ol' 'send an anchovy pizza to a friend' is a classic."

"I know, I know. But he said he was going to come get it himself. So I figured it was probably legit."

"All right, then. But if this guy is a no-show I'm going to make you eat the whole damn thing yourself – in your car. Those things stink to high heaven. Here," he handed the pizza peel to me, a giant spatula used to scoop whole pizzas from the oven, "why don't you box it up?"

"Yes, sir."

"And don't call me Sir, okay? You're not Marcie and I'm not Peppermint Patty." He tried to tone down his rant a bit and give a half-encouraging smile. He hated being an authority as much as he loved it. It seemed he hated it because it didn't fit his philosophy, loved it because he got-off from being an asshole. Dean was like a hippie drill sergeant. "It's busy tonight. Keep on your toes," he yelled to everyone. "Just remember, the less mistakes we make the more money we make."

"Okay," everyone moaned in unison.

"Remember guys, delivery pizzas go on top rack and carry-outs go on the bottom. Don't switch them or you'll screw up somebody's order!" Dean shouted as he returned to the front counter to man the phones.

I scooped the hot pizza from the conveyor belt with the peel, and slid it into the box. The anchovies were arranged on top of the cheese like spokes on a wheel. They had an oily glisten to them that reminded me of salted slugs. I took the pizza cutter and made four deft cuts through the center, remembering to rinse the fish goo off the cutter before setting it back for someone else to use. I wasn't completely stupid. I wished everyone else thought the same.

I turned to the delivery screen to program my next run. It looked like it was going to be a short one. The only orders at the top of the green screen that could be paired together were two deliveries to Eastland Hall, on campus. No problem. The cul-de-sac came right up to the lobby, so I could park and run in quick. If I got back in time, I might be able to get the $90 order that just popped up on the bottom of the screen. It was probably going to the construction workers staying at the Red Carpet Inn. They were working on those new apartment complexes in town. I quickly logged out, pulled my paper receipt, and slid the pizza boxes into a warming sleeve. A stop by the drink cooler for a 2-liter Coke to add to one of the orders, and I was on my way. Another driver coming in passed me at the door as I was leaving.

"Man, what's that smell? Stinks like B.O.!"

*   *   *   *

The advantages of being a delivery guy in a college town were numerous. The amount of tip money to be made, especially on a Saturday night like this, was only limited by how many hours in your shift. I wasn't the best driver, I knew, but for what I lacked in talent I made up for in sheer determination. When I first started working for Papa's Pizza Place, there were only two positions available, dough boy or delivery. The place didn't have a dining area – delivery and pick-up only – and since I had never made a pizza in my life, they only had one position for me. Delivery was baptism by fire. I didn't know any of the street names, didn't know any shortcuts, and I had a penchant for driving too fast. Driving fast wasn't the key to success when you worked delivery, I found out later, it was driving smart, like knowing which back-road curves are banked and which ones will want to throw you over their shoulder, or where to dodge the deep potholes.

I learned one lesson the hard way. When there is a lit pizza sign on top of your car, it is really hard *not* to be an easy target for cops. It's like saying, "look at me – I'm in a hurry!" My first week I got pulled over by a campus cop on River Street, one of the worst places to get pulled if you've got a lead foot. The officer clocked me doing 50 in a 35, and I was so shook up I was in tears. The officer took pity on me, I guess, mainly because I probably looked like a little boy that just skinned his knee. He gave me a lecture about how I wasn't making enough money delivering pizzas to afford getting a speeding ticket.

"How much money do you make a night?" he asked. Not enough, I thought. He left me with a verbal warning. I never mentioned to the others at the store the part about the patronizing speech, or the part about me crying. I was just damn lucky, according to Dean. I played the whole story down like it wasn't a big deal. Better to keep your mouth shut and be thought a fool than to open it and remove all doubt, I've heard someone say.

The run to Eastland Hall was quicker than usual. There weren't any students' cars double parked in front, and I didn't have to call their rooms and wait in the lobby. They were already waiting for me. I liked delivering to the girls' dorms, too. They were usually more courteous and didn't pay in sandwich bags of change, and they often wore skimpy-short pajamas that showed off their legs. On the way back I avoided the stop lights by taking a shortcut up Pine Street, above the Sub Shoppe. Turning in, the hill was steep, and I scraped the underside of my muffler. The transmission whined as I floored it. Once I got to the top and made a right onto Horn in the West, it was a straight shot back to the pizza place. I had that huge order on my mind. Drivers not only get more of a tip with a high-dollar order, but they also receive a percentage, albeit small, of every delivery sale.

Since it was 10:30 on a Saturday night and business was hopping, I left my car running by the side entrance, tossed my empty warming sleeves back under the delivery counter, and logged in. I took a swig of the Sundrop I had set on the unused cutting board in the back, and then returned to the computer. The large delivery was up next! Before I could reach for the keyboard to assign the $90 order to myself, an older delivery guy with thinning hair and a salt-and-pepper goatee muscled his way to the computer.

"Excuse me, man at work here!" he exclaimed as he cursored four lines on the screen and grabbed the large order to Red Carpet Inn, along with two deliveries to Charlotte Anne Lane that hadn't been boxed yet. He spoke with the sharp nasality of someone from up north.

"Uh, Aaron. You know better than I do that we are supposed to check out the oldest orders first, right?" I stated as diplomatically as I could.

"Bite me. I've been getting shit runs all night, having to drive out past Bamboo Road, so don't give me a lecture." My face burned. I knew it to be true, though. The further the run, the longer it takes to get back, and the fewer deliveries you can make. Still, the guy didn't have to be a dick about it. "Pardon me, Greenhorn, I'm coming through!" I had to take two steps back to keep from being bowled over by the man.

"Who are you calling a Greenhorn? I've been working here for almost two months now!" Aaron didn't hear my half-hearted protest as he made his way out the door. I heard him shouting to another driver, whose car door was in his way.

Chris, a manager in training, waved his hand at Aaron in dismissal. "Don't worry about him," he said. "Hang back a few minutes and you can take the four orders to Colbert and Garrison on the West side of campus once they're ready."

"What's that guy's problem?" I asked.

"He's just pissy because he's having to pay child support to his ex-wife, and it's cutting into his tip money." Chris wasn't as uptight and pushy as Dean, but sometimes I thought he could be a better manager if he grew a spine. "Oh yeah. Dean wanted to see you before you made your next run." Chris pointed across the store to the front counter where Dean was making change for a customer.

"Randall, my boy! Guess what?" He motioned for me and then put his arm around me like we were in a football huddle. "Your fish man has five minutes to pick up his pizza before we have to count it as a loss. Someone is going to need some Tic Tacs and a pine-tree air freshener to hang from his rear-view mirror."

"I've got five dollars that says he's a no-show," Craig said to Dean as he slapped some dough back and forth for an extra large pizza. He wore a knitted hat into which he tucked a huge mound of dreadlocks, a contrast to his pale complexion and Midwestern accent. I grimaced. I wished I could just leave with another delivery, that they would just let me get back to work.

"We ain't got time to be placing bets," said Dean, then paused on an afterthought, "but then again – well, alright. I'm with you. Any other takers?"

"I'm in," said Chris, with a good-natured chuckle. "No offense, Randall, but this is easy money. No one's ordered an anchovy pizza and actually bought it in over three months."

"So, Randall. What do you say? For $15 you can match our bet," coaxed Craig. "Any other takers?"

"Well, well. You boys think you're hot shit!" It was Lindsey, who just got back from her delivery run. Her freckles shined on her cheeks, and her dark hair was pulled in a tight ponytail through the back of her hat. She was tall and attractive in a Katherine Hepburn kind of way, and she had a mean streak reserved only for people who really pissed her off. "If Randall's in, I'll double his bet – that he *shows* up. Are you in with me, Randy?" Her vote of confidence was like a shot of adrenaline.

"Fine. I'm in too." I pulled out a crumpled five and a ten from the zippered leg pocket of my khaki pants and slapped it on the counter. "Sometimes you got to know when to hold them, right?" I nervously laughed. I knew I was gambling more than money with this crowd. One stupid mistake and I would be the butt of all jokes from here on out. One guy who got hired the same week I did quit last month. He had such a severe case of acne everyone called him Pizza Face. I thought if he just washed his face more and used a little Clearasil, people would have left him alone. But the dough boys kept running pizzas through the oven for him to catch on the other side in the shape of smiley faces, with pepperonis and green peppers for the eyes and mouth, black olives and feta cheese for the pimples, and called them Pizza-Face Gillespie Specials. He didn't even give his two-week's notice, just disappeared one day. I didn't even see him on campus after that.

Craig chuckled at Lindsey's bet, "Yeah, and you can split that pizza with him, too!"

"I'll split your lip. Go back to beatin' your dough." Lindsey sneered and made a fist with her right hand. Craig mock saluted her and turned back to his counter.

Just then, the door opened with a tinkle of the bell.

"Can I help you?" asked Dean. There was a lull in the kitchen conversation, save for the whirring of the ovens and a few people talking in the far back. An old man in his seventies walked up to the counter. He had a long white beard down to his chest, stained yellow with cigarette smoke, and wearing a raggedy black Harley t-shirt with a brand new pair of Pointer overalls. A hard pack of Marlboros poked out the top of his front zipper pocket.

"Yeah, I'm here to pick up my pizza. I don't think I left my name. It was a double anchovy with extra cheese," replied the old man. Chris went over to the warming counter and pulled the box from where it was sitting by itself. He brought it gingerly to the register, almost comically, like it was a bomb set to explode.

"That'll be $10.59, please," said Dean in a friendly professional tone. The old man pulled the pizza box to him, lifted the lid to look, and took a deep breath.

"Ahh, that's good," said the old man, rather wistfully. "I love a good anchovy pizza every now and then. Smells just like pussy." He paid with exact change, said "Thank you," and shuffled out the door to his green pickup. As soon as the bell dinged twice with the opening and closing of the door, the whole store erupted

8

in laughter. Dean was cackling so hard he couldn't catch his breath, and clutched his ribcage in pain.

Craig's assistant Paul dropped his dough and fell to his knees, clinging to the counter to pull himself back up. His laughter came out in spasms like he was having a seizure. "Did you see that senile grin on his face?" He exclaimed while wiping back tears. "He was smiling like he just got laid!" Craig was laughing as well, but I could tell he was sore from losing his bet. People who were on break came rushing out of the back with their lit cigarettes, asking what was so funny. I just grinned and shook my head in disbelief as people slapped me on the back. Lindsey wasn't laughing, but collected her winnings with a surly smile.

"Dirty ol' man," she muttered under her breath, and winked at me. She handed me $30. "Here ya go, Rocker. Don't spend it all in one place." I smiled, and felt a little energized inside.

"All righty, then!" Dean bellowed. "Listen up people. Let's get this show on the road. Geez, this ain't no lunch-time shift, get moving!" He tried to hold back his amusement with a stern look, before breaking into an exasperated giggle again. "Oh, Randy! Man, that was classic!"

"You're telling me! I was worried for a second that...."

"Get back to work, Marcie."

"Yes, sir! I mean, yeah."

Everyone snapped back to what they were doing before. Pizzas that were piling out of the oven were quickly boxed, cut, shut, and stacked on the warming counter just long enough for the drivers to grab them and head for the door. Craig and Paul went back to slapping and pounding dough, only interrupted with an occasional aftershock of laughter. Wielding a long-handled fork, I popped some dough bubbles on a couple of half-baked pizzas through the front window of the oven and clocked out with a modest run to Cardinal Apartments, letting Lindsey go ahead of me to take four orders to Garrison and Colbert Halls on campus. She pretended not to notice, but pulled out a warming sleeve for me before she left, to be nice. I nodded and smiled. Aaron walked in the door as I walked out with my order and a sly grin on my face.

"What are you so damned jolly about? What did I miss?"

2 _____

There was a faint smell of wood smoke in the air and the rumble of logs being chunked into the stove, followed by the clank of the door and the squeak of the damper. Mom always stoked the fire before she went to bed. I knew I should be asleep, but my mind was so raw with sensory details, how the wind blew around the corner of the house, the draft I felt creep around my blankets and quilts seconds later. But I felt safe. The television murmured from the living room, probably the 11 o'clock news. The floor creaked gently as she walked back up the steps from the basement. It all rushed back to me like a spider building a web in my head, catching the memory so fast it vibrated in the spindly silk with a taste of creosote and oak logs smoldering, keeping the fire burning until morning. But like the elation of getting drunk, the experience was temporary. I held onto it with all my will, that moment between sleep and waking where I was actually there, back home. Then it all faded. The television, the national anthem fading to static, fell through the mist. The incense of the pot-bellied stove gave way to the musty smell of a hotel apartment and the pop of a baseboard heater. It was five in the morning. I had only been asleep for an hour, still wearing my collared shirt with an embroidered pizza slice on the front pocket. Right before fatigue overtook my thoughts, I tried one last time to catch up with the memory, but it was gone. I closed my eyes to a dreamless slumber.

* * * *

I awoke to the sound of church bells ringing from the missionary Baptist church down the road. Almost lunch. My internal clock always got screwed up when I worked a full weekend, especially when I had to work until closing, which was three a.m. on Fridays and Saturdays. It still felt like early morning. As I sat up in my bed I realized I had only managed to kick my shoes and pants off last night before passing out from exhaustion; I was still wearing my collared Papa's Pizza shirt. Though I had to go in again this afternoon at four, at least on Sundays I only had to work until midnight. Business is a little slower then, because it seemed most people didn't throw parties or stay up late when they had to go back to work Monday morning, or had early classes like I did. It amazed me, though, when I first started working that no matter what night of the week it was or what time it was, people ordered pizzas. My mom never made pizza much, except for an occasional cardboard freezer pizza, and Pizza Hut in Galax didn't deliver out where I lived.

My first job in this town was washing dishes at the Daisy Chain Cafe. It was minimum wage, but it paid the bills and my first month's rent. I spent all afternoon and evening scraping food off stacks upon stacks of plates the waitresses brought me, first rinsing them off, then running them through a giant dishwasher sanitizer. Just as I would stack them hot and clean on the shelves, the cooks would snatch them up to use on the next entrée. Another dishwasher who worked the lunch shift told me about delivering pizzas, and that if he had a car he would be rolling in tips. I went out the next day and asked for an application at Domino's, and Papa John's, but nobody was hiring at the time. I later found out that the summer season was slower for deliveries in a college town. Then I went to Papa's Pizza Place, and they hired me on the spot. I told them the next day at the Daisy Chain that I was quitting. The boss wasn't too pleased with my news, but when I picked up my last check I heard that he found someone to take my place that very afternoon. My grandfather always said that as long as there were dishes to be washed in the world, there was always a job to be had.

I put a pot of coffee on to brew and scratched myself, looking around my apartment with bleary eyes. It was only one room, an Efficiency the landlord called it, but more like a hole in the wall. Still, it was good enough for me, and was all I could afford without a roommate. It did have a small kitchenette, a shallow sink and one stove eye, which stood atop a mini refrigerator. The only thing that really ticked me off was that the freezer compartment

11

was only large enough to hold an ice cream sandwich, not even deep or tall enough for a freezer meal. My walls were bare because I didn't feel like wasting my money on decorating the place. Next to my bed stood a nightstand made out of two stacked milk crates and some plywood. Straddling the other side of the room was a desk I found beside a dumpster one night while on delivery. I spotted it behind some ritzy apartments, so I went back after work while it was still dark and wedged it into the trunk of my car with the help of some bungee cords. It was solid, and only one leg was broken, something some wood glue and screws fixed easily. I was still looking for a chair, so I had to do my homework on my bed. The bathroom was so small the door couldn't open completely because the toilet was in the way, and it had a stand-up shower, no tub. Also, the fake linoleum tile on the wall was buckling from prolonged years of moisture. The first day I moved into my apartment I bumped against it and a mushroom fell out from behind it, the ones you normally see growing on sides of trees. I covered the opening with duct tape after that.

I grabbed a can of chicken broth from the cabinet over the sink, and stuffed last night's tips through a slit in the bottom. The can of French Onion soup was already full of cash, and would go to pay next month's rent. An inconspicuous trick of my grandfather's, if someone broke into the apartment, the last thing they'd probably grab was a can of store-brand condensed soup. The money I deposited in the bank I pretended not to have. I was saving that to pay tuition. The coffee pot steamed and gurgled to me that it was finished. I poured a cup with a little cream, I was out of sugar, and pulled a cold piece of pizza wrapped in aluminum foil from the fridge. Taking a bite, I raised my armpit to sniff. Time to do some laundry. I pulled off my uniform shirt, threw it in the basket by the door, kicked off my boxers, and headed for the shower, coffee and pizza still in hand.

* * * *

The clouds congealed in the October sky like milk gravy, and a cold, sharp whiff of moisture in the air reminded me of snow. Still too early yet, I thought. I had put on the sweatshirt my grandfather bought me last spring at the university bookstore when we visited campus. It was gray with black and gold collegiate lettering that read WSU, and then Watauga State University underneath. I threw my basket of dirty clothes and an economy-sized jug of laundry detergent in the back seat. There was always a faint smell of pizza in the upholstery from the night before that lingered like a stale fart. Almost forgetting, I ran back inside for my Walkman. I also grabbed two cassette tapes, the Gin Blossoms, which my ex-girlfriend dubbed for me from a CD back in high school, and a group called Receiving Ravens that I bought at the record store downtown just because I liked their name. I stuck that tape in first.

There were laundromats all over the place, but I liked going to the new one on the edge of town, near the hospital and right next door to a gas station. It wasn't as crowded with college students who walked from campus. Plus, I had a pair of jeans stolen from a laundromat across from Sandford Hall. The little preppy bastards. All I did was go around the corner for a sandwich at the Sub Shoppe and they must've swiped them from my dryer. This place was cleaner, anyway. There were only a few people in the laundromat when I walked in, your typical old lady folding her towels into thirds, a few migrant workers off the tree farms in neatly-starched shirts and dark denim Wranglers, and a girl with strawberry-blonde hair sitting cross-legged and reading a textbook, taking notes as she read. She wore red jogging pants, flip-flops, and a blue parka, the thick collar turned up. I went to the opposite end of the room and claimed a few hard plastic chairs. Quickly, I pushed my sleeves up and went to work. Lights, darks, and towels I separated into three top-loaders. Headphones on, I counted quarters out of a Folgers can and inserted them in the slots. – *Walk out my back door steps into the darkness of the unknown, where not even the porch light shines for me.* – One cup detergent for each load. – *This town, never looks to the horizon much. This time, we're gonna lift our heads up.* – The lead singer moaned sadly. Upon slamming down the last lid, I realized that the girl in the blue parka was standing right across the washers from me, talking and pointing to her ears. I looked at her startled for a few seconds before I pulled my headphones off.

"I'm sorry to bother you, but I couldn't help but overhear your change can rattle. If it's at all possible, if you have some to spare, could I give you a dollar or two for some quarters? The change machine's busted."

13

"Yeah, sure." I stopped my tape player and counted out eight quarters and exchanged them for her two weathered bills, reaching over the back-to-back rows of machines.

"I think a laundromat is one of the worst places to meet people, don't you?" she asked as I handed her the change.

"Huh?"

"I mean, you see it in all those romantic comedies. The ubiquitous scene when the guy and the girl get their underwear mixed up in the dryer or something, and then there's that cheesy, awkward, supposedly-touching moment when they meet."

"Uh, yeah. Really overplayed, I agree." I had no idea what she was talking about.

"So, what year are you at WSU? Sophomore, junior?" I looked at her puzzled. She then points to the sweatshirt I am wearing.

"Yeah. Well, I should be a junior, but I'm actually still a sophomore. I took a year off after high school to travel around, you know, see the country," I lied. The only thing that's worse than being a freshman in the eyes of university students is being a freshman at the community college. I didn't know why I was lying to her, though.

"Cool. I wanted to do something like that, but my parents said they wouldn't pay my way through college if I did, and I'd have to get a real job. Cut the ol' purse strings. Plus, my family lives just out of town, so it's kind of a bummer."

"Yeah. I know what ya mean. Parents breathing down your neck."

She continued, "Well, the reason I asked is I thought you might have been in my Intro to Biology class with Dr. Bonesteel. You look familiar."

"I might've been. Remember how many people were in that class?"

"Yeah, at least 70 or more. Tell me about it! I could never get a word with him afterwards, the line was so long to talk to him."

14

The social interaction was exciting, but she began to make me uncomfortable, as I felt like I was running out of interesting things to say. I wished I brought my homework with me, or a book to retreat to. "So, what's your major?" she asked.

"Well, I'm still undeclared, but I'm thinking about going into Environmental Science or something."

"No rush at this point, until you get all your core classes out of the way. I just settled on majoring in Recreational Management. You know, working with summer camps or resorts. There's tons of them down around Asheville. And I love the outdoors."

"Yeah, me too. I wish I had more time to get out and explore. You know, there's this neat hiking trail just off the Boone Fork I discovered this summer. I can't remember its name. Beavers have built a series of dams along a small stream and literally flooded almost a whole acre of woods." I warmed up to her, and it woke a deep stirring in me.

"I think I know which one you're talking about, but I haven't been on it."

"It starts across the road from a pond near Price Park. You can't miss it. You know, if you want, if you're not busy this week, I could, I mean we...."

"I know which one you are talking about now. My boyfriend and I walked part of it a few weeks ago before the leaves started changing. It intersects the Mountains-to-Sea Trail, doesn't it?"

"Yeah. I think it does."

"Well, I better let you get back to your laundry, and I've got a huge test on Monday to cram for. It was nice talking to you, though."

"Sure. Same here." The girl walked back to her seat, her flip-flops slapping her heels as she went, taunting me.

I put my headphones back on and sat down. I watched her put quarters into two dryers, then looked away from her, out the wide window, past the cars and the gas pumps next door. A pang of rejection grew from my chest and spread hotly to my face. I tried to swallow it back down. The Latino men in their neatly-starched shirts stood just outside, smoking cigarettes and talking soundlessly. — *She told me she climbs the edges where the forest meets the stars.* — The singer smoothly whined. Past the parking lot my eyes caught some far off trees swaying faintly with the wind. — *says she's not far from meeting her savior.* — One of the washers somewhere started into a spin cycle. — *This town, never gives us breath. This time, we're not like the rest.* — I pulled the sleeves of my sweatshirt down to my wrists and crossed my arms tightly until the ache in my chest subsided.

3

I drove to Independence, past the old courthouse, making a left at the stoplight, and followed 221 through Twin Oaks and past miles of cow pastures and creeks. An old iron-grate bridge buzzed as I drove over it in the darkness. The clouds drew a thick curtain over the stars as the fence posts raced past and into the black abyss behind me.

If I had known better, I would have taken 16 through Mouth of Wilson, which was less curvy, but in the midnight dark I didn't have much of an opportunity to look at a road map. I didn't really know if I was going to go through with this or not. I thought at first of going to my Aunt Faith's for the night and then sort it out. But then I thought about the fight Cathy and I had, my father's absence, my mother's drunken indifference, my grandfather's promise, and it made me want to keep driving.

I had it planned in my head for a while now, but planning it and actually doing it seemed like opposite charges. In my mind I knew exactly what to do, how I was going to make-do, but to drive this narrow road with nothing but the unknown ahead was terrifying. I didn't know how my friend James did it, ran away from home. I didn't know if I could really go through with it myself. All I knew was that if I was going to be able to pass for 21 instead of 16, I was going to have to watch myself – act more mature, talk more mature, and keep a low profile. I tried growing a mustache, but it just looked like peach fuzz. I scratched the small dark patch of beard on the end of my chin self-consciously.

I started getting pains in the pit of my stomach, and a thickness in the back of my throat that I couldn't swallow down.

Could I drive all night? My eyes started feeling strained and heavy from peering ahead of my headlights into the soupy pitch beyond. It started drizzling too, a fine mist that my wipers only pushed back and forth. Lightning flashed in the distance and the rain picked up pace. I wanted to stop soon, but I also wanted to put as many miles between me and what I left behind. I passed a sign for New River State Park and thought about parking, I was so tired, but the gates were probably locked. I made it to Jefferson by tightening my leg muscles to push blood back to my head and stretching my eyes open as wide as I could. I stopped at the first gas station I came to and bought a large coffee that must have been slowly cooked down on its hot plate to a consistency of 30-weight oil. I added a little cream and sugar to knock the bitterness off, swirling the cup into gray clouds. The cashier seemed to have needed a cup of coffee himself, as he groggily handed me my change.

Standing outside under the front-door awning, I watched the summer rain fall and heard the thunder rolling through the hills, chasing the next elusive flashes of lightning. I caught a whiff of damp earthiness, as if the ground was alive with night crawlers and grub worms, and it gave me strength. I decided to forge ahead. If I could just make it to Boone before daylight, I could find an inconspicuous place to park and take a short nap. Then I would look for a job, a place to stay, and enroll in the community college there. And if I can do that, albeit under false pretenses, then maybe I can make a new life for myself. In a couple of years who knows what will happen, but by then it won't matter. I'll be free. I just need to remember to take it one day at a time.

I took to the road again, and although the rain had stopped, it was still dark. Here and there I saw distant lights of houses riding the rise of the hills, front porches lit for husbands coming home from a second-shift factory job or for daughters out past curfew, their parents sitting inside on the couch worrying. I passed a mileage sign that read: Boone 20 miles.

4 _____

The road was dark and overhung with low-lying tree limbs, making the street signs hard to spot. I had only been up this way once before, and not at night. I plugged my spotlight into my cigarette lighter and shined its halogen beam on mailboxes as I passed them. It was one of the best investments I made, since most of all the runs were after dark, especially with Daylight Savings Time ending soon. But my lamp wasn't picking up a thing from any of the mailboxes I passed. Just when I thought I had gone too far and was slowing down to make a three-point turn to retrace my steps, I spotted it – a mailbox with the hand-painted address 258 Roby Greene Road, but no name. I only hoped this was the driveway for 258-A.

The broken pavement of the driveway was narrow and lined with overgrown hedges at least eight feet high. At the bottom of the driveway, about 50 yards straight down a hill, burned a lone porch light and a small parking area crammed with three vehicles. The side mirrors of my Grand Am scraped limbs as I drove in, and a tall, skinny man with a ball cap stepped out of one of the doors of the apartment and waved. Not really an apartment, it looked more like a house that had been chopped into three units. I pulled in as far as I could and looked around. Well – hell, I thought. There wasn't three feet in any direction to turn around the way I pulled in. I was going to have to back all the way up the driveway to leave. I jumped out and opened the driver's side back door to get the pizzas. The clear window of the warming sleeve flap sweated with condensation as I double-checked the labels on the boxes. I walked briskly between a Chevy Bronco and a rusting International Scout. The man had his money ready.

"Were you able to find this place all right?" the man asked.

"Not too bad. It's kinda hidden back here, though. You ordered a large double pepperoni and a large half-sausage, half bacon?"

"Sure did."

"That'll be $14.90, please." The man handed me a twenty and a folded slip of paper.

"Keep the change, and I left you a tip, too."

"What's this?" Confused, I shuffled a pamphlet to the top and looked at the cover. It looked just like a check, but read "Your Debt Is Paid in Full" at the top. And the signature line read "Jesus."

"Some reading material that may change your life," he smiled with a confident, yet odd demeanor that I couldn't quite place. He looked like a car salesman about to make a deal. "Do you know how to cash that in?"

"Don't worry. I'm already saved, sir," I assured him, finally catching his drift. "Thank you for the tip, anyway." Here it comes, I thought.

"Do you go to church, son?" I bristled inside. I ain't your son, I thought. I really needed to be going if I was to get back and get any more decent runs tonight.

"Well, no sir. But when you have to work until three in the morning on Sunday, you've got to get some sleep sometime," I exaggerated. Smiling, I took a few steps back toward my car, trying not to be on the defensive.

"Fair enough. I won't keep ya, but if you feel a need for some Christian fellowship, our address is on the back. Brushy Mountain Pentecostal Holiness. We also meet on Wednesday nights. You should be able to find it a lot easier than my house," he joked.

"Well, alright. Have a good night sir, and thank you for ordering from Papa's Pizza." I hastily stepped into my car and backed out of the driveway. Branches squeaked and scraped down the passenger side doors. I cut my steering wheel back to the left.

Thank God my car had decent back up lights. Otherwise, I might have backed my axle up on one of the hedges and gotten stuck.

With much effort, I finally got my Grand Am back on the road and headed in the direction of the store. I wanted to be offended by the man for questioning me like I was some type of heathen, but I thought back to seventh grade and how I went to the altar at Calvary Way Baptist with a guilty heart. I remembered all the songs we sang at summer camp when I thought I knew what they were talking about. I remembered how in vacation bible school they taught all the kids that witnessing to others about God was part of our Christian duty. I just didn't think I would ever be a good enough person to be the light of the world, that city on a hill. Regret and anger began to well up in my throat at the thought, how enraptured and joyful I once felt when the pastor and congregation circled around me, laying hands on me and praying, and how alone and forgotten I felt now. I missed it and resented it at the same time, wondering if what I felt was real or if I just got caught up in the moment. I looked at the slip of paper again. Instead of someone's address in the top left corner of the fake check, it listed some scripture verses, John 3:16 and John 8:32. I stuck the tract between the dashboard and the windshield and reached for the directions receipt to my next delivery, some apartments on this side of Blowing Rock Road.

* * * *

The side parking lot was full of drivers' cars when I returned to the store. Must be a lull in business, I thought. I pulled into the last space, turned off my motor, and popped the hood to disconnect my pizza sign from my car battery. The alternator hadn't been charging well lately. Craig was sitting in his car smoking a cigarette and talking on his cell phone.

"Hey, Dude. You left someone's check on your dash." He pointed with his cigarette as he pocketed his phone.

"What? Oh, this? It's nothing." I'm sure he thinks I'm an idiot, leaving my pizza money out. I reached in and pulled it from the dash. "Here, see? It's not a real check." I gave it to him, and he looked at it puzzled, then laughed.

"Hey, I didn't know Jesus was in our delivery area!"

Inside, several people gathered around the toppings counter, chanting like they were performing some kind of strange ritual. The ovens were whirring, conveyor belts squeaking, but no pizzas. Only a few carryout orders sat under the lamps. The two topping boys, whose names I could never get straight – one was named Sam and the other Eric – were turning up sauce cups of an iridescent green liquid. Both of them looked like they were still in middle school.

"Drink, drink, drink, drink!" the others chanted.

"Randy! You're just in time. We were seeing how much pepper juice cocktail Sam n'Eric can drink before they puke," said Paul.

"Slowed down, huh?"

"You got that right." Craig came in behind me, blowing the last of the smoke from his lungs, and rejoined the small circle.

"Here, you try a shot," shouted Paul, handing a small sauce cup to me.

"I don't know, I think I'll pass. Isn't there some boxes that need folding in the back or something?"

"Oh, come on. Don't be a wuss. It'll put hair on your chest," said Craig.

"You must be hard-up for entertainment," called Lindsey from the back, as she crushed a cigarette in the sink, blowing the last bit of smoke out the corner of her mouth and waving the wisps away. Employees weren't supposed to smoke in the building, but no one really enforced it. She had her coat and backpack with her, and had combed her straight, dark hair out so that it hung down to her shoulders. She had on jeans that hugged her hips instead of the mandatory khaki pants, and looked especially beautiful, like a whole different person.

"Are you leaving early?" I asked her. As I turned, I realized Paul had already placed the cup of pepper juice in my hand.

"Early? I've been here since ten this morning. I'm going home to crash. Catch you later, Rocker."

"Why are you calling him Rocker, anyway?" asked Paul incredulously. His thick, dark hair pushed out from around his ball cap.

"Well, because he rocks out. Give him a couple more months and he'll be out-delivering everyone." I blushed at the compliment, but at the same time felt that was a tall order for me to fill. Part of me also wondered if she was being facetious. "And be careful how much of that stuff you drink, Rocker. If it puts hair on your chest, then Craig must've drank too much. His back's so hairy, it's like he's wearing a wool sweater *under* his shirt."

"You weren't complaining the other night when you were clawing at it!" Craig snapped back, making a thrusting motion with his pelvis. Paul laughed.

"The only way I'd touch *you* is with a set of sheep shears." There was in insuck of breath from the room.

Craig clutched his chest, feigning a heart attack. "Ouch, that hurt!"

"And it wouldn't be your back hair I'd trim!" Turning back to me first with a wink, she spoke to the room with a churlish smile, "See y'all on Wednesday, losers!"

"Yeah, take care." I watched her as she walked out the side door and lit another cigarette on her way to her car. I wondered if Lindsey and Craig really had sex, or if it was just playful banter. The thought lingered too long in my mind, and embarrassed me.

"Well, are you going to drink it or what?" pressed Paul.

I looked at the green cup of juice again. "What is it?"

"Jalapeño and pepperoncini brine." Sam n'Eric held their stomachs with a sweaty, pale look on their faces. They looked to me with doleful eyes and shook their heads in unison. I hesitated, then opened a Red Pepper shaker, sprinkled it into my cup, and tilted my head back like I was taking a shot of cheap bourbon. I poured it down my throat in one gulp.

"Dang!" said Chris, who had just stepped out of the office. "I've got some Pepto if you need it later."

23

Dean leaned out the office door to see what the commotion was. "Randy! In my office," he shouted, and to the others he barked, "and you guys need to be folding some boxes or something." I took a couple of gasping gulps to keep the pepper juice from coming back up, and sheepishly walked in. "Have a seat," said Dean. He took a full look at me from his office chair and casually asked, "What's wrong? You look flushed."

"I'm fine." I staunched a burp with the back of my fist.

"Listen, before the late-night rush starts, I wanted to talk to you about something. You are a hell of a good worker, a little quiet at times, but a good worker. I think you know that. But to tell you the truth, when we hired you it was because we were desperate for a driver, and you had just applied for the job."

"Okay?"

"Well, I'm glad you're on the team, but as policy goes the district manager asks us to check up on all references. You said you worked at Lowe's Foods when you were in high school, but when I called they said they had no record of you working there. Same for Pizza Hut, which was the main thing that made me decide to hire you."

"I'm sorry, Dean. I must have given you a wrong phone number. I worked at the one in Hillsville. I bet I wrote down the number for the one in Galax." I felt hot and lightheaded, but it wasn't from the peppers.

Dean raised an eyebrow. "Did you really work at any of those places?" His gaze cut through me. I hesitated, then stammered in reply.

"Uh, no. No I didn't." It was all over. Busted. I wanted to slip into the cracks of the floor and disappear.

"Hey. It's all right." Dean relaxed some. "So maybe you didn't have any work experience before. It's not the first time somebody's lied on their application. You've already proven your worth here."

"Well, I worked at the Daisy Chain a little while, but I didn't list it because I quit on short notice to come work here. I'm sorry. I wanted this job really bad, that's all."

"Well, no harm, no foul. But everything else on your application is correct, I hope? You aren't some illegal alien or something," Dean half-joked.

"No, sir. And yes, sir. Everything else is correct."

"Don't call me sir."

"Sorry, sir. I mean, okay."

"Better get out there and help them man the ovens. I heard the phones ringing. They'll be some deliveries soon. Just remember one thing," Dean's jovial expression turned deadpan. "Don't screw up, Marcie."

I left the office and took a deep breath. My body seemed heavy for a moment, like cold lead, and I moved in slow motion from the office door to the ovens. It seemed like it was all over. Everything. After I had worked so hard to get to where I was. Then the burn of a pepper-juice burp brought me back to the present, and grabbing the peel I scooped two pizzas from the oven and boxed them, cut them, and slid them under the heat lamp. "Can't screw up," I muttered under my breath.

A few minutes had passed and the green screen blinked with a run to Laurel Fork Apartments, out near the community college's administrative building on the 105 bypass, a straight drive out King Street. Not an exciting run, but at least a chance to get out for a while, maybe stop at a convenience store and get some Rolaids. I was about to check out on the delivery when the door exploded open and an infuriated driver slammed his empty warming sleeves on the counter.

"Where's that son of a bitch at?" he asked me.

"What? Who?" Taken off guard, I just shrugged my shoulders with wide eyes and backed away.

"Ollie!" A few people were still gathered by the toppings counter, and began to disperse. A short, stocky guy with a pock-scarred face stepped around the corner.

"What's your problem now, Tyler?"

"You know damn well what! I know it was you that slashed my tire while I was in Howie Hall. I told you last week I didn't know who took your keys from your car. I wasn't even in town that night. You've crossed the line with me this time!"

Ollie looked older than some of the other drivers, but sometimes didn't act it. He always seemed to keep his cool, but underneath lurked the unpredictable. No one ever questioned his actions or accused him of anything, except Dean, and even then it seemed that Dean was intimidated by his demeanor. Tyler was all jock, from his cock-sure attitude to his over-inflated biceps. Last week Tyler and a bunch of his friends allegedly saw Ollie's car parked in front of one of the Greek houses with the engine running. They thought it would be a funny prank to pull on the bad-ass if someone took the keys out of the ignition and threw them under the car, then hid behind some bushes to watch Ollie search for them. Most people with any sense knew Ollie was one of those people that was a better ally than an enemy.

Ollie walked slowly towards Tyler, away from the toppings counter, eyes unblinking. I stepped away a little more, back toward the ovens. "Listen here. I haven't done a damn thing to you. If I did, you'd know it. You've made enough enemies around here. You don't need another. I wouldn't be slinking around behind people, anyways, and hiding their keys or any shit like that." Ollie spoke with an eerie calmness, like the quiet before a lightning strike. "Why don't you go talk to your little fraternity butt-buddies. They're always playing dumb pranks on one another."

"That's it. No one talks about my friends that way. I'm going to pound your ass in the ground!" Tyler snaps his arm back with a clenched fist. Then suddenly, quicker than anyone noticed, Tyler was lying flat on his back on the tiled floor, eyes wide in astonishment. Ollie had swept Tyler's legs out from under him with a martial arts move. He hit the floor with the force of a falling tree. A stack of empty boxes fell on top of him. In the same quick motion, Ollie put a knee on Tyler's chest and thrust his fist with force to within an inch of Tyler's face.

"Do you see these?" Ollie's fists were striped at the knuckles with silvery scars. "Each cut represents the broken teeth of some dumb bastard that tried picking a fight with me. You understand?" Before Tyler could respond, Dean came running out of the bathroom with his belt undone, trying to tuck his shirt tail in.

"What the hell is going on here? Can't I have five minutes to take a dump without having to play babysitter? Ollie! That's your last strike. Punch out and go home." Ollie smirked at Dean, fist drawn back in the air. "I mean clock out. You're fired." Ollie stood up and looked at Dean, unphased.

"Sure thing, bossman," said Ollie, cutting his gaze back toward Tyler, still on the floor. Ollie got up, went to the green delivery screen, and logged out. He walked out the back door with his jacket.

"Tyler, in my office – now!" and to the rest of us he shouted, "Get back to work! We've got some orders that are blinking overdue on the screen. Damn it, guys! Do you know how many other pizza places there are in town? We can't stay in competition if we can't deliver our pizzas on time. Move it!"

Everyone snapped back to their duties. A few people grumbled, and Craig complained about how he was ready to "quit this dumb-assed job" because he was tired of being yelled at for something he didn't do. I hustled to the computer screen and added one more delivery to my run, an apartment on Water Street, and went to pull them from the oven to box them.

As I made my way through King Street traffic, I thought about community college and the classes I had in the morning. I knew I had only just started, but finishing college seemed like a day that would never come, and going on to the university just a pipe dream. But I couldn't give up. If I did, I might as well go back home – and that was just as inconceivable. I made two mental to-do notes: get an extra car door key to carry in my wallet, and check the air in my spare tire.

5 _____

We drove out old 58 in a white pickup truck, my
grandfather at the wheel and pointing to the new nursing home they
built next to Cliffview Cemetery. The dash of the truck still shined
like it was new. Must have been sprayed with Armor-All, I thought.
Papaw always took care of his vehicles. I stared out the window at
the passing scenery, daydreaming. It was Easter break holiday, and
I didn't have to go back to the high school for a few days.

"I'm planning on skipping that step and going straight to
the dirt nap, if I can help it."

"I'm sorry, what did you say Papaw?

"Why do you think they built the nursing home next to the
cemetery? So you can look out your window and see where you're
headed." He makes a left turn into the wrought-iron gate of the
cemetery grounds. "I want to show you how I fixed some of the
stones at the family plot."

"You know, I haven't been up here since Granny died."
The sun was shining and the air blew sweet and warm from the
freshly-cut spring grass. I hung my arm out the window and let the
breeze squeeze through my fingers.

"Now, I wanted to tell you this before, but decided to wait
until you came to visit."

"What's that?"

"I'm going to be cremated," he stated. I chuckled. "I'm
being serious here. I've decided to be cremated."

"But who'd want to keep your urn on their mantle? I can just see someone tipping it over and the ashes going everywhere. And what about the relatives who want to come visit both you and Granny together?" We drove up the hill and around a line of old cedar trees.

"Well, son, I'm still going to be buried next to your grandmother. They'll just use one of those post-hole drills instead of a back hoe, put me in a coffee can or something, and then tamp me in with a stick." We climbed a steep incline where the pavement turned to dirt as my grandfather put the truck in four-wheel drive.

"Those pink dogwoods finally died after the city kept hitting them with their mowers. Girdled them clean around, eventually. So I got Preston to come help me pull them up. You remember the colored boy that helps me now and again?" I wondered why Preston would still work for the miserly old man all these years, and why he still called him "boy." Preston had to be over 50.

"What's with all this talk about being cremated and stuff? Are you dying soon?"

"Well, first of all, I never did like the idea of strange people putting their hands all over me, drawing my blood, pumping me full of formaldehyde."

"I don't think they use that stuff anymore, Papaw."

"Well, whatever they pickle you with. And you never know, they might cut your peter off or something pre-verted like that." I looked at him startled, but the smirk on his face forced a chuckle from me. He had never spoken so candidly before.

"Would it matter to you if you were already dead?" I asked.

"Hell, it would matter when you have $12,000 invested in the funeral home for burial and services." I whistled in disbelief. "So I asked them about cremation and how much *it* would cost, plus the visitation service and burial I was going to have anyway. The lady I talked to down at Vaughn-Guynn tallied it up and said it would come out to $2,000. And I said, 'Sign me up!' I like it when I can save some money, even if I can't take it with me. You see, I can't get that money back until I kick the bucket anyway."

We stopped at a section of the cemetery where only flat headstones were allowed, and got out of the truck. Plastic flower arrangements dotted the otherwise smooth lawn. "Why'd we stop here, Papaw? This isn't our family plot." My grandfather just kept walking ahead. I followed him to two aluminum signs, temporary funeral home plaques that looked like they were both run over with a mower. One was gnarled and had lost its letters. The other had been repaired with what looked like mail box lettering and hot glue. It read – Carol Ann Wilson Phillips Shumaker.

"I fixed your aunt's marker last year after they ran over it. I hope I outlive ol' Edna Shumaker long enough to have a stone made that has both your aunt's maiden and her first husband's last name etched into it, so all her family will know where she is. Edna's been fighting me ever since they buried your Aunt Carol." Edna was my Uncle Blake's mother and the Shumaker's unappointed matriarch. My grandfather looked solemnly at his daughter's plot, and then took two steps to the left. He proceeded to spit on the ground, and stomp around a time or two on the other grave with his heavy brogans. "I hope you felt that, you no-good son of a bitch!" He looked down at the twisted, nameless sign. "You couldn't honor my daughter's last request, could you?" He spat again.

Though his actions caught me off guard, I knew most of this story in bits and pieces. A couple of years after my Uncle Carl died, my Aunt Carol started seeing this plumber named Blake. He seemed like a good man. But they married late in life and already had health problems and mounting bills, both of them being lifelong smokers. When my aunt became terminally ill with lung cancer, the families began planning where she and Blake should be buried. The Shumakers didn't have a plot in Cliffview, so my grandfather offered to move over to the right of his wife and have Blake and Carol Ann buried on the left of the Wilson name marker. But Blake proved even more proud than his father-in-law and insisted on purchasing his own plot for him and Aunt Carol, down at the bottom of the hill near the road. A month after Carol Ann was in the ground, Blake had a heart attack – in bed with another woman. My grandfather suspected he was using "the little blue pill" and was "over-sexed to death." Now the two families have been constantly bickering over what the inscription on their headstones should read, and who was going to pay for it.

"Come on, Papaw. Let's drive on up to the top of the hill and you can show me how you fixed the headstones," I insisted. He took a deep breath, took off his fedora hat, and wiped his brow with the back of his hand. He moved his lips as if in prayer, or maybe speaking with his daughter beyond the grave.

"Thank God your grandmother died before seeing what had become of her daughter," he spoke aloud as we walked to the truck. He put it in low drive to continue up the hill.

At the top, we stepped out of the truck again and walked toward a large upright stone that read WILSON. A bald man in work gloves and an army surplus coat was working two plots over with a spade, cutting the overgrown sod from around some headstones. He stopped and looked our way, leaning on the handle.

"Why, Gilbert Wilson!" the man said. "Haven't seen you in a while. How are you getting along?"

"Oh, fair to middlin'."

"And that must be your grandson. I don't think I seen him since… Well, it's been a while." He walked over with a limp, took off his right glove, and shook Papaw's hand. His left eye was clouded over with a cataract, and it seemed to look in a different direction from his good eye. He was probably in his late fifties, but years of working in the sun had leathered his face and made him seem older. His left cheek shined with a round bulge of tobacco. He turned to me and said, "And you must be in high school by now. Stout boy like you, I bet you're on the football team." I just smiled sheepishly, waiting for Papaw to say something in reply, so I wouldn't have to.

"How's your family doin'?" Papaw finally asked.

"Well, I'm tending to most of them right now, unfortunately." He spreads his arms out around him. "My wife passed away a couple of months ago."

"I'm sorry to hear that."

31

"She'd been sufferin' for a while," the man continued. "Her mind had gone, and I had to put her in Waddell 'cause I couldn't take care of her. Had diabetes on top of that. I've got a son and some grandkids in Raleigh, but I only see them about once or twice a year." The man spit a big amber stream of juice off to the side.

"Well, I'm sorry things are so hard on ya."

"I get by. Do a little gardening, tend to the family plot."

"Got to keep busy."

"Yeah. Well, it's been good talkin' to ya. I gotta get on back to the house eventually and mow the yard."

"Take care, now."

"Same to ya," he said as he limped over to the row of cedars, where his car was parked.

Once the man was out of earshot, Papaw leaned in to me and said, "For the life of me, I cannot remember who that guy is. He might have worked at Appalachian Power when I was there. I thought if he talked more I would figure it out, but nothing came to me. That's the third time that's happened this month."

"Don't worry about it," I said. "As long as you have lived in this town, and all the people you've met, there's bound to be some folks that you won't remember."

I walked around with Papaw to the front of the Wilson plot. The flat headstones had been recently reset an inch above ground, surrounded with a couple of inches of poured concrete. Little wisps of new grass sprouted through surrounding patches of straw. He pointed out his recent handiwork with the toe of his shoe. "I'm leaving the $10,000 to you when I die, so you can go to college. I don't think I'll be around much longer."

My mind was wandering when my grandfather said this. "Huh?"

"I know it's not much these days, but it would be enough to get you started, and you could get a job or maybe a scholarship." I was dumbstruck. Joy and fear swirled inside me in a stew of confusion.

"Are you sick? Are you dying?"

"No, but I feel it in my bones that my time has about come."

"But what would Mom say about the money?"

"Well, you're my only grandson in a family full of women. Besides, your mom and dad's borrowed enough from me that your Aunt Faith will be getting the rest of it. Even if I tried giving it to your mom, your dad would just waste it on God-knows-what. I know you love him, son, but he ain't never did anything for you except make your life hard."

"Yes, sir. Thank you, sir." I hung my head and stared stonily back at my polished granite reflection in the head marker. I loved my father, and hated myself for resenting him almost as much.

"I just wish that...." He stopped short of finishing his thought. "Hey. You know, since you passed Driver's Ed last month, I figure now is as good a time as any to get your driver's license."

"Really?" I looked up with mild surprise. "But I don't have a car."

"Well, the guys down at the Chevy dealership owe me a few favors I'm calling them on, back when I used to run the taxi cab stand. They've got a Pontiac Grand Am with less than 75,000 miles that was just traded in. I can get it real cheap."

"Stick shift or automatic?"

"Now don't you go lookin' the gift horse in the mouth, son. It's an automatic, and it runs decent. And by the way, you're going to Sparta to get your driver's license."

"Why Sparta?"

"You are going to move your mailing address to your Aunt Faith's house. That and a North Carolina driver's license will get you in-state tuition to that teacher's college down in Boone that you've been talking about. Didn't think your Papaw was that swift, did you? I may be getting senile, but I still have a few good pistons firing."

"It's actually a university now, Papaw."

33

"Same difference." We both smiled with our hands in our pockets, not looking at one another, but staring down at the flat headstones. "I fixed it so the grass won't grow over these stones for a while. No need to edge around them for years."

"I don't know what to say."

" 'Bout the headstones?"

"No, about the money, and college."

"Nothing you need to say. First time a Wilson family member goes to college, you better believe I'm going to help out. C'mon, I want to show you where your great-grandmother Higgins is buried. Have I ever told you about her, and her bob-tailed cats?"

I reached up and placed a hand on my grandfather's knotted shoulder. "Thanks." He reached over and placed his own hand on mine, held it there for longer than a moment, then pulled his hand away. I wanted to hug him, but knew it would only make him uncomfortable.

We got back into the pickup and drove across to the other side of the cemetery. It was almost too surreal to be true, and like so many other things, I didn't want to jinx it. Hope and sadness swung like dance partners on the hardened floor of my heart, and my stomach ached with anticipation. The wind turned cooler and changed direction, not altogether disagreeable, but with a different, unfamiliar smell. A slight smile came across my face without at first realizing what it was. I looked down the hill at the road leading out of town.

6

As I drove up the hill to Watauga County High School, I started feeling uneasy. I knew it wasn't my school, and I didn't know anybody there, but I couldn't help but dread going in. Anxiety swelled in my head, and my cheeks grew hot and flushed. How ridiculous, I thought. I was a college student now, not some high school peon. Somehow I felt, though, that they would smell me out and see through my ruse – that another student would rat on me, or an administrator would grab me and take me to the office. Out front an activity bus opened its doors, and students carrying band instruments began filing in one after the other. I pulled into the first available parking space and waited for the bus to load and drive off before walking inside.

Because the community college campus was so small, some of the classes, including this one, were held at the high school in the evenings. I had English class on Mondays and Wednesdays. Though I tried to get only morning classes so it wouldn't interfere with my job, I waited too late to sign up. Fortunately, weeknights aren't peak business hours at the pizza place. I did not know yet what my major would be, what my expertise was. What would I declare when I transferred to the university? I had worked so hard to get to where I was, I never really thought much about what I would do once I got there. But there was plenty of time to find my niche, I thought. Jack-of-all-trades, but master of none, my father used to call me. But he was right. When I get my Associate's of Arts Degree, all my basic classes out of the way, I hoped to get some sort of inspiration as to what vocation I should take. Nothing in high school interested me except leaving.

As I walked in the front door, the hallways were vacant save for the gym-floor echoes of squeaking sneakers carried over from the other end of the school. I walked as fast as I could without looking like a fool. I'm a college student now, I kept telling myself. The door to the classroom was still open. I slowed down to a casual stroll, book bag slung over one shoulder, and walked into the room. It was a small class. Only 12 students besides me had enrolled. A few were a couple years older than me, and the rest were probably second-career students in their thirties and forties.

The teacher was young, just out of graduate school. She had dark, straight hair and a slender, prominent nose that wasn't unattractive, more like a strong Greek arch. But it was her fair complexion that made me think of my ex-girlfriend from home. It gave me a queasy sense of loss that I tried to shake at the end of each class.

"Glad you could join us, Randall," she said. If it were not for the good-natured tone in her voice, I would have taken her for a smart-ass. If it is one thing I've learned about college professors, they're clever when it comes to being insulting, especially English teachers. Unless you are smart enough or quick enough, you're not likely to realize you've just been made the butt of some metaphorical joke.

"Hey Ms. Belvin. Sorry if I'm late. I had car trouble," I lied as earnestly as possible.

"No. You're just in time. We had begun discussing last week's reading assignment, starting with Faulkner's 'Barn Burning.' So, what's your first impression of it?" Everyone's eyes turned on me as I found my seat among the semi-circle of desks.

"Well, what do you mean?" I asked. "Did I understand what happened in the story, did I like it, what?"

"What's the first response that pops into your head? Anything about it." She had a knack of coming up with the vaguest questions. If I didn't find her so attractive, so down-to-earth friendly, I might have gotten ticked at her persistence.

"Well, to tell you the truth, I didn't much care for the story," I replied with a few seconds of deliberation, trying to look casual in front of 13 pairs of eyes.

"What was it about the story that turned you off?" I opened my mouth, trying to form my thoughts into words. But before I could answer Ms. Belvin's question, another student piped up.

"We read this story in the eleventh grade, and I didn't understand much of it then, but now I realize how Faulkner uses gothic motifs to cast a shadowy atmosphere of shame and hostility." The girl smiled confidently after giving her response.

"What a perfect answer – if you were writing for Cliff Notes. We'll get back to themes later. No, I want *your* impression of the story. How did it make you feel to read it, just off the cuff?"

Another younger man answered, "I didn't quite understand why the boy kept following his father around for so long. I mean, I would've left after a while. Sarty should have ducked out the first chance he got."

"He did leave, at the *end* of the story," I remarked.

"Well, looks like someone didn't finish their assignment," an older Asian man exclaimed. Some of the other students snickered. The boy just flashed a "screw you" look at the man.

"Why didn't you like Faulkner's story?" Ms. Belvin asked again very innocently. "If you don't mind sharing."

"Faulkner doesn't offer much hope to any of his characters," I said finally.

"True. That's Faulkner's nature. What bothers you about that? Is it too idealistic, too true to life?" the teacher asked.

"It's one thing to read his work, to get into the miserable life of Sartoris, then take a step back from it all and breathe a sigh of relief that your own life isn't so messed up, it's another thing to...." I stopped in mid-thought, struggling to put it into words. "Either way Sartoris is damned, whether he stayed with his father or left to face the unknown. If he left his father, he would be betraying Family, his blood. Staying would have only ensured... his demise."

"Very good. You put some thought into this." Too much, I thought. "But isn't there hope in the unknown? The possibility that things will be better?"

I chose my words very carefully. Everyone stared at me as if I were Helen Keller in *The Miracle Worker*, saying "wa-ter" for the first time. It was probably the most I had ever uttered this semester. "I think the unknown is worse because it's beyond one's view, one's control. At least with his father he knew life from one day to the next. I think sometimes people are afraid that change means things could get worse, that uncertainty of the future. They live in fear of it, so they stick with what they know, because it's familiar."

"Excellent. I hadn't thought of it in that manner before. Very astute! Does anybody have anything they'd like to add to that?"

A woman in her late fifties with red hair and a tight perm chimed in. "I agree. It's a vicious cycle that many people get trapped in and not even realize that there is a way out. But do you think that Sartoris' circumstances could provide hope for the reader as well? He might possibly be better off, maybe not. But at least now there is much more that Sartoris has control of – his destiny."

"Wow. Some deep stuff here, and we are only into the first story tonight," Ms. Belvin exclaims. I couldn't stand being the center of attention. So I got the story. So what? I always got better grades in English class in high school, though we never read anything I liked. I prayed someone would say something intelligent and draw the attention away from me.

"Yeah, too bad they didn't have carpet cleaner back then. The dad could've just 'Shout-ed out' the stain and saved a lot of argument, instead of beating it with a rock," a younger girl remarked. A few of the students giggled again, and some of the older adults rolled their eyes, but smiled. I relaxed some, and talk turned back to Faulkner and some other asinine things they brought up, but I didn't care. I was doing the best I could, and that's all that mattered.

*   *   *   *

After the class, the red-haired woman with the tight perm approached me, limping with a cane because of a walking cast she wore. "I just want you to know I enjoyed your addition to the class discussion. Most of the other kids your age are just out of high

38

school, and do nothing but make vulgar remarks about the stories. Don't give up. There are things worth hoping for out there. You've come a long way I bet, and that's worth commending."

What are you talking about? I wanted to say, but instead I replied, "Uh, thank you." The woman just smiled and waddled out a side door where her car was parked right next to the entrance. I walked slowly out to my car. Am I that transparent? The woman's words set in my ears eerily like a strange comfort, and then evaporated. It was well after dark now, and the orange glow of the sodium vapor lights illuminated snowflakes, flurrying around like moths in summer.

As I shook my keys out, looking for the car door key, Ms. Belvin exclaimed from the next car over, "Have a good evening, Randall. Keep up the reading. You are doing well."

"Thanks, Ms. Belvin."

"Think we'll get some accumulation tonight?" she asked.

"You never know," I replied. She smiled quickly, told me to drive safely, and waved before getting into her wood-grained station wagon. God, she was beautiful. I sat down in front of my steering wheel, and watched her as she drove away, feeling a familiar pang of regret as I thought about Cathy, my ex-girlfriend.

It started small, in the back of my head, then moved to the pit of my stomach. I could feel it coming, that drain of energy beginning to overtake me. An emptiness, swallowed by panic, raced to my outer skin, made me feel naked, vulnerable, alone. Quickly, I tried taking a few deep breaths, followed by swallowing a couple of lumps down the back of my throat. It subsided, but still seemed right on the verge of coming back to the surface. I tried to forget. She called me last week, found my number somehow. Cathy wanted to talk to me, see how I was doing. But I blew her off, just stood there with the phone to my ear letting my silent anger swallow everything. Eventually she hung up. All she said was, "Okay. Well, goodbye then," like she was stung by a sweat bee, and in my mind she slowly set her pink Ericofon back down on her desk. I cancelled my phone service the next week.

7

We ran quickly across Highway 52. Her flip-flops slapped the back of her feet as we walked across the gravel parking lot of the produce stand. It was well after nine in the evening, so the sky had let go of the last summer daylight. The place was deserted.

"Where are they?" I asked.

"By the door, under the tables." Cathy pointed to a row of round sugar melons, their green skin glowing with the passing of cars on the highway.

"No. I mean, where are the store owners? Do they know we're stealing their produce?" Everything else had been taken inside for the night – the crates of peaches and apples, and the jars of honey and sorghum that normally sit on the front tables.

"There's no need to whisper. The Warlicks just left for a few days, or I'd knock on their door and pay for them. Their cousins are driving from Dobson to run the place while they're gone. Besides, I used to do this all the time when I was younger, and just pay them back later."

Cathy lived across the road from one of Cana's many produce stands. It was a small storefront compared to some of the other outfits. There was a large produce market and general store down the road called Mountain Man that had several buildings, and had bluegrass on Saturdays, not the flashy stuff but the traditional old-time sound that spoke of sweat and hard ground. Cathy took me there a few times to listen to music and share an order of chili cheese fries from the grill.

It took me 30 minutes to drive from Galax down the mountain to see her. I never minded the drive, though. Sometimes I drove out Piper's Gap and down the sharp, rutted switchbacks through Lambsburg. Sometimes I continued out to Fancy Gap and down Highway 52, past the piles of sand that I never thought could stop a runaway truck. It became a ritual for me. And though I hated leaving her at the end of the evening, I looked forward to driving back up that mountain road, to gain some elevation. She told me I was crazy one time when I swore the air felt different up there.

I rolled out a watermelon from under the table and gave it a thump or two like a drum. "The good an' ripe ones have a hollow sound most of the time." I pulled my pocketknife out and flipped out the large blade.

"You aren't going to cut it open here, are you?" she questioned.

"No, dear. I'm going to plug it to see if it's ripe enough." Sometimes I felt that Cathy and I talked like an old married couple. Though I didn't let on, I kind of enjoyed it.

"And what? If it's not ripe enough leave it with a hole squared into it? Here," she squatted and reached past me, "take this one. It has a larger yellow spot on the bottom where it's sat out in the field longer." She playfully elbowed me in the ribs, enough so I lost my balance from sitting on the balls of my feet, rolling me onto my side. I looked up her long legs to her denim shorts to see her smiling in the dim light of the passing cars, watermelon under one arm and the other reaching down to pull me up.

We ran back across the road with our prize. She cradled the green orb in her arms as if it was a child, or a football. "I'll get some newspapers to spread out and a knife from the kitchen. I think my mom's done with the dishes by now."

"I've got a better idea," I said. "Just bring two spoons."

"All right, but is that pocketknife clean? You haven't been scaling fish with it lately, have you?" I just glared at her comically while I reflexively popped the blade out and inserted it into the firm flesh. It was perfectly ripe, I could tell despite the darkness of her

41

front porch. The cut shot ahead of the knife like a crack of wet lightning, filling the air with an aroma of musky sweetness.

* * * *

There was a small little patch of grass in front of my apartment window, in which I set out a reclining lawn chair to savor the sunlight, a chair like one of those Cathy used in her back yard to sunbathe. It unfolded twice and adjusted for the head and feet. I could hear the cars passing by, but some scraggly-looking bushes screened the view of the road, so I didn't worry about people seeing where I lived. These apartments had once been a mini-motel with five individual "bungalows" lined side-by-side, next to a larger building that must have served as an office and the owner's apartment. Now they served as last-resort residencies for people who can't afford anything else. I didn't know my neighbors personally, and tried to avoid running into them if I could. There was only one person I had actually met – a tall, skinny man in his late forties or early fifties that walked everywhere he went. He had a smile that was disarming, despite the few remaining teeth that hung like pumpkin seeds in his mouth. I saw him clasping a brown bag as he reached the door to his apartment. I threw my hand up to wave at him. He smiled briefly and waved back before staggering into the dark opening and shutting the door.

The early November sun warmed my face as I lay on my back in blue jeans and a white short-sleeved undershirt. When the air didn't stir, it was warm on my body and face. I pulled my chin back for every ray of sun I could catch. I remembered Grandma Spivey telling me how the old-timers used to sit in the sun of a warm winter day as a way to combat the blues. Though the weather forecast called for a chance of snow next week, it could have easily been a cool day in September or May. If only I could crack my head open like a watermelon and fill it with sun, maybe I wouldn't feel so hopeless. Maybe I could air out the demons.

Maybe it was my English teacher, or the perfume of the girl that sat next to me in math class yesterday, or how this strangely warm day reminded me of last summer, before I left Cathy, when the world seemed to make sense and have purpose. It was sweet and crisp, the memory of the two of us sitting on her front porch swing. We ate out of the watermelon halves like bowls, spitting the seeds into the front yard. Her mouth was just as sweet, as we kissed and talked for what seemed like hours, periodically swatting mosquitoes away. We agreed we were saving ourselves for marriage, but I was always a little uncomfortable talking about it. Despite that, Cathy periodically had to swat my hands away from reaching up her shirt when I got relaxed and frisky. I was a breast man, I confessed playfully. She was a good Baptist that way, and I missed that blooming, respectful innocence about her.

Cathy had planned for us to go to Surry Community College together, while she hinted we should get engaged. I wasn't against the idea, but I didn't want to rush into something until I was ready. Also, I envisioned getting out of the county and going to college somewhere far away. Cathy was more of a homebody, and would have been perfectly content with setting a double-wide on the back of her father's property, right behind the old Doughton place, her father's grandfather's house. Some time ago Cathy's family must have run an orchard, but most of the trees were cut down and left in brush piles that were never cleaned up. From the road you couldn't see it, but behind Cathy's house was a ghost town of a farm. Most barns and sheds had already collapsed, but the old house and a large barn still stood. Cathy took me back there on several occasions and showed me what was left of an old cider press and the huge cast iron kettle in which they used to cook apple butter, now sitting under the rusting tin of the barn. They sat gathering dust and barn swallow droppings. The house was vacant, but looked like a happy home at one time. Not much was left inside except some pine lumber someone slid into the front room then forgot about. It strangely had two doors to the front of the house. The one on the right led to the living room, while the one on the left led to a front bedroom. Cathy called it a "courtin' door." A young man could come home late from a night of courting without having to walk through the house and wake the family up. The floors sagged away from the center of the house like an old flower about to lose its petals. I wanted to go upstairs, but the steep steps had collapsed. The linoleum of the kitchen floor had curled like wood shavings, revealing several floorboards missing. Once I got Cathy to walk the inside wall with me to the pantry closet. It still contained rusting cans of King Syrup and a mouse-nibbled block of lye soap.

Cathy's father talked to me one time about how nice it would be to clear the land and plant some apple and peach trees, with the proper help. "It makes a man feel good when he can raise a family from the cultivation of his own land," he stated wistfully, then patted me on the shoulder and said, "Don't you think?"

I did think about it. I felt a warmness in the Doughton home that I didn't experience at my own. Cathy's parents were happy, and seemed to really love one another, especially Cathy and her younger brothers Spencer and Phillip. But Cana wasn't far enough away from Galax for me to forget my own life at home. I loved my mother, and my grandfather always tried to help us out when he could. It was my father that seemed to put a smudge on my family picture. He was rarely home – always looking for work, he said. The furniture factory downtown had laid him off and about a hundred other workers, so he often drove to places like Radford or Wytheville, or even Winston-Salem looking for work, and would be gone for days. When he did come back he had an odd air about him, like smoky bars or incense. My mom worked two part-time jobs to make the rent payment on a little brick house at the other side of Oldtown. At one point Papaw suggested we move in with him and live downstairs, which he could make up like an apartment. My father didn't get along too well with Papaw, though, and he would have been too proud to accept any help, unless it was money. When my father was away, my mother would either sit in front of the television, slumped over from fatigue in a dazed stupor, or cry. I tried taking care of her, doing things for her around the house, but it was like she saw a little bit of my father every time she looked in my face, and it made her even more weary and depressed. That's why I never invited Cathy over to my house. When my father was home, all my mother would do was fight with him over money or where he'd been, or make muffled grunting and rutting noises late at night in their bedroom, followed by my father's raspy snore. It scared me and infuriated me that my mother would just take him back each time. Some nights I would lie awake wishing that I either never had a family or that I had never been born.

My grandfather gave me a little hope when he promised to help me with my college tuition. My life was progressing as I had always dreamed. I especially appreciated the car he bought me, in which Cathy and I took many a scenic afternoon drive. It was like a ticket out of town that could be redeemed at any time. I really tested how that Grand Am handled the night Cathy and I had the fight. I drove up Highway 52 to the Blue Ridge Parkway, cutting curves and weaving between the truck lane and passing lanes of the highway. I had the accelerator to the floor on the Parkway's straight stretches, but she was so upset at me she didn't even flinch.

"What's the problem that you won't talk to me?" I kept asking.

"You know, we don't have to have this conversation. You could have just went home."

"Well, I don't want to. I want to find out what's wrong with us, with you and me. Is it something I said or didn't say? Something I did or didn't do?"

"It's nothing like that," she said, exasperated.

I gripped the steering wheel like it was clay squeezing through my fingers. Out to my left I looked past the breaks in the trees onto the lights of Mount Airy and the piedmont. I could tell Cathy was stifling tears because she began wiping her cheeks with the backs of her hand and rubbing them on her blue jeans.

"What is it then?! How can I possibly make things right if I don't know what it is? It's like you are shutting me out or something."

"Just take me home."

"You know what? Fuck it. We're not going anywhere." I screeched into the next scenic overlook. With one movement of resolution, I grabbed the keys out of the ignition, got out of the car, and walked off, making sure to slam the car door with every bit of my frustration. About ten feet from where I parked, I collapsed on the grassy curb, keys cutting into the palm of my hand. It was quiet on the overlook, and must have rained some time ago. A small breeze carried itself up from the piedmont and over the ridge. Crickets chirped somewhere down in the woods.

This was not how I envisioned it turning out. This was not the plan. How could she expect me to stay, with the way things were at home? How could she possibly understand? Cathy and her parents had always gotten along, and she had lived in the same house her whole life. She had no idea what it was like for me. When I tried explaining once what was happening to me at home, about what my father did, how my mother didn't seem to care about me, I broke down crying. She simply stared blankly down at her feet as she sat beside me on the couch. It felt like she was embarrassed to be with me, or that she was disappointed in me because I wasn't stronger. She might as well have just cut my nuts off.

I took a deep breath of the night air and swallowed hard. I refused to fall apart. I took another deep breath. I was going to be strong. The coolness of my face and neck from the evaporating tears made me shiver. I looked up from the lights of the distant communities to the summer sky. The clouds had passed and I could see the stars, like pin pricks in a black tarp. I stared searchingly at their patterns, wishing I knew their names. The Big Dipper punctuated the darkness, but stood empty. To the right, the end of its ladle pointed out the North Star, the same way it always has for sailors and explorers since the beginning of time. But it had nothing to show me, no direction to point me toward. All the other star clusters were just clumps without form, without stories, spinning in arcs of vacuous bliss. I wanted to raise my hands and scream at God, reach in with my fingers and pull the heavens to a grinding halt, for my body to be crushed by the cogs and gear teeth, but the slow constellations wheeled on.

I was exhausted, tired of holding things together when everyone else was willing to let it fall apart. I knew what I had to do, but I watched the sky just a little longer for a sign, to see if Cathy was going to come out of the car to sit or talk to me, or at least check on me. But she didn't, and I decided that was reason enough. I reached into my shirt for the chain I wore. I pulled so hard at her class ring that the chain cut into my neck. On the second pull I was successful in breaking it, and when I came back to the car I tossed both ring and chain on the dash board in front of her. It fell into the air vent. Damn, I thought, as I sat back in the driver's seat.

Cathy didn't look at me, but she knew what I slung at her. "So it's over, then?" she said without emotion.

"Well, you leave me no choice, don't you?"

"I can't go with you, Randall. I'm tired of going around in circles trying to convince you otherwise. I'm not going to ask you to stay anymore, either."

"Good, because my mind's made up. I'm leaving tonight. My stuff's already packed. I can't stay." There was a long pause where all that could be heard was our labored breaths and the aching chasm growing with each wordless moment.

"Look. I really am sorry your grandfather died. I know you loved him a lot. But it's not my fault your father ran off with your college tuition money and that girl from Sylvatus...." She stopped abruptly. "You need to let it go and get on with your life."

"That's what I intend to do."

"You have a life here. What about your mother?"

"My mother – is just a shell of a person! She left *me* a long time ago," I burst out in disgust, spittle flying from my mouth. I stopped. The more I talked, the more I felt like I was turning into something worse than my father, a ball of excuses and pent-up rage. No. I was making a clean break. Right now.

I started the ignition and spun the car around, over the curb and the little mound of grass, and skidded onto the Parkway. After that, I didn't speak another word or take a curve too sharp in anger. Sensing the finality of my actions, Cathy sat quietly in the passenger's seat all the way back to her house.

8 _____

I just finished wiping down my station and boxing a few pick-up orders when Craig asked me.

"Rocker! Why don't you give me a ride up to the corner store for some smokes? It's almost closing. You probably won't get any more deliveries tonight, anyway." Craig wiped down his counter as he spoke over his shoulder at me.

It had been a slow night again. I hadn't made more than $40 in tips. I'm sure some other larger pizza chain had some deal going, or had been passing out flyers around campus or something. I always thought we might get more business at Papa's Pizza if we advertised more.

"You want me to drive you where?"

"To the corner store for some smokes."

"Why don't I just pick up a pack for you on my way back in from a run?"

"I can't wait that long, Dude! Besides, if someone orders something right before closing they deserve to wait. Come on."

I looked around for Dean. He must have been in the back. I looked at my watch, which read 12:45. We would be closing in 15 minutes. Though we were not supposed to be goofing off this close to closing, I didn't want to be seen as a goody two-shoes either. "Okay," I said, "but I want to get back in time to help the guys clean up."

"You mean help Lindsey?" He leaned in close and spoke under his breath. "It's alright by me if you want to do her mopping job for her, just don't expect to get anything in return. She's out of your league, Dude."

I began to blush. "I don't know what you're talking about. I just like to make sure I'm pulling my weight around here."

I drove him up to the top of the hill to an old gas station, next to an auto parts store that looked like it had been closed for years. I decided to walk in there with him and get a Coca-Cola in a glass bottle – which tastes better than in the plastic ones – and a pack of Nabs. The convenience store had a greenish glow about it, an air that smelled of dust and dry dog food, and drink coolers that rattled like they were about to die. Craig sauntered in ahead of me and went to the front, dropping his money on the counter. Some of his dreads hung out of his knitted cap.

"Yes, I'll have two packets of Salem Lights."

I grabbed my 10 ounce bottle of Coke, and decided on a pack of red-skinned peanuts. When I approached the counter, the cashier and her husband were in an intense conversation. Her husband, a tall, skinny man with balding hair and liver spots sat on a stool off to the side of the register.

"The signs are all around us, you know. Trouble brewin' in the Middle East. Famines. All you got to do is turn on the TV and see the signs."

"That's right," said the old lady pulling down the packs of cigarettes from their overhead slot, cutting a strange look at Craig. Craig had an impatient, exasperated look on his face.

The old man continued, "Why, it's just like it says in Revelations about the New World Order and the end of days.

"You said it, Ned," the old lady chimed in again, smiling faintly and handing Craig the change. "Armageddon could even be here with the new millennium."

"It's called Revelation," said Craig. "And besides, people have been thinking the end's coming soon ever since the first century. Nobody knows when the world is going to end," and then under his breath, "least of all some dried-up old geezer like you."

"Excuse me, young man?" The old man looked at us, wide-eyed. "I think I know my Bible pretty well, *especially* the book of Revelations. Who do you think you are?"

"Craig, let's just go!" I pleaded under my breath. I wanted to pretend I didn't know him, drive off and leave him there.

"No, no, Randall," he said without taking his eyes off the old man. "I get sick of all these smug, ignorant, self-righteous people who think they have all the answers."

"Velma, get my bible!" the old man ordered his wife. With a perturbed look, she stepped behind a doorway and came back out with a tattered, black leather-bound book. "Son, I've been readin' the word of God since I was called at 14. I think I know what I'm talking about." He held his bible out in front of him and shook as he talked.

"Well, you go ahead and check it. I know there's no 's' on Revelation," said Craig. "There's only one."

I paid for my drink and peanuts. The old man flipped with discerning fervor. He stopped and opened his mouth to speak, then shut it again. "Get out of here before I call the cops on you, you smart ass."

"Hey, that's Mother-Fuckin' Smart Ass to you, buddy!"

"Come on, Craig!" I said. "You proved your point."

When we walked out the door, I quietly asked, "What was that all about in there? We were in our uniforms and everything. I hope they don't call Dean and say we were harassing them or something."

"Chill out! That old bag of farts was snubbing me, I could tell. And that woman looked at my hat and my dreads and crinkled her nose like she was afraid she might catch something from the air I was bringing in. That just pissed me off, and then they got to talkin' 'bout religion, like I really wanted to hear about it. Don't worry." Unwrapping the cellophane, he popped the lid open with his thumb and pulled a cigarette out of the hard pack with his lips, extending the pack to me. "Wanna cig, before we get back to work?"

"No thanks. I'm trying to quit."

"Yeah. It's a dirty habit," he laughed. I chuckled along with him, and hoped he didn't realize how embarrassed I felt. The woman reminded me of a great aunt I might've had back home.

Lindsey was already mopping when we got back. I washed all the utensils and empty topping tubs after wiping down my station again. Dean let a few people off early since it wasn't going to take everybody to clean shop. The health inspector came a few weeks ago and gave us a 98.5. Dean told me that it was because of all the extra work I had been doing lately.

"Wipe your feet, Rocker," said Lindsey, my arms elbow-deep in soapy water.

"What?"

"Step on the mop and wipe your feet so you won't leave dirty wet footprints all over my newly-mopped floor." I awkwardly stepped up on her mop head while trying to rinse a set of tongs. "Hey, could you be a dear and go over the floor one more time with a dry mop for me? I'll pay you back sometime, I promise. I gotta get home and get a good night's sleep. I am beat, and I got a test tomorrow." She tucked a dark strand of hair behind her pink ear and smiled, then adjusted her cap.

"Well, okay. Since you asked so nicely."

"Thanks, Rocker. You're a peach." She gave me a little pinch on the back of my elbow. I looked over to see the other guys standing around the prep counter. Craig looked at me and smirked with raised eyebrows. I went back to washing dishes, and decided Craig would just have to bum a ride for cigs off someone else next time.

9

This week I was scheduled for several day shifts, and today was my last one. I didn't have to work the next day, and my only class then was in the early afternoon, so I wasn't in a hurry to get home after a slow day of deliveries. Day shifts were the worst for tips, and sometimes didn't make up for all the gas you used. I usually changed out of my uniform before leaving the store if I had some errands to run, to save a trip to my apartment. Today was no different. I hated getting those out-of-place looks from other people for still having my work clothes on in some other place of business, like I was wearing scuba gear on a ski slope or something.

Driving through evening town traffic, I decided to stop at a grocery store for a few things: coffee, Ramen Noodles, a loaf of bread, and some peanut butter. Maybe I'd splurge and get a steak. The atmosphere in the supermarket was soothing, almost ethereal, with the background music and the sanitizing fluorescent lights. It made me feel normal. Shopping was something everyone did. It was communal. I could push the cart around for a half hour, saying "excuse me" if I was in anyone's way, and feel like I belonged to a group of human beings here on earth for the same purpose. I started in the produce section, slowly walking around like I was checking out every banana or head of lettuce. Then I made my way through the deli and bakery. I was starting to get hungry; everything smelled so good.

As I pushed my rickety buggy up the frozen foods aisle in the center of the store, I saw Lindsey and a few other girls walk in. I stopped slouching over the handles and straightened my back to try to look more confident, yet casual as I pushed my few groceries around, feigning not to have noticed their entrance, hoping they didn't see me just the same. A brunette and an unnaturally-looking blonde accompanied her.

"Hey Rocker! Is that you?" Lindsey exclaimed as the three of them filed through a closed checkout line.

"Oh, hey Lindsey."

"Is that his real name?" asked the blonde, incredulously.

"That's his nickname at the pizza place. He's cool. Works too hard, though." Lindsey stepped up on the end of the buggy, grabbing the front like a little girl about to go for a ride. "Listen, Randy, how'd you like to check out this party with us above King Street?"

I was caught off guard by the question, and didn't know quite how to respond. "Well, I didn't have any immediate plans for the night."

The brunette chimed in, "Yeah, and it's a BYOB party."

"A what?"

"Bring your own booze. You don't get out much, do you?" The blonde smirked.

I imagined running over the blonde with my shopping cart when Lindsey added, "Give him a break, Felicity," and then turning to me, "what we are *trying* to get at is that Felicity and I didn't bring our ID's, and Megan here won't turn 21 until next month. Let us grab a couple of 12-packs of Bud Light and we'll chip in to buy your groceries. I owe you a little anyway for helping me win some money last weekend in that 30-dollar bet, and putting a few of those guys in their places."

"I should be thanking you. I felt like I was drowning in there before you came in. I...." I then realized what she was asking. "You want me to buy beer for you?" I scratched the whiskers on the end of my chin nervously.

"If it wouldn't be too much trouble? You could leave your car here and ride with us." The two other girls glanced at each other with raised eyebrows. Lindsey leaned over the cart toward me, tilting her low-cut collar in my direction. Her cleavage was milky-white and smooth, with a few freckles dotted evenly between them. I looked up quickly, wondering if she noticed where my eyes wandered.

"Well, okay. No problem."

"Awesome! You're a peach, Randy." Lindsey came around the shopping cart and playfully punched me in the ribs, then grabbed the handle bar out of my grasp. "C'mon, let's jet." I followed the girls to the front corner of the store, past the dairy section. They loaded two cases of Bud Light and a six-pack of Zima. I wondered what being a peach meant to her.

"Okay, Rocker. We're going to hang back a little bit so we don't look like we're with you. Then we'll come in behind you with a few things. We'll be out of here in no time." She handed me three twenties and gave the cart back to me.

There was only one register open out of eight in the small grocery store, and a girl about my age stood behind the counter. I pushed the cart to her register and she started pulling things out and ringing them up.

"Did you find everything you were looking for?" She asked mechanically without looking at me.

"Yes, just fine. Thanks." She rang up the first case of beer, and an off-key beep resounded from the register.

"Can I see your driver's license, please?"

I reached into my back pocket for my wallet and pulled it out.

The cashier looked at the birth date and the photo. She looked at me, and then back at the card, then back at me. She stopped and picked at the corner of the laminate with her thumbnail.

"I'm going to have to get a supervisor to confirm this."

"What do you mean? What's the problem?" Hot panic swelled in my throat. The cashier didn't answer me, but picked up the receiver of her telephone and paged the office.

"What the hell's taking so long?" Lindsey complained, obviously playing the role of the disgruntled shopper, and gave me a half-conspiring, half-quizzical look.

"Do you really want to know?" The cashier cocked her head toward Lindsey, then rolled her eyes in annoyance, phone in hand. "First, this laminate job is crappy. Second, the mustache in his photo? I mean, come on. Look at him!"

Lindsey grabbed the phone and slammed it back down on the hook. "Look, I haven't got time for this shit!" She flashed a box of O.B.'s in front of the cashier's face. "I am way overdue for changing my tampon, and I can feel my uterus draining as we speak. Send him the hell on, or else you're going to ruin one of my best pairs of designer jeans, and I'm going to take it out of your till!"

Wide-eyed and miffed, the cashier typed in some numbers. She looked at Lindsey, then me, and turned her eyes to the empty office at the front of the store. I prayed the manager wouldn't show up. I felt like I was robbing a bank or something. The cashier punched some more numbers, then proceeded to ring up the other case of beer and the rest of the groceries. "Better not try this again if you know what's good for you," she muttered to me. I pushed the groceries out the door without looking back. Lindsey and her friends caught up with me halfway to my car.

"Hail Lindsey, the Drama Queen!" shouted Felicity.

"You almost had me convinced you *were* on the rag!" said Megan.

"You are soooo lucky!" said Lindsey, sidling up to me. "Let me see your license."

"What for?" I asked.

"C'mon, it's okay. Let me see it," she said again. I turned the cart around to keep it from rolling into my car and pulled it out from my front pocket. Lindsey and the others looked closely. "Well, if I knew that you had such a bad fake ID, I wouldn't have asked you." The other two girls snickered.

"Is that one of those fake 70's porno mustaches?" Felicity held the laminated card close to their faces in the dark parking lot.

"So you weren't really born in 1974? How old are you, really? asked Lindsey.

"I'm 20," I lied. "I was just tired of not being able to do what I wanted to do." The two girls looked at me skeptically, then grabbed the beer out of my cart and walked four spaces over to Lindsey's car, whispering and giggling as they went. I felt their distance in the cold wind blowing down from Howards Knob, and it made my face burn. I hated those types of prissy debutants.

After I dropped my few bags of groceries into my trunk, Lindsey slipped her hand around the crook of my arm and walked me to her car. "Don't worry about it. I know where you're coming from. Last year I couldn't wait to turn 21, but once I did it wasn't such a big deal at all. Like losing your virginity. I'm sorry I didn't have my ID." She flicked the card back to me, holding it between her fingers. I tucked it into my back pocket. "Who made that for you?"

"I made it myself. James, a guy I knew from high school, showed me how to do it." Still, I didn't think I did too badly with a Polaroid camera and laminating kit.

"I think it's the fake mustache that gave it away. You look old enough without it, and more handsome, anyway," she stated matter-of-factly. I blushed at the compliment. I could not believe a girl five years older was flirting with me! Then I remembered. I couldn't act like I was 16, so I tried subduing what I'm sure was a goofy adolescent smile on my face.

The other girls already had the car started and the heater running full blast. I took the back seat with the brunette, much to her dismay. Lindsey got behind the wheel, and the four of us pulled out into Highland Street traffic.

"I don't know how you can stand to live up here, Lindsey. It's too fucking cold!" said the brunette as she shivered.

I smiled to myself over these girls being such sissies, so different from Lindsey. "So, where are you from, uh...," I asked the brunette, trying to remember.

"It's Megan, again by the way. We drove up from Chapel Hill for the week to raise a little hell with our BFF, Lindsey."

"Yeah, that stands for Best Friends Forever," she said to me, and then to Lindsey, "and every time I try calling you, you're at work or something."

"Well, I got to pay the bills, Felicity. My financial aid will only cover tuition. I'm sure your daddy's money only goes so far, doesn't it?" Felicity gives a playful "screw you" look at Lindsey as she checked her makeup in the rearview mirror. "Your tuition probably doesn't set you back too much, does it, Randy?" Lindsey says over her shoulder, trying to include me in the conversation.

"What do you mean?"

"You go to the community college, don't you?"

Yeah, that's my plan for now." I was caught off guard by her probing question, and a little embarrassed in front of these rich Chapel Hill friends of hers.

"My younger brother went there because his grades weren't so hot, and is transferring to WSU in the spring. It's easier to get in when you transfer than coming in as a freshman anyway."

"Oh, please," said Megan. "It is so easy to get into WSU, period. Everyone I know that goes here couldn't get accepted anywhere else! No offense, Lindsey."

"None taken. I shouldn't have goofed off and partied so much in high school, or I'd be walking down Franklin Street right now with you guys, and a Carolina frat boy on each arm."

"Yeah, and if you had given a blow job to your SAT administrator, maybe!" joked Felicity.

Lindsey flicked Felicity on the end of her nose as she drove. "You hateful cunt!" she laughed.

I was a little startled by their rough language. I had heard girls drop the "f" bomb before, but this was a little more than I was used to, and it was strangely exciting. I was not to be put off by Megan's comment, though. "My grades were fine. I just couldn't pay the tuition for WSU, but I'm saving up for it. It's a long story." Inside I was kicking myself for running my mouth too much in the first place and letting these girls get under my skin. They probably already thought I was just some local hick from the hills since I first opened my mouth.

57

Lindsey made a right off King Street and up Grand Boulevard. She passed a few streets that ran laterally to the main street until I saw a bunch of cars, and parked down from where all the activity was, almost blocking someone's driveway. I thought about my own car left in the grocery parking lot, my only means of making a decent wage. If they tow it, I'm screwed because I won't be able to get it out of impound in time to get to class tomorrow afternoon, unless I walked five miles to the main campus or waited an hour for the transit system. We got out with beer in tote, and headed up the street.

"So, what are you majoring in?" I asked Lindsey, trying to make conversation as we walked. I couldn't help but notice how her breasts jumped slightly as she swung her arms.

"Besides partying?" Megan laughed.

"You're one to talk. The last party you went to had a clown that made funny balloon animals!"

"It was my niece's birthday, okay?" The three girls laughed like they were already tipsy.

"Listen, Randy," coached Lindsey. "This isn't a big affair, so just relax and be yourself. You'll probably meet some people from work here, too. Paul will probably be here, maybe even Ollie. I hear he's got a job over at Domino's now." I wondered before if my nervousness showed through, until Lindsey's comments confirmed it. She shifted the beer to her other arm and gave me a little squeeze on the shoulder. It sent warm shivers down my back. "You work too hard, Rocker. You need to *relax!*"

The sound of raucous laughter and muffled, throbbing bass came from inside. It sounded like gangster rap, but I wasn't sure. Some people were out on the porch, while others sauntered around in the yard, talking in little groups. Its dirt and weed-mottled yard was already littered with red and blue plastic drinking cups.

"Lindsey, is that you? Get your fine ass over here!" came a voice from the front porch. "Have you lost some weight?"

"Warren, how the hell are you?" Lindsey shot back. A slightly pudgy guy neatly dressed in jeans and a sweater came down from the steps waving a cigarette between his fingers with much drama. The other girls motioned with the beer and proceeded to the kitchen to put it on ice.

"Warren, this is Randy. He works with me at the pizza place. Randy, this is my very gay friend, Warren." I tried to stifle my surprise before extending my hand to shake.

"Just because I'm on the market, Lindsey, doesn't mean you have to advertise it to everyone!" he said in an exasperated huff.

"Nice to meet you," I said.

"My, what a strong grip you have! Is this one taken?" Warren took my hand, giving a wink to Lindsey.

"Oh, Randy is pretty straight, I do believe," Lindsey replied. "Sorry to disappoint you."

"Uh, yeah. No hard feelings." I tried laughing. I was made a little uneasy by Warren's flamboyant display, maybe not so much because he was gay but because I had never met a gay guy before, I guess, and didn't know how to act. I replayed Lindsey's "straight" comment in my head and wondered if she noticed me staring at her boobs.

"Oh, what a waste, what a waste," replied Warren, with a sigh and more than an air of melodrama. "Shall we?" he asked. Lindsey and Warren linked arms like Dorothy and the Scarecrow and skipped inside. I stared at the porch steps, then to the groups of people congregating inside. I wasn't really into parties much in high school, and this was definitely not a high school party. I thought about turning around and retreating. Do I dare? I took a deep breath and stepped through the threshold.

* * * *

The house was much smaller than it looked from the outside, with 40 or more people hovering in little groups or three or four, sitting on the couches and chairs, going up and down the stairs, or making their way to the back kitchen, where I noticed a couple of kegs of beer in trash cans of ice. The whir of a blender filled the air as some people made frozen drinks.

"What'll it be, Chief?" asked a guy in a Blind Melon t-shirt. He was filling red Dixie cups from a nozzle attached to a keg.

"Cans and bottles are in coolers on the back porch, and we've got Budweiser and Rolling Rock on tap."

"How much?" I asked.

"How much?!" He chuckled, and looked at the guy standing next to him. "For one night only, it's all you can drink for the low, low price of your momma's ass."

"Hell, man, give him a break," the other guy said. "The only thing *you're* going to be tapping tonight is the next keg!" He turned back to me and handed me a cup. "One King of Beers it is. And when you need refills, help yourself. Don't let this dumbass serve you again." I took the plastic cup from him and wandered off.

After a few drinks of social lubricant, I was feeling pretty good. More people arrived as the night progressed, but it was still early, only a little after eleven. I mostly made small talk with the guys from work, trying to avoid Lindsey's girlfriends. Lindsey had been doing her own thing, talking with others, making rounds from room to room, but had bumped in to me every now and then to introduce me to someone she knew or to ask me if she could get me a refill. There was a thin air of anxiety still hovering around me. Most of these people I didn't know, and they didn't seem too interested in striking up a conversation with me. The only one I really knew, Lindsey, had seemingly lost interest in me. I had a hard time reading her. Did she just use me to buy beer? I kept getting urges to just leave the party and go back to get my car. Maybe I should, I thought.

From the stereo in the living room came a slow reggae beat with the singer repeating "Keeeep it stirred." It was infectious, though I had never heard the song before. Some of the other workers from the pizza place gathered on a sofa and a few encircled chairs. I sat down to join them.

"So, is Ollie still around? I wanted to get some tips on how I could out-maneuver ol' Aaron next time he tried beating me back to the store for the best runs!"

Paul, who had his arm around Lindsey's friend, Felicity, spoke up. "Nah, you just missed him about an hour ago. He didn't stay too long, just came to make a delivery."

"A delivery of what?" slurred Megan, who was well past three-sheets-to-the-wind, looking around. "Where's the pizza?"

Paul answered in hushed tones. "Shhh. He's got some good home-grown connections, does some 'gardening.' Mostly though, his family is an old-school supplier of hooch." No reply from the Chapel Hill girls. "You know, moonshine, white lightning. What do you think is in your Daiquiri, by the way?"

Grandma Spivey, my dad's mom, used to tell me stories – how the thin blue smoke from the stills would rise from the back-wood hollows below her house on cold mornings. You could never find where they made it, she said, but you knew they were out there.

"Have you got any straight?" I asked.

"Woo-hoo! That's what I'm talking about! Somebody get this man a jar," shouted Paul. Craig came out of the kitchen with a narrow-mouthed, quart jar. His matted dreadlocks were hanging loosely from his head.

Lindsey smirked at me and handed me the jar after taking herself a swig. "Smooth! Here you go, Rocker. Go easy."

I held the corn liquor up to the light and swished it around until a few balls, like quicksilver bubbles, rolled along the surface tension of the alcohol before quickly dropping back in. "Beads good," I replied, and took a long sip. Lindsey's friends looked on in wonder.

"What did you just do, Rocker?" asked Megan.

"Oh, I was just checking the quality of it, and let me tell you," I paused and sipped again, "this is well over 100 proof, the real deal," trying to impress the others with this small knowledge. "It's good you keep this in a glass jar. This would eat through the bottom of a plastic jug before too long."

"See, I told you I didn't drink that half gallon jug you kept under the sink at my apartment! It must've leaked out," Paul said to Craig.

I remembered the story about Grandpa Spivey's secret still. He kept it at one point in the dairy parlor. There was so much machinery for collecting and refrigerating the milk, as well as milk cans, and a stovepipe that went out one of the side windows, that it was kept well camouflaged. No one questioned the smoke rising from it. But what my grandmother never told me was how it tasted. I found that out for the first time at the age of 12, when I came across a few jars hidden behind some old canned sausage in her root cellar. Grandpa Spivey must have thought no one would look behind the dusty glass jars of fat-congealed meat. That didn't stop my curiosity, though. I don't remember how many sips I took, but I sure remember puking my toenails up in the calving barn. With a little less reservation this time, I tilted the jar back against my lips and took a larger swig. It started like water on the back of my tongue, and then followed with the burn in my chest. It was as if I had just swallowed a hot, candy-coated campfire coal.

"Whoo! That's good! Right down the gullet!" I handed it across to Paul who, not to be outdone, took an even longer swig. I started to feel it within minutes, and with it, a welling of confidence. Still, I kept reminding myself not to act like an idiot. I didn't want to forget how fine the line between cool and social outcast was for me.

"You're not kidding, Rocker!" exclaimed Paul. "This is some good shit!"

*   *   *   *

The night progressed. After I tied on a good buzz with everyone else, I began to loosen up. These people, who were just acquaintances from work, began to seem like old friends. I liked it more than I allowed myself to let on, lest I seem like a novice at this. Going to parties and drinking wasn't something Cathy condoned, and though it didn't matter at the time, now it was different. Inside I craved this fellowship, especially the attention Lindsey had now been heaping on me. It filled a void that was empty since I left home.

The stereo was playing another reggae song. It was warm and almost spiritual. – *One body, in communion, give love and praise to the Almighty, because He's on high* – Things felt all right. I was trying not to go overboard, so I retired from the corn liquor and was nursing a beer. – *Is there hope for the lost and forsaken?* – What was that old saying, liquor before beer, never fear? I couldn't remember, but I didn't feel sick, far from it. – *From the beginning, the word also was* – Paul and Craig were hanging all over Lindsey's friends, Felicity and

Megan. Lindsey was sitting close to me, laughing and putting her hand on my thigh every time I told a joke, a cigarette in the other hand.

"'I asked for a million bucks, not a million ducks!' And the bartender said, 'Yeah, and do you think I rubbed this lamp asking for a 12-inch pianist?'" I had Paul rolling in the floor.

Warren had joined our group sometime ago, and sat on the other side of Lindsey. I was amazed that, under all that flamboyant act he put on, he was just as normal as everyone else in the group. I noticed some of the other groups at the party were thinning out. I was afraid that if too many people started going home, this moment would be cut short. I was having such a good time; I didn't want it to end. It was around two o'clock, and I wasn't a bit tired. Craig and Megan got up to get a drink, but didn't come back. I was even afraid at first that if I went to the bathroom upstairs to take a leak, I would come back down to find everyone else gone, but I got over that after the first couple of trips to the john. I thought I might have a little hangover in the morning, which would make getting ready for my afternoon P.E. class especially rough. Maybe I could catch up on my sleep afterwards, I thought.

"And I told my advisor to kiss my ass! So that's how I was able to switch out of Mr. Goldwater's class." Paul was finishing one of his many stories about successfully slacking his way through college. "Hey, guys, Felicity and I are going to go out and get some smokes down the street. You need anything, Rocker?"

"Naw, I'm fine." I tried all night not to let on that I didn't smoke. "I'm trying to quit."

"It's a shame I didn't get any weed tonight, or I'd roll you a real fat one," said Paul. You need anything, Warren? Lindsey?"

"I'm good," she said, and then to her friend, "Felicity, you watch out for this guy. He's a wolf in sheep's clothing." Felicity just giggled as Paul pulled her to him and let out a half-hearted howl. After all their talk about frat boys, it was funny to see Megan and Felicity become less picky by the end of the night, ultimately ending up with a couple of pie slingers. When they got up, I realized that Lindsey, Warren, and I were the only ones left in our group. "You know, Rocker? I've worked with you for over two months and we've never got to sit down and get to know each other," Lindsey exclaimed as if it was a great travesty. She was clearly drunk, maybe more than I was, but still in control of her faculties it seemed. "So tell me a little about yourself." Lindsey put her chin on her hand and leaned forward, letting her straight, dark hair cascade around her shoulders, and batted her hazel eyes at me.

"Well, there's really not much to tell. I grew up my whole life in a little factory town northeast of here in Virginia, called Galax."

"Gay-lax? Lindsey giggled at its pronunciation. Sounds like a laxative Warren would take!" She laughed again and elbowed Warren in the ribs. My eyes got wide as I turned to Warren for his response. Warren just rolled his eyes and got up to leave in mock offense.

"You're just jealous because I get more dick than you do," he said.

"You are probably right, if you count the times you five-knuckle shuffle!"

Warren's mouth dropped. "Oh no you didn't! You know my date didn't show up tonight. That was harsh."

"Warren, I'm sorry." Lindsey got up to hug him, trying not to laugh through the pouty look on her face. "I promise sometime next week we'll go out together to see a movie at the dollar theater down the street."

"Yeah, and you're buying the popcorn and Milk Duds, bitch!" Warren faked and attitude, then immediately smiled. "See you two kids later," and with that, he kissed Lindsey on the cheek, took a bow, and left with a flourish.

"Yeah, see ya Warren." I got a little sidetracked from the conversation, and wanted to return to it. "Galax is actually named after a leaf that people collect and use in the winter for making ornamental wreaths and stuff." Lindsey looked at me and nodded with a smile, but didn't seem to recognize what I was referring to, so I changed the topic. "So where are you originally from?"

"Oh, I lived most of my life in Winston-Salem, and a few years of high school with my mother in Greensboro when my parents divorced. I would love to have gone to Wake Forest, but definitely didn't have the grades, and both Wake and UNC-Greensboro was just too close to home. I had to get away from my parents, you know what I mean?"

"More than you know."

"Did your parents divorce, too?" My buzz began to fade with her sobering question.

I sighed deeply. "No. My father ran off with another woman, but my mother is still waiting for him to get tired of the slut and return so she can take him back for the umpteenth time. The slut." I tilted my beer and chugged the remains, tossing the can in the corner. "My dad's an idiot."

"Sounds fucked up." Lindsey pulled out the remains of the moonshine jar and two shot glasses from a side table. After wiping the inside of the shot glasses with her shirttail, she poured us two drinks with an air of formality. "Here's to fucked-up parents!" She raised her glass, and I quickly followed suit. We both tossed back our drinks. This shot didn't go down as good as the others, and I wondered if I should stop drinking for the night altogether.

Someone had shuffled the CD changer to play "Party Hardy," a Brooklyn Boys song I recognized from the fourth grade. I used to play it in the juke box at the roller skating rink.

"Turn it up!" I heard someone say, which they quickly did.

"Hey! Paaarty haaaaardeeee!" a few revelers chanted the chorus.

"So, Rocker, how do you come to know so much about nature and stuff? You don't seem like one of those hippie granola types." Lindsey's question surprised me. I didn't think she was paying attention.

"Well, my grandmother on my father's side was what the old folks called a 'wildcrafter.' She used to collect roots and bark of certain plants to sell to pharmacies for a little extra money, I mean income. But that was a long time ago. I bet she knew the names of over 100 different herbs, flowers, and stuff."

The bass seemed to get even more pronounced. "Damn, they turned that music up way too much, you can't even hear yourself think!" Lindsey stood up and held a hand out to me. "Let's go outside where it's not so loud."

With that, I gave my hand to her to pull me off the couch, then pulled a little too much, bringing me to stumble into her. Though she smelled a little like cigarettes, her hair wafted of flowery shampoo. "Whoa! You okay?"

"Yeah. No problem," I tried to conceal the flood of emotions I felt from being so close to her. I wondered if I should call it a night.

"Let's go out the back door. I know a really cool place I think you'd like to check out." Lindsey took my hand and pulled me through the living room, past a couple of guys holding a girl's legs up to do a keg stand. She wore a skirt, and it had flipped down to reveal a pair of pink panties with little red hearts. I turned my face in modesty, my ears flushed with heat. The boys kept chanting 'Chug! Chug! Chug!' as the two of us walked out the back door.

The air was cold and sharp, but the wind off Howards Knob had subsided. Also, there was a tall hedge circling the house's small back yard. "Where are we going?" I asked, trying not to sound anxious. She just grinned and led me through the row of cedars to the neighbor's back yard directly behind.

There was a greenhouse about the size of a one-car garage, made of glass with a steel frame. It was dark inside, but I could see condensation collecting in the upper panes. "Come on, you gotta see this!" Lindsey beckoned. I was unsure about trespassing in this person's back yard, even more so about breaking and entering, but her tight grip on my hand and her warm smile urged me to oblige her. She quietly turned the handle of the door to see if it was locked, found that it wasn't, and peeked her head inside like she was checking for something. We slid in quietly and latched the door behind us.

"Wow!" I exclaimed. Inside, the greenhouse was warm, but not completely dark. The reflection of the downtown lights in the air above gave the room a faint glow. On several tables stood rows and rows of Poinsettias, some red, some white, and some a rosy pink. Christmas was just a little over a month away. There was a slightly bitter, almost medicinal smell to the air inside. I walked up to one of the tables and picked up a pot for closer inspection. "I haven't seen this many Poinsettias at one time, ever! I wonder if this guy sells them for a living."

"I told you you'd like it." She clutched my hand again. "It's very cozy in here, isn't it?" With that, she leaned into me, putting one hand on the small of my back and the other around my shoulder. I gasped, startled. She muffled it with a kiss.

My body arced with an electrical charge. Her advance caught me off guard. I stepped back a little from her grasp, too shocked at first of my own arousal. She broke her kiss, but stood looking straight into my eyes. "Lindsey," I stammered, "I... had no idea you thought... I mean...."

"Been a while? Don't be so modest." She took one of my hands that held her waist and moved it lower, guiding it to the back of her thigh. She brought her face close to mine again, slower this time, allowing me to draw her closer. My mind was reeling, never having a girl come on to me before. I was feeling the effects of that last shot of moonshine, my inhibitions loosening. I kissed her passionately. It had been so long! She purred and brought her hand between our bodies, trying to grasp the growing erection through my jeans.

There was more than alcohol coursing through my head, an adrenaline high like I had never experienced. This older girl I barely knew was now making out with *me*, and wanting it, without hesitation, without pushing me away in modesty. Still kissing, I explored with my hands, reaching around her waist and up under her shirt, a little higher, to the bra strap in the middle of her back, following it under her arm to the softness of her breast. Lindsey pulled me closer, pushing her pubic bone against me. A jolt of electricity coursed through my brain again, the current running down, then back up to my giddy head, completing the circuit. I was afraid I might pass out.

How many minutes had passed, I had no idea. I didn't remember undoing her bra or hiking up her shirt. All I knew at that moment was soft skin, firm kisses, perspiration, and a growing euphoria. Without saying a word, Lindsey pulled me down on top of her to a pile of flattened cardboard boxes that were spread out. The concrete floor seemed to give way from under us.

Questions like "how far?" and "should I stop?" barely made a sound in my mind over the rushing crescendo of testosterone and blood pressure billowing inside me. My legs were caught between hers as she rolled on top of me, pressing herself against me. My consciousness began to float out of my skin, hovering in the air just above us. I ran my hands over her, enveloped my face between her breasts, caressed her neck with kisses.

"Oh Rocker, yes!" she whispered in my ear, holding tightly to my shoulders, thrusting against me. "Do you have a condom? God, I want you to fuck me *so* bad!"

The force of a shotgun blast went off in the back of my head, followed by several recoils in the depths of my abdomen. My lips went numb. All at once extreme pleasure collided with extreme panic. I knew what had happened. Lindsey sensed me tighten, the spasms running through my body. Looking down at my crotch confirmed what she already knew.

"You must be joking!" she exclaimed, breaking from the moment. I froze in complete, utter embarrassment. I didn't even notice Lindsey reaching into my pants and down the front of my boxers. She pulled her hand out and rubbed her thumb and forefinger together, then smiled with dismay. "I've been told I was a cock tease, but if I didn't know any better, Randy, I'd say this was your first time. You're already going soft." She smirked and looked at me from under her long bangs in playful disappointment.

Something had changed in her eyes. It was as if I stood naked in front of her, not just bare skinned, but all my heart and genitals spread out in broad daylight for her and the world to see. Yes, I'm a 16-year-old virgin, yes, I'm inexperienced, and yes, you are the first girl I've been this far with, I wanted to confess, to scream at her. But I was mortified and angered all at once. My waning manhood was on exhibition. I felt robbed of my masculinity, leaving nothing but a premature-ejaculating, pubescent boy in its place. I stumbled to my feet, knocking over a potted plant.

"Wait, where are you going, Randy?" she asked, seemingly concerned, but I couldn't speak. Not saying a word for fear my voice would crack and send me back to the eighth grade, I got up, my eyes still trapped by her playful look, and staggered backwards out of the greenhouse. She said something else to me, but I didn't catch it.

I wanted to run as fast as I could, but was afraid to draw attention to myself from the other party-goers, who were probably lurking in the bushes, huddled from the cold and consumed by their own experienced lusts, watching me walk shamefully back to King Street. I had left my jacket on the couch, and my teeth began to chatter. The wind blew sharply through my flannel shirt, half-unbuttoned, as I set my mind toward retrieving my car. Even when I was out of sight of the house, I still felt eyes on me, condescending eyes, from the dark apartment windows hovering over the street, from my own eyes looking back at me through the reflection in the dark shop windows. A lump began to tighten in my throat, and I couldn't swallow it down. Then a sharp pain grew in the back of my head, followed by a wave of emptiness and panic. I saw sparkling spots in front of me and felt a loss of strength in my legs. Taking a deep breath, I tried to regain my composure, but lightheadedness turned to nausea as I stopped to vomit into someone's empty, store-front flower pot.

I looked ahead, and up the sidewalk I saw Paul and Megan walking back to the party, smoking cigarettes and carrying plastic grocery bags. I walked quickly in a panic and turned the corner down Appalachian Street, cutting behind an apartment complex parking lot. I hoped they didn't spot me, my face red, streamed with angry tears. Oh God, were they watching me? Did they know? Are You watching me in disgust, in disappointment? Are You punishing me? Do you even care? The spots in my eyes disappeared, but the emptiness remained. There was no response to my questions it seemed, just the gravel crunching under my feet as I braced against the cold wind.

10

The Japanese Hornets were thick in late summer. They swarmed through the apple trees and buzzed in circles around porch lights. It was a Friday night, and I was reading Spider-Man comics by my bedside lamp. I opened my window to let in a faint breeze. All was quiet except for the infernal racket those hornets kept making. They must have been attracted to the light in my room. I could hear them scratching and rattling the metal screen of my window, trying to get in. It sounded like they were chewing through it with their little mandible jaws, and would cut through any moment and be swarming around me. They could have been tiny raccoons trying to scratch open garbage can lids, they were so loud. One lone cricket, every now and then, would send up a chirp and gently touch the back of my mind.

I wasn't reading much, just couldn't get to sleep. Buzz – thump. Buzz – thump. Buzz – thump, rattle. Those hornets kept at my window screen like someone flipping it with their fingers. Buzz – thump. I was almost back into reading when the thumping became more rhythmic and not in time with the buzzing. I sat straight up in my bed like I was stung. Thump, thump, thump, in quick succession. Someone *was* at my window. "Who's there?" I asked.

"Pssst! Randall, were you asleep? It's me, James."

"Well, if I was, I'm not now. You scared me half to death, though! What are you doing out there in the middle of the night?"

"Beatin' my meat. What do you think? My mom kicked me out of the house again. Let me in, will ya?"

James had thick, dark curly hair and almost a full goatee, not the peach fuzz that most guys tried to grow when they hit puberty. He lived down the street from me in the community of Old Town, across from a set of vacant lots in a housing development that was never finished. My parents might have fought a lot, but they weren't near as messed up as his. Either his dad was home and his mom wasn't, or his mom was home and his dad wasn't, or no one was home and he was by himself taking care of Chad, his six-year-old younger brother, who went everywhere he went when he wasn't at school. When his parents were home, they all fought. Since James was the oldest, I guess he took the brunt of it.

The summer of our ninth-grade year James' parents were out of town almost every weekend. He would throw these huge parties in the basement, making Chad stay up in his room and watch *Teenage Mutant Ninja Turtles*. James became a popular guy. Even some girls came, but they were usually with their boyfriends or had absolutely no interest in someone fresh out of middle school. We'd all watch horror movies like *Hellraiser* and *A Nightmare on Elm Street* on VHS and order pizzas. Some older boys would bring beer and charge two dollars a can, except for the girls, who never had to pay. One time James swore he bought beer at the convenience store down the road with his dad's driver's license, and if he wanted to he could easily make a fake license for himself, and could show me how to do it. I didn't believe him at first, but James did look just like his father, and was a year and a half older than me, too. I didn't know where his parents were during those times, but James' mother eventually caught on about the parties after the neighbors complained about the noise. When he got into fights with his parents, he would end up coming over to my house to cool down, and we would play Nintendo or shoot basketball at a hoop someone nailed to a light pole at the end of the street. That was usually during the day, though.

"Shhh! James, you know I can't let you in. My dad's home. He's been in a stinky mood all evening. He'd kill me if he knew you were here banging outside my window, much less staying over. What happened?" I tried talking as quietly as I could, hoping my parents' window wasn't open. James' voice was only one volume, full blast.

71

"My mom found out I was skimming money out of her purse. I tried telling her it was for school lunch, since there wasn't a damn thing in the house to eat for me or my brother, but she didn't believe me. Then I called her a selfish bitch and said I was going to call social services on her." He said this calmly, but I could tell he was rattled. I did remember a time that his mom accused him of taking money out of a change jar on top of the refrigerator to buy dirty magazines. She had found them between his mattress and bedsprings, not the smartest place to hide them. He had since resorted to hiding them in the woods in some of his mom's Tupperware containers after that. "Speaking of food, have you got anything to eat? I'm starving."

"Keep it down, will you? Hold on a minute. Stay here, and I'll be right back. And don't make any noise!" I didn't want him coming around to the back door because my parents' bedroom was adjacent to it, and they'd hear the door opening. I crept slowly, trying to remember where the squeaks in the floor joists were, in hopes of stepping over and missing them. I hit one as I walked past their door, but both of them kept snoring. I came to a kitchen cabinet and took spittle on my finger to grease the hinges so they wouldn't squeak. It was the one with all the canned goods. I couldn't make out what most of them were in the dark by touch, and I didn't want to give him a can of sauerkraut or something like that. I finally came upon a square can of corned beef. Good. It still had the key attached to the top of it. He wouldn't need a can opener that way. I grabbed the remains of a loaf of bread, heels and a few slices in between, and tiptoed back to my room. James had his glasses off and his face pressed against the window screen. He looked quite comical, his nose and cheeks flattened against it like those bank robbers that wear panty hose on their heads. The Japanese Hornets swarmed around him.

"Man, you've got an insect problem out here, for sure!"

"Better not let one of those things sting you."

He just chuckled, pulling away from the screen and looking down at his feet. I pulled in the screen latches and slowly wiggled it up as little as I could. It made a slight grating sound. Some hornets flew into my room and began buzzing around the inside of my lampshade by my bed.

"This is all I could get you without it being missed. Sorry I couldn't help you out more." I passed the bread bag and can to him through the opening in the window. As an afterthought, I ducked under my bed and pulled out a spare army surplus blanket, then fed it to him through the crack as well.

"No problemo," he replied, and then "Thanks." I shut the window back before any more hornets let themselves in.

"Are you gonna be okay? Maybe you could find somewhere to camp out, maybe down by the river against one of the cliffs in case it rains. I got me a box of campfire matches you can have."

"No thanks. I've got a cigarette lighter if I need it."

"Well, if you're around in the morning, come by and we'll go bike riding or something."

"Sure thing." He held up his provisions, which he had rolled into the blanket. "See ya, man, and thanks again." He stepped backwards into the darkness and was gone. I could hear his footsteps for another couple of seconds in the dry grass before all was quiet again, save for the buzzing of the Japanese Hornets against the screen. The couple that made it into my room had burned their wings against the light bulb of my bedside lamp. They spun around in circles on my nightstand, trying to fly again. I squished them with the heel of a shoe I picked up, turned the light out, and tried to sleep.

*   *   *   *

The next day after my chores, I asked my mom if I could go bike riding.

"Did you stack that firewood on the ends like I told you to?" My father asked.

"Yes, sir."

"If it collapses I'm going to make you restack every stick of it, you hear me?"

"Yes, sir." My father stretched out on his recliner, and turned back to the television. A Clint Eastwood western was on, guns blazing and ricocheting.

"School will be starting soon," my mom added. "Maybe this afternoon we can go to Family Dollar in town and get you some school supplies. For the new year."

"Sure, Mom. Oh, and I'll be starting Driver's Ed in the fall or spring sometime, too."

"You ain't old enough to be learning to drive," my father said. "You can't even steer the riding mower without leaving patches of unmowed grass around every turn." His voice always wore pointed-toe cowboy boots, as if I was a cockroach in the corner. I kept my mouth shut, for fear of riling him up further.

"Be home by lunch," my mother said. I heard her rattle the ice in her glass of Southern Comfort, setting it back on the windowsill above the sink.

I rode my bike down to the New River, about a mile from my house. I thought if James *did* camp out down there, it would be along a stretch where there was a large patch of river sand deposited from the last flood. The weeds were shoulder high along the river, though, and they smacked against my handlebars, stinging my knuckles. There was a faint smell of fish slime from the deep, slow water along the bank. Out in the middle of the river huge slabs of rocks rose from the surface. The currents made a constant rushing sound around them. A snapping turtle sunned itself on a driftwood log; it slipped into the water with a plop when I passed by. I caught a whiff of smoke, and decided to follow it. Among tall stalks of Pokeweed hanging heavy with purple berries was a small trail that looked recently trampled. When followed, it led to an overhanging rock cliff. James was standing over a small fire with something on the end of a stick.

"Hey! What's shakin'?" I called out. James jumped about a foot in the air.

"Damn it! Don't startle me like that, you big dork! You made me drop my catfish in the fire." He gingerly pulled a half-charred fish out of the hot coals, and tried to skewer it back on the end of his roasting stick.

"Serves you right for scaring me last night. Did you not like the corned beef?"

"Eh, I ate that right away. I was starving. I caught this beauty just this morning with a ball of bread dough." He turned his hip toward me to show off his Rambo survival knife looped on his belt and tied to his leg. "I knew when I bought this last year at the flea market it would come in handy. It had a place for a hook and line built right into the handle, along with room for some waterproof matches and a wire saw. You should have bought you one."

I noticed the blanket and a pile of small pine boughs under a rock overhang. He must have slept there last night, I thought, and my heart sank. "So, how are ya doin'?"

"Fair to middlin'. I got to tell you somethin' Randy. I'm thinking about running away." He looked into the fire with stern resolve. "For real."

"What?"

"I may go back home one more time, then I'm hitting the road. I already got my license, and almost got my Chevy Nova running, by the way, and every bit of that car's mine. Let my mom try to take it away from me."

"Hey, did you know 'no va' in Spanish means 'it doesn't go?' But that's a Chevy for ya."

"Quit being a smartass. I'm serious. I'm going to leave this piece of shit town."

I looked at him for a few seconds more just to see if he was joking or not. "What about school?"

"Every community college's got some program to finish your high school diploma. I could have aced every one of my classes if I wanted to. My auto mechanics teacher, Mr. Huffman, always told me that, and I'm good in math. If I just hadn't missed so many days of school."

I could tell James was serious at that point. He had an astigmatism, but his eyes were steely calm through his thick glasses. "Where will you go?" I asked.

"Somewhere out west. Maybe California. Or Alaska. I heard from one of my cousins that there was always jobs at these big fish canneries. And they had room and board, too."

I sat down with him while he finished cooking and eating his catfish. He let me have a few chunks of meat from it, then picked the bones clean. Afterwards, we found a grape vine to swing on that James hacked in two, after much effort and cussing, with his Rambo knife. We climbed a little ways up an adjacent rock and pushed off, coming back around in a circle after our legs dangled out in the air for a few seconds. Sometimes we hit our backs on the cliff rocks if we got turned around. I lost track of how many times we did that, swinging out into space like we were craving the freedom of flight. Close to lunchtime I told him I had to go back home, and asked him if his little brother would be okay with him gone.

"Chad'll be fine. I know my mom would stay home if she had to take care of him. They always liked him better, anyways."

We hung out a few more times after that, at his place when his folks weren't home. He didn't mention about running away, so I thought maybe he forgot about it. I saw him at lunch the first week back at school. Then I didn't see him anymore. None of the teachers knew anything, despite how small our city school was. I thought he might have just been playing hooky, and watched his house from across the abandoned lot on a few afternoons, hoping to see him mowing the yard or working on his car. The carport was empty, though. I was afraid to go by his house and ask if he was home, for fear his parents might try to interrogate me to find out where he went. He was one of the only real friends I had, and now he was gone. In my mind I wished him good luck and hoped he was happy, wherever he was.

11 _____

Ever since my grandfather told me of his intentions to send me to college, I started taking school a little more seriously. I saw it as a golden ticket out of there. My mom was happy about my renewed interest for school, but I felt my dad resented it. "I never had to work so hard in school, and I did just fine for myself," my father always said. "I don't know why you have so much homework." I couldn't get him to understand that maybe school is different than it was then, and I eventually became ashamed of admitting that I wanted to go to college. It felt as if he couldn't stand me being happy or successful at anything, even if it was just school.

I was originally glad they signed me up for Mr. Carpenter's sixth-period study hall because I knew he didn't care what you did in there. It was a great class to goof off or take a nap. For the first half of the year, I mainly read comic books or doodled. If I tried doing schoolwork the rougher kids, usually from the other side of Chestnut Creek, would use me and my open book as spit-wad target practice. I realized I had to get out of that zoo of a classroom, though, especially if I was going to bring my grade point average up. With reluctance, I knew I had to go see the tenth-grade guidance counselor. She had to be at least 65, but her thin, frail body made her look tired and even more weathered. She was also in charge of student records. Her office was the filing room – a windowless, dimly-lit closet that looked like a bank vault with filing cabinets. Everyone at school called her the Crypt Keeper. She rarely smiled. She seemed hateful and stressed, and at times she bit her thin lower lip so tight she had a permanent groove of teeth marks on it. I called her Ms. Green.

Swallowing my fears of her, I told her my grievance as respectfully as I could and threw myself at her mercy. She said I couldn't switch to another study hall because they were all full and it was so late in the school year, but she offered to make a special case for me by making me her assistant. At first I didn't know if I would like the idea, sharing such close company to someone who smelled like lotion and moth balls. Then she assured me that I would help her file records only on occasion, and I could work on my homework for the majority of the time in her office or in an empty conference room. I warmed up to the idea. I just made sure that no other students knew of my arrangement, or I would really get a ribbing. It amazed me how students I didn't even know thought it was their business to know my business.

It turned out that Ms. Green knew my Granny Wilson, who was a nurse at the old hospital downtown. My grandmother also volunteered at the high school before my parents attended there, treating sprained ankles, taking temperatures, and giving vaccinations to students. I had no idea Ms. Green was good friends with her since their childhood.

"Before your grandmother married, we used to be the best of friends. Thick as thieves," she told me in her crackly voice one day, her upper front teeth pressing into the groove in her lower lip, like she was part chipmunk. I tried not to stare when she talked to me, but I couldn't help it. Her lips squeezed through the gap in her front teeth so much that when she opened her mouth to talk, her lower lip had an impression that looked like that little thing that hung upside down in the back of your throat, only it was right side up. "We'd go down to the drug store on Main Street, order two vanilla cokes from the soda jerk, and flirt with the boys." I couldn't picture this woman as a teenager, winking at guys, but I began to realize that she had a special affinity to my grandmother that carried on to me. She must not have had anyone else to talk to, because she was always gabbing with me as if I was a member of her quilting club.

One day while I helped her affix new labels to student record folders, she talked in great detail about Granny. "When our husbands were in the Navy during the Second World War, we spent a lot of time together. Ginny was all I had during that time. My parents moved to Norfolk with my younger sister because my father got a job working in the shipyards. I stayed here with my husband and his family – never had any children. His family didn't care too much for me, neither. They thought I acted too high and mighty for their taste, I suppose. Did your grandpa ever tell you about being sent to teach submarine school?"

"A little," I replied. "He said he was in the Navy. He was stationed in Key West and taught people to pilot the old diesel-powered submarines."

"Well, I was always envious of your grandmother because your grandpa managed to get such safe assignments on account that his brother John was killed in early combat. They tried to make sure the mothers weren't left without at least one surviving son. My late husband Charles seemed always to be on the front. He was good at what he did, though. He was one of the many who landed on the beach at Normandy on D-Day. Many good men were lost that day, including my dear Charles."

"I'm sorry to hear that."

"Well, it was a long time ago," she said as she touched sticker labels to folders. Her eyes got a little wet, but she continued. "Before I first got the news that he was missing in action, I knew it in my heart, like I had a premonition that God had taken him home. I was washing dishes at the sink that day when I thought I saw something out the window from the corner of my eye. I looked up and saw Charles in uniform waving at me, just like he did when he first left, but when I blinked the motion of his arm turned into a crow taking off from my front yard. I dropped a dish and ran to the front porch just as I was met by another man in uniform, a stranger, with the letter stating he had been killed." She looked at me, smiling. "But your grandmother, she was right there for me. She was the only one I told at the time about what I saw. She came over almost every day with your Aunt Carol, who was just a toddler at the time. Well, if it weren't for your grandmother I would have never made it through that ordeal." I never knew this about Granny. I wished especially at that moment that I could have talked with her more when she was alive.

"You were only five when she passed away, but I remember your mom holding you on her lap during the service. All those

79

years smoking. I was probably the one who got her started, sharing my Lucky Strikes with her." As she talked, I remembered the funeral, not understanding what was going on, why Granny was asleep and wouldn't wake up. Ms. Green continued talking. "Even when we vowed to stop smoking during the times of rationing, she picked the habit right back up. Was it the emphysema or pneumonia? I can't remember."

"I'm not sure." My head was beginning to feel congested, and my throat lumpy. "Where do you want me to put these?" I asked, holding up a stack of newly-labeled folders, concealing the clouds in my eyes.

*　*　*　*

As the weeks progressed toward the end of my junior year, I began thinking about what I needed to be doing to apply for college. Nobody in my family had ever been, so I was hesitant about asking my parents for help. Ms. Green continued to talk my ear off, mostly about her childhood growing up during the Great Depression. I told her about my grandfather's plan to help me financially with college, and how he worked it out for me to get in-state tuition so I could go to Watauga State. I didn't tell her the part about how he was going to save the money by being cremated. She was very pleased, and immediately signed me up for the SAT in May. "Your grandmother would be so proud. She had wanted to go back to get a higher degree, but children just took precedence over everything else."

"When do I need to request a transcript?" I asked, sitting in her cramped, windowless office.

"Well, it's usually good to send it as soon as the beginning of your senior year. You might want to take the SAT a couple of times, and combine scores. See this form here?" She pulled out a blank form from one of her desk drawers. "One of these days they'll have these printed on computers. I'm sure some schools probably already do, but I hope to be gone before I have to learn how to use one. It's really quite simple now." She put one of the forms into her typewriter and turned the platen knob on the side, making a clacking sound. "All I do is feed this through the roller and line up the empty fields." She showed me how to line up the point indicator with the blank line. "See? This would be a good idea in filling out your college application. It would make it more professional looking."

"So, that's all you have to do to send a transcript?" I asked.

"Of course, after I type it I sign it to make it official. We don't give students transcripts, but send it straight to the college. Sometimes the parents ask for it sealed in an envelope and then send it to the college themselves." Ms. Green pulled the form from the typewriter. I watched her as she carefully placed the form back in a folder in her desk drawer. "I don't have any pressing jobs for you today, so you are welcome to sit here at my desk for the remaining 20 minutes of sixth period."

"Thank you, Ms. Green. I sure do appreciate it. I think I'll be finishing up the school year with all A's and one B."

"I knew you could do it. Your grandmother would be so proud!"

"Do you think I could use your typewriter to type a paper for my Social Studies class?"

"Why, sure. Typing paper is in one of the side drawers of my desk."

"Thanks!"

She turned away. As I heard her steps get fainter down the office corridor, I cracked her metal desk drawer open to look for typing paper, and instead spotted the folder labeled *Transcript Forms* in red marker. I pulled a blank form out, slid it into my Social Studies notebook, and quietly closed the drawer back.

12 _____

I hated when the professor got into discussions like this. It never failed; the reaction was the same every time. That was one reason why I sat at the back of the amphitheater. With about a hundred students, I knew if I sat at the back I wouldn't be pulled into the classroom conversations, which always made me nervous. Also, I was at WSU's campus, sitting in on a class in which I wasn't enrolled.

The Social Psychology professor lectured in a booming, cynical voice. "When the average woman aged 19-25 looks at a man favorably she, whether instinctually or she consciously realizes it, looks at how self-sufficient he is. She instinctively sizes him up as to how good of a father he would be, how dependable he would be, how much of a provider he would be, whether she is seriously looking for a mate or not. However, with guys it is a different story." There is a rise of murmurs from the class as if they are expecting what he is about to say. "Regardless whether he is looking for a girlfriend or a wife, the average male, upon looking at a person of the opposite sex, immediately sizes her up as a sexual partner. To put it plainly, the college-age male instinctively looks for 'a good lay.' It is how men are wired."

The room broke out with snickers and a host of responses. I overheard one girl in front of me exclaim, "Girl, ain't that the truth!" while another responded, "That's all they think about," and shook her head disapprovingly with her friends, like she had the whole race of men figured out. Most of the guys just laughed, some were elbowed by their female friends at something lewd they must have added to the professor's words, until the professor raised his hand for everyone's attention. A few guys patted each other on the back in recognition of some shared secret conquest as the professor continued his lecture. I could not join in the celebration of hormones, though. The memory of my embarrassing incident with Lindsey still stung in my mind. Since the day before yesterday, I wanted to forget about it, to think with a clear mind. There was a part of me, however, that knew there was truth to what the professor was saying, and it made me feel helpless. The professor continued to lecture, giving key terms for people to look up and define later, but I was lost in my thoughts.

On days I didn't have classes at the community college, I parked my car behind the pizza place, then took the Appalcart bus to the university campus. Part of me knew that there was something dishonest about taking a class you didn't pay tuition for, but there was something inside of me that felt like I was supposed to be there. It wasn't entitlement. I needed to be there. I got a hold of a list of classes offered, found out which ones were the largest, and picked a couple that fit my schedule. I discovered the key to being anonymous was to walk in when the class was about to start behind a group of students, then find a seat almost, but not all the way, in the back. Come too early and the professor or the early-bird students might try to strike up a conversation with you. Too late, and the professor might try to identify what slacker would dare show up at the last second. I took notes, but only for my own interest, and did some reading of suggested books in the library, but only when it didn't interfere with my *actual* classes. Plus, when I got to the university I figured I would already be ahead of the others a little.

I did have legitimate reasons to be on campus as well. The satellite campus of the community college here in Boone had only a very sparse collection of books in a room they called a "library," housed at the administration offices on the other side of town. I found my way around Bell Library on the university campus fairly quickly, though, and found it much more conducive to research and quiet time. There were lots of tables and couches one could camp at and study, uninterrupted for the most part by any other students sitting around or walking by. It was a good place to study or kill time. After Social Psychology class, I had five hours to kill before I had to go to work. I did not want to go today, though.

It was just after eleven, so instead of the library I decided to walk to the Student Union in hopes to find a soft chair where I could sit and read *Huckleberry Finn* for English, and maybe do a few practice worksheets for my Applied Algebra test at the end of the week. I patted the book bag at my side to make sure I brought all my work with me. Final exams were coming up soon, and I didn't want to drop the ball.

The professor's lecture on the male and female biological drives still reverberated in my head. Where other guys accepted their sexual desires as the dominant animal part of them, I seemed to grapple with it. It was like an alien being in me that Lindsey awakened, working separately with my logical, conscious mind, my conscience. I could not anticipate its moves. It was becoming more of a distraction. I thought I knew what urges were with Cathy; she was very attractive. Maybe the temptation wasn't there, pushing itself against me like Lindsey. What did she say to all her friends about me after the party? I didn't want to imagine, for fear I would choke on another wave of shame. How could I show my face this evening at work? All the effort I put into fitting in, of building a rapport with the other workers, would be gone as soon as Lindsey told everyone that I was an inexperienced, premature-ejaculating virgin. Part of me wished I could have gone all the way with her. But would I have felt any less empty than I do now? Who would I want to brag my conquest to?

It was not love, but lust that lurked inside me, and women had the upper hand on both sides. My mind struggled to make sense of it. Girls know how easily a man's desire can be aroused, so they know they can manipulate it and use it to their advantage when that is what *they* desire. On the other hand, those same girls can turn off their own desire easily, and then look down their noses at men's knuckle-dragging animalism when they want to feel superior. As I continued toward the center of campus, a girl walked out of the library toward me. Her hurried pace, and her backpack straps, seemed to animate her breasts under her wool turtleneck sweater, and the cold brought them to attention. For a second I imagined them, bare in my upturned palms. But what are breasts, some mammary glands encased in fatty tissue, a means of feeding a mother's infant child? But no means of rationalizing lessened the memory of Lindsey. The sensation of her breasts in my hands was

84

like a phantom limb as I watched this girl walk toward me. She met my wandering eyes with a cold stare as she passed me on the sidewalk. "Damn!" I cursed myself for allowing one more girl to confirm the professor's theory, that men are just erections with arms and legs. "I am not," I said under my breath, "a walking penis." I looked around to see if anyone heard me.

Coffee Exchange was the only coffee house on campus, and was different from the Jumping Bean uptown, which was dank and always had a smoky haze hanging just below the ceiling. It was located between the old half of the student union and the newly-finished commons area. The place was decorated like an oil change garage, with enameled advertisements for Sinclair gas and shadow boxes of NASCAR memorabilia on the walls. I walked inside the coffee shop and was met by the savory, earthy smell of fresh-ground coffee and the whir of the espresso grinder. People quietly chatted, low enough that I could read my book and study, but not so quiet that I could hear my ears ring. Sometimes the library felt lonely and sterile, and although I didn't care to chat with anyone, there was a camaraderie that seemed warm and inviting. We were all there for a common purpose, to drink coffee and maybe feel intellectual.

Over in the far right corner of the room was a raised area above the main floor with a couch, a coffee table made from racing tires, and a couple of overstuffed armchairs. I slung my book bag down on the one facing away from the rest of the room, laid my coat on the arm, and opened up a couple of my notebooks to make it look like I had been there a while. This deterred anyone from simply moving my bag and taking the seat while I went to the counter. I never tried an espresso because they seemed really expensive for such a small cup, and to me the cappuccino had more milk and foam than coffee, so I always got an X-Grande size regular coffee, and added cream and sugar to my liking at the side bar.

I returned to my seat, still saved, and sat my coffee and honey bun down while I got out my book. I had barely begun *Huckleberry Finn* when three people, a guy and two girls, came up and started laying their book bags and coats down.

"It was so nice of you to save this big couch just for me," she said. It took a few seconds to realize that the comment was directed toward me. I looked up from my book to see a full-faced, rather attractive girl with curly dark hair, a red toboggan, and Osh Kosh overalls. "You really shouldn't have," she said quite dramatically.

Realizing that maybe she was just trying to be friendly in a flirtatious way, I answered, "Well, you're welcome. Just make yourselves at...." Before I could finish being coyly polite, she had already left with her friends to go order something from the counter. I went back to my reading, trying not to think much else of it.

Several pages later they were back with their French presses, some fancy cup used to brew tea without using teabags. They pushed the little plungers down to compress their tea leaves. I tried not to listen in on their conversation, but the girl with the red toboggan spoke in such a raised tone that I wondered if she *wanted* everyone within earshot to hear her. Her dark curls bounced from under her toboggan while she continued chatting with her friends. The other girl had amber hair and small, metal-rimmed glasses that looked like Ben Franklin spectacles. The guy had a dark scraggly beard and straight-cut bangs like someone sat a bowl on his head and trimmed around it. There was a sweetly-strange fragrance in the air of black pepper mixed with Murphy's Oil Soap.

For a while I tried to read over the sound of their conversation, but their voices were so audible and animated I eventually had to resort to reading every page twice. I thought, surely they knew they were disturbing me. I cleared my throat to remind them I was there. No change in their volume. It wasn't a library, but still, everyone else understood that the tone of conversations should be hushed in here. Maybe that was what they were intending, to run me off so they could take my seat, but if I got up immediately they would think I was leaving *because* of them and probably feel victorious in their effort to annoy me. I just let my ears be immersed in their banter.

They talked about their parents' professions and their allowances while Toboggan Girl got a backrub from Bearded Guy. In between her incessant moaning and grunting over her "masseur's magical fingers," which gave me tingles down the back of my neck, discussions ensued over where to get the best herbal teas, and the aromatherapy oil she had at her apartment that she just had to get Bearded Guy to use on her back later. I gathered that Glasses Girl's parents had friends in some Latin-American country that would always send her gifts of expensive wine, and Toboggan Girl's parents must have had a summer home or something in northern California.

Toboggan Girl kept making comments on how she needed "a big, soft, warm man" to keep her cozy this winter. Bearded Guy and the other girl tried to convince her she needed to get a German Shepherd instead. I couldn't figure them out, especially Toboggan Girl. One moment she was talking about getting naked when she got back to her pad and letting Bearded Guy oil her body down, and the next she was talking about wanting a man to keep her warm this winter, all in the same manner as one would order pizza over the phone.

"What's your name?" she asked.

"Huh?" I looked up from my book, startled and lost in rereading a page. I realized she was talking to me again. "Oh. Uh, my name's Randall," I answered, still in bewilderment at such a random request, especially after I had been sitting here ignored for almost half an hour.

"This is Emily. She pointed at the other girl, "and this is Dennis," hiking her thumb behind her as Dennis was finishing his back rub. "And my name's Gwenhwyfar." She lifted her hand to me in a small wave as if we were sitting across the room from each other and not across a coffee table. "Wave back to me. Don't leave me hanging!" I was still trying to shake the stun of her abrupt introductions to collect my thoughts as I raised my hand in response.

"I'm sorry, I was just – I have never heard anyone by that name before. I just wasn't sure I heard you right." I realized I was still waving at her, and dropped my hand.

"It is a unique name, isn't it? It's 'Gwen' – G-W-E-N – 'eh' – and 'Far' – F-A-R, as in 'far out.'" She wasn't kidding, I thought. "I've been called Gwendy, Guinevere, Gwendolin, and Guano."

"Don't forget Gwenofart." Emily added.

"Gee, thanks! I was trying to forget that one."

"So where are y'all from?" I asked, trying to warm up to the conversation.

"Emily's from Wilmington, Dennis is from Raleigh...."

"Cary, actually," he interjected.

"And I'm currently from Carolina Beach, which is near Wilmington, by way of California. I ran away from home one summer, and from the beach made my way up to the mountains, where I joined a commune called Turtle Island, then decided to go to college."

I heard about Turtle Island from my English teacher. It was run by a man named Eustace, somewhere in the mountains out of town. I forgot his last name. He taught people how to live off the land and in harmony with nature, but I couldn't picture this girl hunting squirrels or taking baths by a campfire. She looked too pampered. I said, "Well, if you liked the communal atmosphere, I heard there's a place down near Asheville called Warren Wilson College. I heard you could work and...."

"Oh, yeah," Dennis interrupted. "It's in Swanna-'nowhere', isn't it?"

"Yes, I believe so," Emily agreed.

"I thought it was pronounced Swannanoa," I said, then immediately got the joke.

"It's in the middle of nowhere," Dennis stated.

"Where are you from, Randall? Do you go by Randy?" asked Emily.

"Sometimes."

"How about Rand-meister? Rand-aroni?" asked Gwenhwyfar.

"Uh, no."

"The Randster?" she continued.

"I'm from a little city just northeast of here, across the Virginia border, called Galax. You've probably never heard of it."

"Oh, yes. I know where it is," said Gwenhwyfar.

"It's the only city in the country by that name, my high school History teacher told me. Despite how small the city is, you could mail a letter without the state or zip code and it would still get there. It's spelled G-A-L-A-X, by the way."

"How interesting," Gwenhwyfar commented. "So, Emily, I tried calling you last night, but you didn't pick up the phone. Were you screening your calls?"

Maybe I wasn't as interesting as she first thought I was. Was she just talking to me to shop for her big, soft man, and put me back like a green piece of fruit at the produce stand? I looked at my belly and noticed I had a little paunch over my belt, and then noticed how plainly dressed I was: flannel shirt, blue jeans, and work boots. I went back to my book in order not to look foolish, not like I was *waiting* for one of them to let me back into the conversation, but inside I was thoroughly irritated at how they made me feel – like a simple-minded country bumpkin. Well, if Gwenhwyfar wanted interesting, if she thought I was just some dull-witted hillbilly, I'd give her interesting. Who was I trying to impress, anyway?

At this point they were talking about how different answering machines made their voices sound. "I always hate to call my dad's voice mail when he's off traveling because I just know I sound like I'm drunk. Then I tell him later when he questions me that I always wait until I'm sober to call him," Gwenhwyfar said to Dennis.

"Well, sometimes you *are* drunk when you call me!" he replied.

"I have trouble makin' outgoing messages on my answerin' machine because I always think I sound like Forrest Gump. Know what I mean?" I added, making sure to thicken my mountain accent just a little more.

"Oh, I loved that movie! Did you know they filmed a lot of it near Wilmington? All the scenes with the big plantation houses, that's around where I'm from," Emily said. She looked at me and seemed to smile like she just noticed me for the first time, but Gwenhwyfar was ready to reclaim the lead.

"Ever see *Singles*? When I lived out west, my friends and I drove to Seattle and got a part as extras in the movie. You can see the back of my head in one of the street scenes."

"I wanted to see that, but at the time we didn't have a movie thee-ater in Galax. You had to drive down the mountain to Mount Airy." I then turned back to Emily. "Oh, I do know of another movie scene, Emily. If you've ever been to Grandfather Mountain, you'll recognize the scene in *Forrest Gump* where he's joggin' up a really curvy, steep hill with that herd of people followin' him. There's also a scene where he's runnin' past a split-rail fence. They filmed that up on the Parkway somewhere." I tried to speak more to Emily, who seemed genuinely interested in what I had to say, despite my playing the fool.

Talk turned back to Gwenofar's search for a big, soft man. "Can you believe they want me to get a German Shepherd?" she asked me.

"I tell ya," I promptly added, "those *are* some big dogs. They sure do eat a lot."

"Do you have a dog?" Gwenhwyfar asked.

"I didn't bring any of them with me to school, the dog boxes in the back of my pick-up truck wouldn't hold them all, you know, so I left them with my parents. They're still mine, and pretty valuable, but I don't have much use for them here," I lied.

"Valuable? What kind of dogs do you have, purebreds?"

"Yep. Pure-bred coon dogs, five of them – Daisy, Bo, Luke, and Roscoe. But my favorite dog has half an ear missing, no tail, and only one eye. His name's Lucky." Emily smirked, but the other two just stared blankly. I continued to lay it thick. "But I don't have much time to go coon huntin' since I started here at WSU. I also had a good bear dog once, 'til he got kilt."

"How did it die?" Emily asked, engrossed in my story.

"A bear gored it. Awfulest bunch of racket you ever seen and heard, fur flying everywhere. And I would've killed the bear, too, exceptin' that it had two cubs, and it was out of season, so I ran the bear off with a few warnin' shots, then had to put the dog out of its misery."

"Oh that poor dog! How inhumane! Couldn't there have been some other way?" asked Gwenhwyfar.

"So what's your major?" Dennis asked, laughing, "Appalachian Studies?"

Pause. "No. I'm majorin' in Environmental Science, but I may switch to Recreational Management."

"Is that what you're reading that book for?" Gwenhwyfar asked. I held up the cover of the book, and she blinked a few times and looked back at me like she didn't believe I could even read a book.

"No. It's for an English class, but I've been having trouble readin' it today."

"Well, if school's too hard for you, you should take off and do something else. I got tired of living at home, and so I ran off to go join a commune. I got tired of trying to live up to my parents' expectations of me. I wanted to get as far away from their bourgeois lifestyles as possible. You know, go off on my own, do my own thing, be independent."

"At least your parents have some expectations for you, and they have the means to help you, don't they?" I said.

"Why do you ask?" Gwenhwyfar realized I might have heard more of their earlier conversation than she thought.

"Well, my mother works at Dairy Queen and my dad lost his factory job over a year ago. I'm the first in all of my family to ever go to college, and ever-one's looking to see if I'm going to make it or go back home with my tail 'tween my legs. I have all of this weight on me; it's like, like...." I was surprised at what I was saying, at how angry I was getting.

"Like wanting to succeed for your whole family, yet feeling guilty that you might just do so?" Dennis said.

"Yeah. Something like that."

Dennis continued. "My parents are old-school, grass-roots hippies. Hated the Capitalist economy. They used to teach at Carolina. When they learned that I was studying business and wanted to work on Wall Street, they flipped their lid. They thought I was betraying everything they believed in."

I remembered how my grandfather and Aunt Faith were the only ones who showed interest in my dream of going to college. "My mother humored me at first, but I don't think she knew how to help me. My father laughed and said we could never afford it, that I should just get me a job down at the factory where he worked or at a lumber yard and make some real money."

"Well, I've figured out how to beat that," said Gwenhwyfar, sipping on her tea. "Just cut off all communication to your family for three or four years like I did. Don't even go home to visit. Then you won't feel so pressured to succeed, and you'd be free to do whatever you please instead of trying to please your parents."

"That's all fine and good, but what if your family's all you got?" I said.

"Well, I'm sorry for you."

"Don't be," I said. "Ever heard the saying, 'blood is thicker than water?'" I was so livid by the conversation, I scarcely knew what I was talking about at this point.

"Or in your case herbal tea!" Dennis interrupted.

"Speaking of tea," Gwenhwyfar chirped while subtly changing the subject, "this green tea they use here is absolutely horrible. I've drunk better dishwater."

"You drink dishwater? What did you do, run out of booze?" Dennis joked. I had been grappling with them and Gwenhwyfar's back-handed snobbery long enough. I wanted to tell them where to go, but anything I said would just make me look like a hot-headed fool, and them even more smug and self-righteous.

"Tastes too much like parsley?"

"No, no, Emily. Parsley is actually good. I drink it all the time as a diuretic."

The talk turned randomly back to pets, how Emily's Dachshund looked more like a sewer rat, and where the best vegetarian restaurant in town was. It was like trying to have a conversation at the Mad Hatter's tea party. I was exasperated. I was just about to give up, to let them have their circle of chairs and leave them to their asinine conversations, when someone tapped me on the shoulder. I was so lost in self-loathing I startled, turning quickly around to see who it was. It was a girl with strawberry-blonde hair. She looked familiar, but I couldn't remember from where, until she spoke.

"Well, there you are! Did you forget where we were supposed to meet? I've been waiting at the high tables on the other side of the room for you. I thought for a few minutes you had forgotten," she said. It was the girl from the laundromat. It took a couple of seconds for me to recognize her, because she had her bangs cut. I had no idea what she was talking about, but her disarming smile made me want to humor her, and anything was better than the social snubbing I had been receiving.

"Hey!" I said. "Sorry about that. Let me get my things together and we'll go," and then to Gwenhwyfar, "Well, I reckon I ought to be going. It's been a pleasure."

Gwenhwyfar picked up a newspaper from the coffee table, "Ooh, Calvin and Hobbes!" she exclaimed, pulling out the comics section. She immediately engrossed herself in its front page.

Dennis pulled it out of her hands, "Hey, let me read the middle page at least. Don't be a comics hog!"

As I rose to leave, Emily turned to me, "I'll speak for the rest of them since it seems they're preoccupied. It was nice to meet you too, and I hope we'll meet again."

"Likewise," said the laundromat girl, then turning to Gwenhwyfar, "See ya later, *Jennifer*." Gwenhwyfar didn't reply, but her eyes peeked over the top of her comics. She did not look amused.

The girl from the laundromat gave me her arm and gestured for me to lead the way out the door. When we left the soft-lit coffee shop, she added, "I guess the funny papers weren't as funny as she thought they would be."

"Do you know those people?" I asked.

"Oh, yes. Unfortunately. They go to the Wesley Foundation with me, the Methodist student center. They're harmless enough, full of hot air, but a huge pain in the butt if you have to work with them much. Jennifer is her real name. She *hates* being called that!"

"By the way, I wanted to say thanks." We walked out the front of the Student Union and down the steps to Sandford Mall.

"Don't mention it. Those three just love to mess with people. I saw you trapped over there, trying to read your book. Thought you needed an exit strategy. There's a black hole that surrounds them, you know. Very few people's self-esteem can escape their gravitational pull." She smiled. "Besides, coffee shops are one of the worst places to meet people."

"Yeah. I've heard the same about laundromats, too."

"About that," she pauses. "I believe I owe you an apology. I'm just really squeamish about meeting strangers in public places." She smiled uncomfortably. "It's hard to explain."

"My name's Randall Spivey, by the way."

"Cassandra Miller, but everyone calls me Cassie."

"See? Now we ain't strangers anymore."

Cassie smiled broadly and nodded her head in agreement. "I've got a class to go to in a few minutes, but maybe you'd like to join me for a bite to eat later this week? I heard the cafeteria is serving Christmas dinner before the holiday break. Not as good as Mom would make, I'm sure."

"I've got to work tonight, but yes. That would be cool. Would your boyfriend mind?"

"What? Oh," she blushes. "We broke up last month."

"I'm sorry."

"It's okay. Water under the bridge." She pulled out a slip of paper and a pen from her jacket pocket, tore the paper in half, and quickly scribbled. "Here's my apartment phone number, if you don't miss me before I leave for break. Don't leave a message with any of my roommates. I'd never get it." She wrote while she talked. "And here is my home number. My family lives in Sugar Grove, just out of town. Let me get your number so it won't be any one person's responsibility to call first. You know, no big deal, no rush."

"To tell ya the truth, I haven't got a phone right now. Dispute with some billing issues." That was a dumb thing to have to lie about, I thought. I haven't had phone service since Cathy last called, when I cancelled it. "How about I give you my work number? There is sometimes a lull in business from two to five p.m." I sounded so lame! Inside I was kicking myself. Here I was, 16, feeling like I was 13, instead of the 21-year-old I was pretending to be.

She handed me the pen and paper scrap, and I quickly scribbled the number on it as best I could, using my hand as backing. As soon as I gave it to her, she smiled. "Where do ya work at?"

"Papa's Pizza. That little plaza across from the lumber yard."

"I might have to order there sometime, then. See ya. Have fun at work." She turned, and then quickly disappeared into a crowd of people walking toward Sandford Hall. Her hair lilted, and she had a bounce in her retreating steps that made me smile. It was two hours until I had to go to work, and for the first time today work was the last thing on my mind.

13

I dreaded this. The shot of courage from that phone number in my wallet was wearing off quickly as I stepped off the Appalcart bus in front of Papa's Pizza and walked around to my car in back. A cold breeze cut down my collar. I saw Lindsey on the phone taking an order. She probably didn't see me through the window, as it was getting darker outside. I knew I had better go in and get changed or I'd be late for work, and Dean would have a fit. I sneaked into the side entrance and made my way to the bathroom without anyone noticing me. I had been rehearsing over and over, wondering what I would say to her, or to them, and how they would react, how much Lindsey might have told them. I couldn't run from this, as much as I wanted to. I needed this job. I thought back to every dollar of tip money I squirreled away so far, how much money I had in the bank, and how it would all be gone within a couple of months if I quit.

The bathroom smelled of urine and hand soap. I hung my backpack on a hook and got out my work clothes, trying not to let anything touch the floor as I struggled to get into my work pants and shoes. Okay. There wasn't anything else for me to do but walk to the front and clock in. I tucked in my shirttail, put on my best poker face, and opened the bathroom door. My legs were moving, but my body felt shrunken and separated from the floor.

"Rocker! What's up?" asked Paul, who was slinging an extra-large disk of dough between his hands. Corn meal powder dusted the air.

"Hey Paul," I said casually.

"Have you recouped from the party?"

"For the most part." So far so good, I thought. Lindsey was boxing a couple of pizzas that just came out of the oven as I clocked in. The convection fans whirred over the sound of a ringing phone. I thought, maybe I should say something to her first. I opened my mouth, but felt disembodied, like someone else was speaking through me.

"Hey, Lindsey."

"Oh, hey Randy," she replied. "By the way, you left your jacket at the party. I hung it in the back room over a chair."

"Oh, thanks. I didn't realize I forgot it." I thought at that moment that maybe later, when things died down, that I might talk to her one-on-one, to apologize for acting so juvenile, to maybe get some sort of consolation from her. I checked the oven for dough bubbles and set out a box for an upcoming pizza.

It seemed at first no one else knew what happened until Craig, who had been manning the phones before, was ready on the trigger. He fired, "So, Rocker! I heard you and Lindsey hooked up this weekend. Care to share the details? I heard things ended a little... premature."

Without looking at me, Lindsey turned on Craig. "Quit being an asshole! What's your problem? You worried about how you measure up? You want me to tell everyone you've got a pencil dick in comparison? Randy's a nice guy. Leave him the hell alone!"

"Hey! That hurt my feeling!" Craig said, and then turned to me. "That's okay, Dude. I've seen your little Jesus fish on the back of your car. I know what you're all about. Think you're so pious, but deep down you are just a hypocrite like all the rest of them bible beaters." He folded his arms and smiled cunningly, like he was looking right through me at some sad, ugly truth. All eyes were on me.

I didn't know where this attack came from. I was dumbfounded. It took me a few seconds to catch on to what he referred to, something Cathy had gotten for me in high school, a decal from the bible bookstore in Mount Airy. What did I do to offend him? I was a sorry excuse for a Christian; I knew it. I didn't act self-righteous about it, and sometimes I didn't even know where I stood. So what the hell was his problem? I felt a welling of anger that seemed to bloom hotly in my chest. I walked casually up to Craig, feigning a smile.

"Sorry, Chief. I know I am *far* from perfect, but I don't kiss and tell. And, by the way, that's 'Mother-Fucking Hypocrite' to you!"

There were a few seconds, which seemed like more than a minute, when I looked straight into his face and his blank, dumbfounded stare back at me. My ears were deaf to every other sound but my pulse, racing as if I had just run a sprint. Here it comes. I was ready to get knocked down, to hit the floor like a falling tree. Craig's mouth curled up into a surly smile, and a chuckle erupted deep within his chest.

"Man, you're one crazy motherfucker," he laughed.

"Looks like you got served, Craig!" said Dean.

"Sh-sh-sh-shot down!" shouted Paul, holding his hands out in imitation of firing a machine gun.

I wasn't sure if Craig was pissed at me or not, but if he was he didn't show it. He just kept smiling at the others' ribbing and looking at me from the corner of his eye as he got back to stretching some dough, squinting like he was still trying to figure me out. I tried not to look rattled, and turned around to check the screen for my first delivery while a host of smiling, congratulatory faces met mine.

"We're not worthy!" chanted Sam n'Eric, bowing in unison, arms overhead.

I noticed Lindsey was gone. Her shift must have been over, for her time receipt was left on the counter from clocking out. I picked up a campus delivery to Johnson dorm and Moretz Street, and headed outside. A few cars over from mine, Lindsey was throwing her duffel bag into her back seat. I swallowed my hesitancy and decided now was the time to clear the air.

"Lindsey," I called, looking around to see if anyone else was out in the parking lot as I approached her. My teeth were chattering. "I've been wanting t-to apologize about this past weekend, I...."

"Look, it's okay," she paused. "There's nothing to be sorry for, Randy. We had fun." She patted me on the shoulder and smiled. "And don't worry about Craig. We share some old history, that's all." There was a slight, awkward pause. "You're a good guy, and a good friend. It's not you." She looked at me with warmth and a little disappointment, then leaned in and kissed me on the cheek. "And don't worry. I swear I didn't tell anyone."

"Thanks," I blushed.

"You better get going. Your pizzas are going to get cold sitting on the trunk of your car."

I looked around to see the flaps of the warming sleeves were unfastened and rattling in the wind. "Oh, crap! I guess I'll s-see ya... whenever." I took a few steps backward and turned around to my car.

"See ya Randy."

A strange pang of disappointment and relief twisted in my gut. I pulled my sign out from the back seat and popped it down on my roof. After months of reattaching the sign to my car, the magnets had buffed soft white scratches into the blue paint. I never noticed that before now.

* * * *

One of the last deliveries I made that night was to Candler Hall. Some college students claimed they found an ant in their pizza and wanted us to send them a fresh one as compensation. Dean was a little wary of the call and suspected it was a hoax, but didn't want the students to call the complaint hotline and have the franchise owner chewing out the managers. He sent me specific orders for dealing with the guys.

"Okay, Rocker. Don't forget they must return the pizza under complaint, but before you take it and give them the fresh one, check the label. There's a date on it. If it wasn't purchased today then I wouldn't accept it. They are probably trying to get a free pizza out of us because they're a bunch of broke losers. I mean, an ant? It's the middle of winter. I wouldn't be surprised if someone has one of those mail-order ant farms up in his dorm room. It would seem almost believable if they had said a cockroach."

"Gotcha. Check the label."

The first week I started delivering I was tricked by a couple of guys in Howie Hall. They complained about their order being wrong, then ate over half of the pizza they were to return. Well, it never occurred to me at the time that if someone didn't want a pizza they wouldn't have eaten it. So it didn't dawn on me until later that those guys filled their bellies with the first pizza they ordered, and then traded a few slices back for a whole, free pizza.

I pulled into the parking lot in front of the dorm, locked my doors, and walked in with their order. A tall, skinny guy in baggy pants and a sleeveless t-shirt was waiting with the pizza box, chomping at the bit to tell his whopper lie. "Here's the bug-infested pizza we told you about." He opens the lid to the box, "See?" and points to a tiny little speck with legs. He wasn't looking me in the eye. I glanced inside the box, three pieces were left, and inspected the side sticker. Bingo. The pizza was delivered two weeks ago. I peeled the sticker off his box, which he still held out to me in ready exchange.

"I'm sorry, but I can't accept this return."

"Why the hell not?"

"Well, first – you've eaten over half the pizza. Second – where'd you get an ant in the middle of winter? Third – this pizza was purchased from us the week before last. The last reason alone is enough to deny your request. I'm sorry."

He hesitated for a few seconds. "Well, all I know is that my roommate said he bought this pizza about an hour ago, and sent me down here to return this... and he'll be calling your manager." His face reddened and I could tell he knew I caught him.

"The phone number's on the box. Ask for Dean." I smiled as politely as I could, then turned and walked out with the pizza, still steaming in its warming sleeve. I kept the pizza label from his box for Dean as proof. I made one more delivery to a small apartment complex on Woodland Drive, then circled back to Horn Avenue and back to the store. Dean was waiting for me to return.

"What did you tell that guy? He called back complaining that you cussed him out and called him a liar."

"He what? Ugh! I'm sorry sir, but I was *very* professional. I did exactly what you told me to do. The pizza in question was two weeks old. I have the sticker to prove it." I could not believe this guy. Some people think that if they perpetuate a lie enough, it will become the truth. Dean took the sticker from me and looked at it.

"Don't call me sir," he said, almost perfunctory, then looked at the sticker again. "Well, as much as you and I would like to tell this ass-hat to 'get bent,' he's raising so much of a stink we're going to have to give him the pizza."

"What?"

"The last thing I need is a customer calling the Health Department to get us in trouble. What was it, a Mighty Meat? There's a fresh one coming out of the oven right now. Box it up for them and take it back over there in exchange for the one you originally took over there. We don't want to mess this one up."

"Me? I just told him we *weren't* going to give him the pizza." I looked around, but remembered we were short a delivery driver tonight and everyone else was currently on a run.

"I'm sorry, Rocker. You're just going to have to swallow your pride and take one for the team." I was fuming. On top of the night I've already had, I did *not* want to face this guy again.

"Yes, sir."

"Geez, Marcie. Stop calling me sir."

"Sorry," I apologized, then chuckled self-consciously. Dean looked at me in mock disgust, then smiled and walked over to answer the phone. I was beginning to feel that maybe inside he wasn't such an asshole after all, just wanted everybody to think he was.

As I walked back to my drop box to slip some cash into it, I heard Craig and two other guys talking and laughing in hushed tones.

"The girl told me she was on the rag, so instead I got her to go down on me in the back of someone else's car."

"Damn!" one of the other guys said in admiration.

"Then I saw Lindsey leading Rocker through the bushes out back, and I knew she was about to get freaky on him. But then he comes stumbling out about five minutes later and runs away. When Lindsey and her friends left the party not long after that, Lindsey asked me if I'd seen that little twerp. She's wasting her time if you ask me."

I wanted to go in there and tell him off again, but my confidence had left me. Only shame remained, and it settled in the pit of my stomach like river sand. I turned around and pretended not to hear him.

I picked up another delivery to a house on Pinnacle Drive, a curvy, steep dead-end road off West King Street, and headed back out. As I drove out of the parking lot, I thought how smug Ant Guy would probably act when I came back, and looked at the pizza in its warming sleeve beside me in the passenger seat. A delightful thought crept into my head, a desire to open the box and hawk a big gummy wad of phlegm right in the middle of it, so everyone who got a slice would bite into it first thing. My throat had been scratchy for the past two days. Maybe I could spread a few cold germs their way. I was feeling awfully mean. Then my conscience took over, and I shook the thought off. I would just be stooping to their level.

The same guy with the baggy jeans was waiting for me, and now a few of his buddies were with him.

"Yeah! That's what I thought!" he said to me, an air of victory in his voice. "See, you guys? I told you the customer is *always* right."

"One Mighty Meat pizza? Here you go. Have a good evening, and Merry Christmas." I gave them my best fake, car-salesman smile, and turned to walk away.

"Hey, wait a minute. I asked for *extra* cheese!" I heard Ant Guy say, the others laughing. I just kept walking, and thought about what Jesus said about turning the other cheek, but it didn't make me feel much better. If it was my pimply ass cheek, and I told them to kiss it, maybe that would have made me feel better.

14 _____

The scent of creosote and wood ash filled my sinuses. It
made me feel empty, but how I missed it. My dreams curled like
smoke from the furnace door when the fire's not drawing well. It
must be really cold outside. The North wind whistled around the
corner of my apartment like blowing into a Coke bottle, across the
chimney top that stirred the ashes in my head. I closed the furnace
door quickly to the orange glow and all went dark again.

On the other side, my mother sat with her back to the wood
furnace like she was drying her hair. She sat so still that I tried to
walk around for a glimpse of her face, to see if she was asleep, but I
couldn't. Everything spun with each step as if on a giant turntable,
the furnace, my mother. She sat in her ladder-backed chair with her
back constantly toward me. There was a brush on a stool next to
her. I went to reach for the brush, but someone else picked it up. I
could only see his hands – larger than bear's paws. His fingers were
thick, palms muscled and calloused as if from years of field work.
His sleeves were rolled up, and I couldn't see any other part of him,
not even his face. In the warm smoky darkness of the basement, I
became aware of a growing sense of insignificance, a smallness of
existence, and I knew who held the brush. It was God Almighty.

I felt he knew I was there, yet his face wasn't turned toward
me. I was glad I couldn't see him, for when I tried looking into the
darkness for his face I shook in fear. I wanted to say something to
him, wanted to make a plea for strength, but before my thoughts
could manifest themselves into words God lifted my mother's hair
up in his large hands to brush the first strand. I could tell it was my
mother by the way her wet hair shined by the light of the wood

furnace vent, her ear peeking out from under it. God ran the brush through her hair, and it was long, longer than I had ever seen it. It cascaded out from her head in thick drapes like Rapunzel and climbed up the basement stairs, which disappeared into nothing. God was so gentle with her hair, brushing the strands, combing out knots into a silky sheen. I tried to ask him what he was doing with my mother, to call to her, but only silence and air came out of my mouth. I tried screaming, crying to Him, to her, but to no effect. I was struck mute.

He spoke to her. "Your locks are still growing. Some may fall out. Others will be strong enough to hold his weight, but you must trust me."

"I'll try," she replied. What were they talking about?

God continued brushing her wet hair, until it came to a knot where several strands of hair crossed paths and tangled. He said, "But first this must be straightened out." God pulled on it slowly and firmly with the plastic-handled brush. I felt a pain like my own hair being pulled from the root-core of my brain. I woke up to my alarm clock. The pain soon subsided, and my head cleared. Only a scratchiness in the back of my throat remained. Dumbfounded and bewildered, I got out of bed and yawned, but no sound came from my mouth. I tried to clear my throat, but my vocal chords seized up. The only sound that came out of my mouth was that of air passing through a broken whistle. Then it hit me, a rush of guilt washing over me, weighing me down like quilted lead. I didn't want to do it. No. But a strong push compelled me to reconsider. The weight slackened just enough for me to straighten up and catch my breath.

* * * *

I didn't know how I was going to be able to work tonight without the use of my voice, but I was going to have to try. If I concentrated enough, I was able to move my lips and manipulate an almost audible whisper. If I tried to say anything louder, only noiseless air escaped my throat. A doctor wouldn't do me any good. Besides, I didn't have any insurance. Maybe if it was just a cold I could wait it out, but I knew better.

The minute I walked into the delivery entrance could see I was in for it. The place was hopping with activity. Craig and Paul were slamming dough furiously onto the stainless-steel counter, sending wisps of flour into the air. Sam n'Eric spread cheese like their life depended on it, one occasionally stepping on the other's foot, the other whining about it. The most alarming thing was the beep-beep-beep of orders that were overdue to be cleared from the prep screen. The delivery screen was overloaded as well. It was the week of exams, and many college students were calling in for deliveries. Chris approached me with a look of anxiety.

"Thank God you showed up, Randy. Two of our drivers called in sick, and Dean's out of town, so it's just me managing the place."

"Who all in see?" I mouthed.

"What?" he asked, screwing up his face, and leaning in closer.

"Who seeck?" I breathed again, and stuck my tongue out, holding the back of my hand to my forehead.

"Oh! It was Aaron and the new guy we hired to replace Lindsey. She quit the other day. Man, sounds like *you're* sick for real. Make sure to wash your hands and don't sneeze on the pizzas. Hurry up and clock in – you and Ollie have your work cut out for you. Check the ovens for dough bubbles to pop. Some pizzas have been coming out looking like the Astrodome."

I must have stood there with a dumbstruck look on my face for a few seconds more than I should have. So Lindsey quit. I wondered why. I hoped it didn't have anything to do with me.

"Well, don't just stand there." Chris said.

Ollie walked up to me with a stack of warming sleeves. He was just checking out with a delivery as I was checking in. I figured I could ask him later why Lindsey quit. He would know. "Boy, I'm glad to see you. The day shift guy clocked out too early, and I've been on my own for almost an hour. Here's the plan. Take as many orders as you can to any one section of town: Northeast, Southeast, Southwest, and Northwest and Campus. If you can wait a few minutes for a pizza to come out of the oven to add it to an existing run before you go, do so. Otherwise, we need to keep moving." Under his breath he muttered, "The owner Walt left ol' Limp-Dick in charge, and he doesn't know what the Hell he's doing most of the time, so we've got to ask ourselves, 'What Would Dean Do?'"

After Tyler quit several weeks ago, Dean rehired Ollie on a trial basis. I guess he must have been a good worker. I hadn't worked with Ollie much, and when I did he usually checked in, grabbed his next delivery, and was gone. He didn't hang around to talk when he could help it. I didn't understand all of his instructions, but didn't want him to have to explain it all again, so I quickly made a hand gesture with thumb and index finger and mouthed "Okay."

"What've you got, Laryngitis? I've got some 'cough syrup' that might fix that right up. It's in the side pocket of my backpack." With that, he winked, collected his warming sleeves, and rushed toward the door. Halfway out he stopped, shouting, "Expect a few people to be pissed about late orders, but don't sweat it. We'll let management worry about that!"

It was hard to tell how old Ollie was. He could be 25 or 40. Though his face was scarred from acne as a teenager, he had this ageless quality about him, like he lived on his own time. He wore the usual green shirt and khaki pants, but they always looked new. My shirt was already starting to fade a little. He also slicked his hair back with some type of pomade, like Buddy Holly without the glasses. What really made him stand out from the other drivers was his car. Most drivers run them into the ground. My Pontiac Grand Am had already racked up almost 10,000 more miles since I started working here, and I was going to have to replace the shocks soon on account that my tires have been grating the inside of the wheel wells when I go over big pot holes. Ollie's car, however, was a classic – a blue 1965 Ford Mustang Shelby GT 350. It's definitely not a show car, mind you. But I overheard him talking to Aaron one time that he was planning on painting it a glossy black, and finishing the job with a metallic gold stripe kit. I've never known much about engines, but Ollie must have kept that thing regularly tuned, because that V-8 purred like a tiger when it idled. One time I checked out a delivery right after him in the same direction, and followed him out Blowing Rock Road past the hospital. Ollie took a right out Payne Branch and, with a rumble, just disappeared into the night like a ghost. I felt like I was driving a pedal car behind him.

Thankfully, the seven-to-ten rush was fairly routine. Just as Ollie said, some customers were irate over their orders being more than 30-45 minutes late, but I tried making it up to them by giving them their drink or breadsticks for free. One guy pitched a fit because I grabbed a two-liter Pepsi instead of a 20 ounce, even though I was giving him more drink. "It gets flat too quick," he said. I just shrugged my shoulders and gave him an "I'm sorry" look. In communicating the price of the pizzas to the customers, I had to point to the sticker on the box. That was where I wished I had my voice back. A couple of times some customers even thought I gave them the wrong change because I couldn't count it back to them out loud, the way bank tellers usually do when you cash a check. I never realized what a difference that made until I couldn't do it. I didn't care how much tip money I made tonight, though. I had too much sitting cold and greasy on the back burners of my mind, and as long as I came out in the plus by closing, I was okay.

At around 11:00, the skies let loose with an unexpected snow. The forecast only called for a chance of flurries. It was slow at first, then gradually steadier, until there was about two inches on the back streets, with the main roads getting slushier by the minute. Ollie suggested to Chris that he enact the "limited delivery range" on account of the weather, which did alleviate some of the longer hauls to the edge of town that killed our delivery time turnarounds. Still, it was slick out there. I put cables around my front tires, but then I got careless. On one delivery to the East part of campus, I came down the hill on Oak Street a little too fast. When I braked for the stop sign at Clement, I started to skid. The chains didn't do a bit of good for stopping. I had to make a quick choice, slide out into the intersection and possibly across the street into someone's car, or hit the stop sign. I chose the stop sign. I let off my brakes just enough to steer, and aimed for the post dead center of my front bumper. I folded that metal sign post over like a bendy straw. After I came to a complete stop, I got out and looked around. The stop sign was two feet from touching the ground, I had bent it over so much. No cops, no witnesses. My bumper had a chunk scraped out of it, showing the yellow plastic underneath, but nothing major. I jumped up and down on the sign to bend it off my bumper a little, then hopped back in my car and put it in reverse. I spun a little grass and gravel out in front of me, but managed to pull myself free. Then I got out of the car again, bent the post back up as best I could, and got in my car and took off. The signpost sat a little cock-eyed now, but not terribly so.

It got quieter around midnight. There were no more delivery calls. The snow turned to big, fat flakes the size of silver dollars before tapering off, but that six inches of snow seemed to muffle the sounds of town, save for the hiss of cars driving through pasty road slush in front of the store or the occasional jangle of tire chains. I reluctantly helped Craig ladle sauce on some pies for carryout while Sam n'Eric took a bathroom break.

Ollie was leaning up against the wall in the back, smoking a cigarette. Though I didn't like the smell of smoke, I grabbed a Sun Drop and sat in the back as well. Craig and the others were wiping down their stations. I already cleaned mine twice, so it could wait until closing.

"So, Randy. How was your night?"

I held my hand out like I was playing with a toy car, making puttering noises with my lips, and held my arm up like a stop sign. "Pwoosh." I whispered. I made the pretend car hit the pretend sign, knocking it down.

"You hit a telephone pole?" He asked.

I shook my head.

"Timmy fell in the well again and got trapped?"

I gave him a "What the hell" look and searched for a pen in my pocket. I wrote on the back of a coupon flyer, "Hit a stop sign."

"Well, I hope it didn't mess your bumper up too bad. They don't make them like they used to. Did you get a chance to try my throat remedy?"

I shook my head and pointed at my watch. "No time," I mouthed.

"Well, let Dr. Ollie get you a sample." He took half a step over to a bag hanging on a hook on the wall, and pulled out a small jelly jar of light amber-colored liquid. He looked around to see if anyone else was in the room. "Take a quick swig of that, but hurry. Dean don't care, but I don't trust that weasel Chris."

I gave him an inquisitive look as I unscrewed the lid and took a sniff. I wanted to make sure it wasn't turpentine or kerosene or something like that.

"You know what it is. It's my granddad's best 'shine. Been soaking peaches in it since the summer. Don't be shy, take a big gulp. That'll lube your throat."

I would have rather eaten the peaches, but filled my mouth and swallowed all at once. It was smooth and faintly sweet, with a hint of fruit and spice. Then the burn came like a wave, all the way down my throat to my stomach. I shivered and handed it back to him. That stuff was much stronger than what Lindsey and I drank at the party.

"This stuff's been distilled three times. My granddad doesn't do that hardly ever, only once in a while when he's caught up on his orders."

I pounded my chest, nodded my head, and mouthed the words, "Good." But my voice didn't come back. I tried clearing my throat, but it was almost as if I was missing my vocal chords altogether.

Ollie smiled, "You're a good guy, Randy. So I feel I can trust you. And if you double-cross me, I'll break your legs." My eyes must have gotten wide at that remark, because he went from a serious face, to one of mirth. "You're a hoot, man! You always take things so seriously. You need to lighten up sometimes. What I was saying is," and here he took a drag on his cigarette, blowing the smoke to the side, then in a lowered voice, "I have a little business selling 'shine for my dad and my granddad, but I get busy this time of year with other things. You could deliver a few small orders for me if you wanted to, less than two dozen quart jars, during the holidays and make a little extra spending cash. More than you would delivering a few pizzas."

I always thought the story of moonshine runners was romantic, almost heroic, like Junior Johnson. If it weren't for bootleggers we wouldn't have stock car racing today. Still, I remembered that I heard somewhere he also sold pot, among other things, which made me a little nervous at the thought. I pointed to my throat and made like I wanted to talk to him about it, but just shrugged my shoulders at its evident futility.

"You think about it. Sorry my home remedy didn't help you much. You must really have it bad." I tried handing the jar back to him. "Stick that in your duffel bag. You can keep it. Get back to me later on that little proposal when you feel better."

I grabbed an old pizza box, brushed the crumbs off, and with my pocket pen scribbled "Lindsey?" on the top, then, "What's the story?" beneath it.

"Oh, Lindsey? Well, I can't say there's much to tell. I think she said something about being tired of working with a bunch of immature boys."

I pointed at myself with a quizzical look on my face.

"You? Y'all were buddies, weren't you? No, I think she got tired of the 'Dough Boys' Craig and Paul, but mainly Craig. They had some bad history together, I think. She took a job waiting tables at the Caribbean Café. You should go see her sometime. They have good wings there." A wave of longing for Lindsey passed through me, so I thought of Cassie's phone number in my wallet instead, but I didn't know when I should call her, or if she would still want to go out with me. I festered with inaction, and it frustrated me.

Chris stuck his head into the break room. "Guys, we have a few pizzas to box up and deliver. Let's get back to it."

"Don't get your panties in a wad," said Ollie, crushing a cigarette out in an old pizza box. He turned to me. "I'll let you take whatever shorter run there is, and I'll take the edge of town run. That'll give you a chance to make another run before I get back."

I wondered how he could know what deliveries were up before even looking at the screen. But then again, he is a good driver. He knows what he's doing. Sure enough, when I helped him box the pizzas, I checked the labels, two to Meadow Hill apartments and one to Swampbox Road. Chris looked at the green screen as we packed our warming sleeves.

"Swampbox? Someone should have told them we weren't delivering that far on account of the roads."

"It's not a problem, Chris. I've got it. The roads aren't that bad now."

"I delivered to Swampbox Road when I used to be a driver," Chris said. "It's got to be the roughest trailer park in the whole county. I had a man one time cuss me out, and throw an ashtray at me because I wouldn't step in his door and lay the pizzas on the bar for him. The idiot was too stoned to get out of his easy chair, but I was afraid someone was waiting behind the door with a baseball bat to mug me."

"Well, you were probably acting like a prick," Ollie muttered.

"What did you say?"

"Nothing, boss." Ollie grabbed his printed receipt and walked briskly to his car.

∗   ∗   ∗   ∗

The pizzas I had to deliver to Meadow Hill were two separate orders to the same address. The apartment complex wasn't hard to spot. It was the one with the three-unit party going on. Despite the cold, people were spilling out of the sliding doors and standing around on the balconies. After delivering the first order to apartment 204 to a guy in boxers who scowled at me, handing me a check for the exact amount, I instinctually made my way to the party. The door was already open when I made it to 211. I waved and smiled at the first group of people I saw.

"Pizza's here!" a red-headed girl with freckles called out to the larger group. A group of four partygoers made their way to the door, all very drunk and wearing their coats and toboggans. The red-headed girl spoke again, her speech loose but not slurred. "We have an odd proposition for you. I hope you'll hear us out." She took a few steps closer to me, and I could smell a mixture of heavy perfume and cigarette smoke. She put her hand on my shoulder. "My friends and I live in Watauga Village Apartments."

"The up-one on the hill, next the dealership-cars," one of the two guys in the group slurred.

"Frank, calm down and let me explain," she said to him, and then turning back to me, "We were wondering – if you were heading back to Papa's Pizza – could you give us a ride? It's just up the hill from your store, and on the way. We'll pay for the pizzas regardless." She ran her hand over my arm that held the warming sleeve, smiled and batted her eyes. "My, you must lift more than just pizzas to have biceps like this." I could feel her finger nails through my long-sleeve thermal undershirt.

I knew she was laying it on thick. But what could I say? Absolutely nothing, with my voice gone like it was. I scratched my head through my ball cap and screwed my face up like I was thinking about it.

"Please, please, pretty please!" a thick-haired girl with dark eyebrows pleaded, folding her hands and sticking her lower lip out in a pout.

I made like I was going to talk, but gestured to my throat.

"You're deaf? I'm sorry, I didn't know," said the red head, speaking louder.

I shook my head no.

"Would you – please give – us a ride?" yelled Frank, mouthing the words slowly.

I could tell there wasn't a way I could gracefully back out of this one, so I rolled my eyes in mock impatience and nodded my head yes.

"All right, man. You the man!" the other guy exclaimed.

It was a tight fit in my Grand Am. We all waited around for five more minutes for another girl who decided to join the group, to make six total. I sure hoped no cops spotted us all stuffed in here like a clown car, driving up King Street. Four fit in the backseat, with one holding the warming sleeve and lying across everyone's laps, while the red-headed girl sat on the lap of the girl with dark eyebrows in the front. And they all reeked of liquor. As I drove, I hoped no one ended up puking in my car between here and there. The redhead dug clumsily into the front pocket of her tight jeans.

"Here's a 20 for the pizza, but that's all I got. Have any of you back there got anything for tip or taxi fare?" A few people fidgeted in the back, but no one made a real effort to cough up any more dough. I figured in my head that I would probably make a $1.62 tip on this run, and wished I could just dump everyone out and make them walk their drunk asses the rest of the way home.

"I think we're all broke back here!" a few of them laughed.

"You broke something, with your bony ass!" one said to the other, still laughing.

"Listen, I'm really sorry, Pizza Guy. It's really sweet of you to give us a ride home, especially on a night like this. Here," the redhead grabbed my delivery receipt for their order and read my name off it. "Okay, Randall S. Next time I drive past the store I'll stop and leave you some tip money with the manager. How does that sound?"

I doubted the sincerity of her promise, seeing she was clearly on her way to becoming wasted with a few more wine coolers. But I nodded my head and tried mouthing "thank you" to her as I watched the road.

It was a little slick, but the tire cables gripped well as I pulled onto Robin Lane.

"Just drop us off at that one there," said the dark-eyebrowed girl sitting under the redhead, pointing to a set of steps leading up the hill.

"Aw, we always go back to your place," said the red-headed girl.

"Your roommate's probably already asleep," she cooed, leaning in and kissing the redhead briskly on the lips. With much grunting and struggling, they all wiggled and crawled out of my car.

"Thanks again, Pizza Guy!" a few of them shouted from outside. The red-headed girl waved and blew me a kiss through the front windshield, and then turned and walked away with the rest of the group, who were all laughing and stumbling over one another. They also walked away with my warming sleeve.

I would have normally been flattered, blushing even, but feeling like a tool was just the icing on the cake of this crummy night. I would be lucky to make $20 on tips, this detour probably costing me some delivery time, and I knew the store would be closing in about 30 minutes. After parking my car, though, I spotted something in the back seat. It was a folded ten-dollar bill and some ones that must have fallen out of someone's pocket. There's my taxi fare, I thought. Without any ID, I had no way of knowing who dropped it, so I chalked it up to a blessing of divine intervention. When I bent down to get it, I noticed something else in the floor one of them must have dropped. I picked it up. It was a prepaid phone card. My throat tightened and swelled, and I immediately knew what I needed to do with it.

* * * *

The next day, I stopped at the gas station near the community college on my way to class. I was anxious, not so much from the fact that I was about to take a final exam as what I was about to do first. There was a pay phone out by the air compressor, but how could I use the phone when I couldn't talk? I felt in my front pocket for the card I found the night before. It was still there, and as I tried clearing my throat I felt a slight hum return. The afternoon rays were bright, but when the sun wasn't looking the December wind bit into my cheeks. I thought again about calling Cassie, but that would have to wait for now. I didn't know if the university's Christmas break started earlier, if she would be in her apartment or already at home. I was drowning in guilt and regret, and I wanted to be free of it. I took a swig of a flat Sun Drop left in my car from the night before and tried to clear my throat again. Another small hum came from the recesses of my vocal chords. I took a long drink.

The final exam in Algebra was in 45 minutes, so I knew I couldn't talk long. What would I say? What if she wasn't home? What if my dad picked up? I still didn't care if I ever talked to *him* again. I felt my throat closing up more, and tried clearing my mind of it. I wanted to sound happy and well. I didn't want her to worry. I took a few deep breaths and dialed the card's numbers.

The recording said there were 12 minutes left on it. I then dialed my number. It rang, four, five, six times. I was about to hang up when it stopped, and a voice I hadn't heard in a while came over the line.

"Hello?" I had almost forgotten what she sounded like.

"Hey Mom," my voice cracked.

"Randall?! Is that you? Oh God, where have you been?"

"Relax, Mom, relax. Listen, I'm fine. I'm doing well. School and work's going good." I coughed and cleared my throat.

"Where are you? You sound different."

"I'm okay. I'm at a pay phone, and I'm getting over a sore throat. I've got a final exam soon that I need to take, so I don't have long to chat. I just wanted to tell you I'm doing just great. You would be proud of me. No need to worry."

"Son, please come home."

"I haven't planned on it, and I can't right now anyway. I've gotta work over Christmas, save my money."

"Son...," she quietly pleaded.

My throat thickened. I felt pressure building behind my eyes. "Mom, I love you. Know that, but I gotta go."

"Okay, but wait..." I hung up the phone, and immediately a dam burst in me of pent-up emotion.

I jumped into my car and drove as I was overcome with a wave of shuddering sobs. I tried holding it in, but that only created sharp pains in my chest. I turned into the road to the community college, but drove past it, up the switch-back hill where the earth movers were grading to build rows of new apartments. I stopped at an empty lot of rutted, dried mud and put my car in park just before another wave of sobs ripped through me. I cried like a little boy being held down to get a tooth pulled too early, angry for the twisting, cutting pain.

"Why are you doing this to me?" I screamed, gripping the steering wheel. "I'm not a child anymore!"

I got out of my car into the last of the cold afternoon sun before it dipped behind the far hill. Tucked in its shadow hummed a rock quarry, its conveyor belts carrying crushed stone under the road to the other side to be further processed. Every now and again there was a faraway clank of metal against metal, like the grinding, sharp coldness inside me. I resented how I felt, how she made me feel. I wiped my face on my sleeve, then rubbed the wet snot in. I took a few deep breaths as I tried to control the spasms still welling up from my chest as sniffled huffs. I took a few more deep breaths and looked down at the college sitting in the valley below as the wetness evaporated from my face, drying in icy wisps with the passing breeze. My throat loosened and my head cleared.

Something in the distance caught my eye. On the road below, a car had run over a plastic grocery bag, sending it into the air. The wind picked it up further, and it continued to swirl and climb, sinking for a bit, and then climbing further. Perhaps it was the heat from the quarry machines that pushed it. It seemed so white and small in the distance as it rose to the level of the hill I stood on. I thought if I took my eyes off it for a second, I would lose it. It kept floating higher and further away, off toward the river, until it melded into the sun and haze of the distance.

I grew tired, wondering if I was on the edge of defeat, if I should just give up, just pack my car and leave it all, follow the grocery bag. Then I wondered when it would come back down, knowing everything eventually does. I cleared my throat and looked at my watch. My exam started five minutes ago.

15 _____

The fall quarter ended last week, so I was finished with classes until the second of January. Final exams were over for the university as well, and the throng of college students had already descended from the mountain. It surprised me how quiet and less congested Boone was, as thousands of people seemed to evacuate to go visit their families for Christmas break. Dean was excited when I told him I was staying here for the holidays, and he didn't ask me why I wasn't going home. Pizza deliveries were slower, but I was still making good tips because some of our drivers went home for vacation as well. Tonight was a cold and especially slow night, the first official day of winter, but it seemed like it had already been here for a while. I was sharing delivery runs with two veteran drivers, Aaron and Ollie. When there were no deliveries or pizzas to make, we stood around folding boxes and talking. Ollie was pretty cool, but Aaron was a prick as usual.

"So my ex-wife has the gall to ask me for 50 bucks two weeks after I sent her a child support check! The nerve of that bitch! If she wouldn't buy our daughter's clothes at those designer stores at the mall, maybe she would have more money, know what I'm sayin'?"

"I can't help you there, man. I learned a long time ago that when it comes to women you're better off to love 'em and leave 'em – and wear a condom," Ollie said.

"How old is your daughter?" I asked Aaron.

"She's about 13 now. It used to be great, my wife and I, but she kept bugging me and bugging me that we should have a kid. It would bring us closer together, I guess she thought. It got to the point that I eventually gave in when I realized it was the only way I was going to get laid. I should've dropped her for a new piece of tail." He moved the stack of pizza boxes he had been folding onto a shelf above us.

I was glad that I wasn't the butt of every snide remark he made now, but I still had trouble stomaching how he talked about the mother of his daughter. One of these days when I started a family of my own, I thought, I wouldn't be that way. I would make sure I was the best husband and father I could be. But who knows how or when that's ever going to happen. Sometimes I thought God forgot about me. I felt like a dead leaf swirling down an icy creek, tumbling and hitting every rock along the way.

Dean was taking some time off for Christmas, so Chris was in charge again tonight. He wasn't giving orders much, just sat in the office on the phone. Paul was slinging the dough, and Sam n'Eric worked the sauce and toppings. I found out later that these two guys were sophomores in high school and actually brothers, the grandchildren of Walt Groves, the owner of the store. At the moment they mainly stood around and played with the toppings, making little pizzas out of scraps of breadstick dough and sending them through the oven. Something wasn't right, though. Without some of the others working, like Dean or Lindsey, the social chemistry was off. My chest and neck felt suddenly flush. I spaced out, and my thoughts found their way back to Cathy, the only one I'd ever fallen in love with before.

I tried to change my course of thought, to keep from spiraling into a funk. Cassie. She was gorgeous, and seemed to like me. I had already floundered with indecision, though, foolishly waiting too late to call her. She had already left for home. I was on a pay phone a few days ago at a gas station near my apartment when I called her, and I hung up before leaving a message on her answering machine. What would her parents think of some strange boy calling their daughter at home from a pay phone, anyway? She probably already thinks I'm not interested. The more I thought about it, the more hesitant I was about calling her again. I couldn't take any more rejection right now.

"Randy? – Hey Rocker!" Ollie was snapping his fingers, trying to get my attention. "It's your turn to take the delivery, Chief."

"Sorry. I was zoning out there. Where's it to?" I approached the delivery screen. Ollie shrugged his shoulders as he walked into the back room, putting a cigarette in his mouth and reaching into his pants pocket for a lighter. I looked on the green-hued screen to see it was Crocker Road.

"Ha! Rocker's got Crocker! Have a fun climb," Aaron chuckled as he looked over my shoulder.

"Yeah, you're a regular poet," I said. Crocker Road was off Highway 321 past the edge of town. Though not the farthest road we delivered, definitely one of the steepest. The switchback curves were so sharp you could look out your driver's side window and wave at the people in the back seat.

It was a single-pizza delivery, pepperoni and mushroom. I wouldn't be getting much of a tip on this one, but at least it got me out of the store for a while. The Country radio station here in Boone played too much Christmas music, so I popped in a cassette tape of Chuck Denson's Band. It reminded me of the times James and I would sit on his carport and listen to his boom box while I helped him tinker with his Chevy Nova. – *I ain't gonna ask a thing from you, I can survive just fine on my own* – I turned up the volume about as loud as I could without rattling the back-window speakers. – *And if you don't like my country style, why don't you just kiss my ass and go the hell on home* – I turned off 321 and drove past a builder's supply store. Though I learned how to drive a stick shift on my dad's truck, I was glad my Grand Am was an automatic. As small and sporty as it was, the transmission seemed to hold up good under the strain.

There were many roads that forked and came to dead ends at the head of this steep hollow, and Crocker Road didn't have a street sign. I knew I was on the right road, however, when I saw the zig-zagging switchback up the hill ahead of me. I looked at the number on the address and then flashed my spotlight on the mailboxes. It had to be at the top, near the small apartment complex, I thought. There weren't any numbers on the houses, but as I drove past the mailboxes I spotted the number on the front lid, and pulled into a short, steep driveway. I wondered how anyone

119

got down this road, or even out of their driveway, when it came a good snow. I pulled my emergency brake handle as hard as I could, and got out with the pizza. It was a brick house. The porch light was on, and several terra cotta pots filled with dead flowers lined the front steps. I rang the doorbell, just as a brisk blast of wind shot across the ridge and rattled the treetops above.

"Come on in, ith's freezing outside," the young woman said as she opened the door. I always felt awkward stepping in someone's house, but Dean assured me it was okay if they invited you in. There wasn't a storm door, so I closed the heavy door behind me with my free hand to keep out the wind.

"You ordered a large pepperoni and mushroom, ma'am?" She was short and slight of build with long brunette hair, and wore a silky, pink nightgown with red lace fringe around the edges. It looked a little large on her where it hung around her shoulders, except where her breasts filled it in. I tried not to stare at her exposed cleavage, so I kept my eyes toward the floor. She wore matching slippers and a metal brace on her left leg, and spoke to me with a slight lisp.

"I hope ith's not too hot in here for you. I keep the heat turned up in the winter, but I sthill feel cold. I think I ordered a medium pizza." She gestured to the large pizza in my hand.

I looked at the sticker on the box. "Well, I do know we have a special right now on a large three topping pizza for the price of a medium, so I guess one of the guys rang it up as a large."

"Well, okay. It'll all go to my thighs, though." She patted her leg through the thin gown, then looked back at me. "I got in a bad car accident three months ago," she said.

"I'm sorry to hear that, ma'am." I looked fleetingly into her eyes and smiled. She wasn't old, maybe in her late 30s.

"Does this gown look good on me? Give me your honesth opinion. I just got it in the mail today from Frederick's." She took a step with her good leg like a model posing. "When I hit the stheering wheel, it broke my jaw in four places and knocked three teeth out, so I had to get porcelains, see?" She limped a few steps closer to me, brushed her hair back and, tilting her chin up, revealed a long, dark red scar from her ear to right under her chin. I looked

120

at it closely at her request, and I could feel her eyes on me. She moistened her lips with the tip of her tongue. Aside from her scar, her face was radiant and flawless, and her green eyes bore right into me. "Ever thince the accident, and my boyfriend leaving me, I've felt so unattractive."

"I'm sorry to hear that." It *was* warm in the house, and the perfume she wore drifted into my nose and mouth. It had a sweet fragrance, like vanilla and flowers. "It's not very noticeable, ma'am. The scar. I heard that rubbing Vitamin E oil will help get rid of them almost completely after a while." I then added, "You look very beautiful, ma'am."

"Really? You're sweet. The doctor thaid I broke my thibia and fibula in ten different places, told me that in a few more months I could get the rods and stheel pins out of my leg, but I might have to wear a brace longer. Even so, they said I may never walk without a limp." Pretending to be coy, she pulled back her gown as she spoke and stuck her injured leg out to reveal her metal brace and most of her smooth, white upper thigh.

I felt sorry for her predicament, and her loneliness. I wanted to reach out to her, tell her everything was going to be fine, like she seemed to be reaching out to me. I felt awkward, her eyes searching me, a desire rising in me, but remembering I was on the clock, wearing my green, collared Papa's Pizza shirt with the pizza slice emblem and matching ball cap, I regained composure. "The pizza is $7.89 with tax, ma'am," I said politely, my face hot. I set the box down on the bar.

"The money's on the table by the door." She pulled her gown around her neck and tightened her sash. Her eyes turned downward, away from me. I was about to turn around to leave, when instead I turned to her. I grasped her hand as she was about to turn away and gently squeezed it. I looked into her eyes intently, swallowed my hesitancy, and scarcely knew what I was about to say next.

"Anyone should be able to see you are an attractive, sexy, warm and caring woman," I stated. "Trust me. And one of these days you are going to make some man extremely happy, I know it. Don't feel so down." I leaned down and kissed her hand.

"That ith the sweetest thing anyone's said to me in a long time." She tilted her head and looked into my face searchingly. "I knew it. You already have thomeone elth in your life, don't you?"

"Well, I guess you could say so." I blushed and thought about Cassie's phone number in my wallet.

"Sthay no more! I know where you are coming from. I should have known, thince you weren't wearing a wedding band, that someone so sensitive to a woman's feelings had to be either married or gay. And all of us *sthraight* people complain how hard it is to find love these days!"

What?!

I bristled inside. Where in the hell did that come from? I'm not gay, I thought. Why would she think that? What did I do to make her think that? Then I looked at how she was smiling at me, how she still held my hand, how relieved she seemed that my rejection of her advances wasn't the result of her undesirability.

"Please don't say anything," I said in a hushed tone of embarrassment. "I'm not really 'out' yet." I couldn't believe what I was saying.

"Oh, Thweetie. It'll be okay. You're still young. You have plenty of time. I feel things are gonna change. One day you won't have to live in fear or shame for how you feel. Stay strong, Honey."

"Now look who's trying to make who feel better!" I smiled. She limped closer and leaned up to give me a hug, and I felt her taut breasts press against me through her gown. "I better get along now, before the boss wonders where I'm at." I felt an erection growing, and held the pizza-warming sleeve in front of me. "I hope your pizza's not cold."

"Ith's okay. I'll reheat it. Ith's freezing in this house anyway. Don't forget your money."

I walked to the front door and picked up a 20-dollar bill, then looked back at her. "You want change?

"No, take it," she smiled at me. "Merry Christhmas."

"Thank you. Merry Christmas to you, too." I walked out the front door quickly to keep the cold wind from blowing in, but also because I didn't know how much longer I could keep the ruse going. I *could* have accepted her advances, I thought as I got in my car. I knew how it went now. If things were different, if I were a different man. But it wouldn't have been love. It wouldn't have been real. I prayed to God that she would find happiness in her life, which felt good to do. I should probably do that more often, praying.

They did ask me what took me so long when I got back. Ollie and Aaron had both made short delivery runs to some apartments in town, and were standing around doing nothing. I told them about the woman, how she was dressed, and how she acted toward me, but not about the part where she thought I was gay.

"She *was* pretty, but I felt like I would just be, you know, using her if I gave in to her advances. And I didn't want to *hurt* her feelings, you know, if she was hoping for more of a relationship." I tried explaining as casual as I could, as if strange women threw themselves at me all the time.

Aaron chimes in, "Yeah, not to mention she was a cripple. I wouldn't want to fuck a cripple. There's something creepy about that. I'd be afraid of breaking her back and getting sued, or getting something pinched in her leg brace. Were her jaws wired shut, by the way?" He poked the side of his cheek out with his tongue while moving his circled fingers back and forth against the other corner of his open mouth. His was a malevolent brand of rudeness. I liked it better when he and I weren't on speaking terms.

"I think I delivered a pizza to her once a few weeks back," Ollie said. "Long brunette hair, about five-five, lives in a small brick house?"

"That's her," I nodded.

"Yeah. I remember. She seemed like a lonely woman. Her pain was more than physical. When you come across a woman who's more lovelorn than horny, it's best to pass them by and save them the heartache."

123

"What kind of advice is that to give? You are one to talk, Mr. Gigolo," Aaron said.

Ollie gave Aaron a stern look. "Fuck you."

16 _____

The rumble of thunder and soft patter of rain against the roof was soothing as I lay in my bed, staring at the textured ceiling, tracing the patterns in the thin cobwebs that hung in the corners. It had been a dry winter, and even the spring rains weren't enough to soak deep into the parched ground. I tried digging a flowerbed in the front yard for my mother, to cheer her up. I even bought some marigold seeds at the hardware store downtown. The orange dirt was tough, though, like hacking through cowhide leather with my mattock. But tonight I imagined the ground was soaking it in slowly, without the sun or the June heat wave to wick it away in evaporation. It would also make it easier for the city workers to dig Papaw's grave, even if it was just a small hole.

I wasn't there when it happened. I planned to go see Cathy that day, since school let out a few days before, so I stayed at home to wash my car while my mother went to check on him. He hadn't been feeling well. Having just gotten my driver's license the month before, the thrill of being independent was still fresh in my lungs. Mom found Papaw at the bottom of the steps, hunched over with a sweat rag in his hand and grass clippings stuck to his pants leg. He managed to finish all of the back yard except for two passes in the middle with the push mower. He refused to hire someone to mow for him. They said he must have had chest pains and went inside to sit in the cool basement, and just never got back up. I should've gone over there and mowed the yard for him that day. I knew he would fuss about it if I did, and he would never ask me unless it was something he wanted to teach me how to do, like sharpen and balance the blades. If I had helped him, maybe he would have been alive for a little longer.

When I saw the look on my mother's face as she walked in the door of our house, I already knew what had happened. I ran to my room and cried into my pillow for what seemed like an hour. I couldn't stop it, couldn't fight it. Afterwards, I felt a little bit of a release at the thought that he was no longer in pain from his arthritis, no longer had to keep track of his prescription medicines every day or look around the sink for his misplaced partials. He was in a better place. Papaw wasn't a saint or a church-going man, but I knew he loved the Lord, so I couldn't see how he'd be anywhere else but in Heaven, with Granny.

Papaw did arrange to have his body cremated, and at his request he skipped the visitation at the funeral home and paid only for a graveside service. As soon as Mom found him dead, she called Vaughn-Gwynn and arranged for them to pick him up. They then immediately sent him to Radford to be cremated at a special facility, shipping his ashes back two days later. The next day was the service.

I didn't have a suit, had only one pair of pants that wasn't blue jeans, and I wore a clip-on tie I got at Easter years ago that was too short, with a blue long-sleeve shirt. I drove my mother to Cliffview cemetery, having just gotten my license on May 20, my birthday. She didn't like the idea of my North Carolina driver's license, but she couldn't argue against her father, who assured her beforehand it was perfectly legal in order for me to get in-state tuition at WSU. But now he was not around to assure my mother that everything was going to work out fine.

It had stopped raining long enough to hold the service. Many people showed up, some friends and some family, but most I didn't know at all. Without Papaw to introduce them or point them out for me, I knew very little of them. Aunt Faith came and gave my mom and me a hug, then mentioned she had some mail for me at her house. "Looked like junk mail, to me," she chuckled, and then nervously looked to my mom, who simply turned her head away. It was a short service, and I didn't pay attention to what the pastor said. I just kept staring at the huge hole they dug for Papaw, even though his urn was not much larger than a six-pack Igloo cooler. The large mound of dirt hunched under the carpet of artificial turf bothered me, like they were embarrassed to expose so much of that naked, raw ground to the light. Who cares about the stupid dirt, I thought. My mother stood next to me and cried. I wanted to hold her hand, but both her fists were full of tissues. Dad was nowhere to be found.

"Mom. Where's Dad at?" I whispered.

She shuddered, then gave me a quiet reply. "I don't know, dear. Maybe he's at the funeral home finishing some paperwork." When she said this, I felt a sudden voiding of my insides, like something sank in my gut. No one had seen him all day, I knew. If Cathy was there to stand beside me, I might have felt a little stronger. Her church had vacation bible school that week, and she was in charge of the children's music. She wanted to come, but I told her she needed to be there for the kids, when in fact I was just embarrassed for her to meet my family in our disjointed state.

The pastor had just finished his eulogy. I asked my mother again, "Where is Dad at? What about my college tuition money?"

"Now's not the time to be talking about money," she replied as people approached to shake her hand and offer condolences.

*   *   *   *

Mom sat in the living room with the television off, staring at nothing, a glass of Southern Comfort on ice in her hand. It had to be at least her third glass. I knew it had to do with more than just the death of her father. About three weeks before this, my dad got a job hauling produce for a trucking company, and was away on overnight runs at least a few times a week. Now we rarely saw him. He was gone all the time, only coming home on Saturday nights. He talked to me very little when he came home, mainly to tell me to do my chores or fuss at me for little pissy things like wiping toothpaste on the hand towels or not using coasters on the living room table. It was like every little thing I did summed up what a big disappointment I was to him. I don't think he talked to my mother much, either. I no longer heard their muffled, hurried lovemaking in the other room on late nights.

"Mom?"

"What is it, dear?"

127

"Did you get the refund from the funeral home yet? The $10,000 that Papaw said the funeral home had?" She just closed her eyes and placed her thumb and forefinger to her temples. "I got to thinking that if we put it in a CD account for at least six months, we could draw some in interest. That alone might pay for my meals on campus for a semester."

My mother sighed weakly. "Randall, there is no money."

"What do you mean? Did the funeral cost more than he thought?"

"No. Your father. Your father took the money. He ran off with another woman."

A ringing in my ears started, quiet at first, then gaining in force like a jet plane coming in for a landing. My mother just sat there, staring at the living room floor with no expression. "Well, where is he?" I yelled. "Maybe *you're* mistaken. How do you know? Maybe he's just on a long run. He wouldn't do this to me, to us!" She wouldn't look at me. "How could he do this to us?!"

"He did. He just did."

I became angry with her. "What did he tell you? Did he leave a note? Did y'all have another fight?

She said nothing, as if she didn't hear me.

"Well, what are we going to do?" I asked. "What am I going to do about college now? Do you want me to stay here and do nothing?"

Her eyes had an ethereal quality to them, like she was only half there, and half in another world. "I don't know what to do. Now leave me alone, please." She stared at the dark television and took another drink. The ice clinked mockingly in her glass.

17

I sat at my desk – having finally bought a chair – and flipped through the December issue of *Playboy* while drinking a beer, but Farrah Fawcett wasn't doing anything for me. A few days ago, I went to the usual gas station on the end of town, small and out of the way, so the chances of someone catching me buying a copy were slim. If there was a woman behind the counter, though, I would just buy a pack of gum and come back another time. This instance a tall college-aged guy stood behind the register. I got a Sundrop and a bag of Doritos, and placed them on the counter.

"And the Christmas issue of *Playboy*, please." I said nonchalantly as I could.

He turned around to the special rack behind him, the top magazines covered with cardboard, showing only the titles. "Hey, man. Did you drive past the killer party down the road? I heard it's right out front of some apartment complex. Some dudes were tellin' me about it, came in and bought all my cases of Bud Light!"

"No," I said, full of self-pity. "I haven't been invited to any 'killer' parties this Christmas. I'm just a lowly Freshman."

The guy grabbed the plastic-wrapped magazine and laid it on the counter. "Yeah, you must be pretty lonely," he chuckled. It took me a few seconds to realize what he was referring to.

"I said *lowly* Freshman, not lonely. I got a girl!"

"Sure you do. Merry Christmas." He smirked and handed my items to me in a brown paper bag.

"Asshole," I murmured as I walked out of the store.

It was Christmas Eve, and I had the night off. I used to love the holidays growing up, but not now. I *was* lonely. Those I knew from work were only acquaintances, not really friends. Friends would invite you over for hot chocolate or a beer, or to play Nintendo or something. No one at work even asked me my plans except Dean, who was just glad I could work over Christmas break. I tried thinking of fond memories from past holidays, but resentment just came rushing back to fill the aching, empty spaces.

I wondered how long it would take people to miss me, if for some reason I ceased to exist. Landlord – two months, after the rent due notices piled up. Work – they'd just hire some other poor sap to wear the green shirt and cap. No one even questioned my fake ID when I bought beer at the grocery store this afternoon. I'm just a stone in a road. If I were to get run over and popped into a side ditch, who would miss me? My mom? I wondered if I was causing her pain. I ached worse at that thought. Would she be better off if she never had me?

Ollie's jelly jar of moonshine sat on my desk as well, and I had the radio tuned to a talk news station because all the other stations were playing stupid Christmas music or the same top-40 crap. There was some drivel about solar power or alternative fuels that I wasn't quite following. I took a long sip, and felt the burn. I chased it down with half a beer and gave my magazine a toss under the bed, where the others lay in a box. I chucked the empty can across the room towards the trashcan.

What am I doing here? What is my purpose on this mud ball of a world? I didn't have any special talents to devote myself to. I wasn't an artist. I wasn't that good at writing. I tried writing a poem in the ninth grade, but I burned it soon afterwards in the wood stove. I didn't want anyone else to see how bad it was. I'm not even good with computers. So why am I bothering with college? I didn't know how to express my inadequacy. All I knew was that something was missing in me, and I was beginning to doubt that I would find it here. I needed something to smother the pain, but there was nothing out there that would cure what I had, this empty gall husk inside me.

I had something here that would sure alleviate some symptoms, at least for tonight. I took another swig, and felt the lightness in my head, chased it with another beer, then opened a third. The commentator on the radio discussed something about pig manure being made into diesel fuel on the eastern end of the state.

"Poop!" I said out loud. I took another sip of moonshine, and saw a glimpse of the bottom of the jelly jar. "Now that just won't do," I spoke to the jar. "You need to experience life a little more, feel the air rushing inside you, instead of keeping all those secrets bottled up. I'll help you get them out." I took another swig, and finished the third beer. I remembered that old Jimmy Stuart movie, *It's a Wonderful Life.* That was the most depressing Christmas movie in the world. That angel saving him at the last minute from jumping off a bridge didn't make up for how crappy his life was, despite all the hard work he put into making his life something, all the dreams he gave up for everyone else. No angel is going to save me here. I'm not worth it. I wondered if it would even matter if I saw the sun come up the next day or not, if I should just numb myself and embrace the darkness. But – if I actually had to *ask* myself that question, then maybe I wasn't ready for the end just yet. I was thinking about it too much. I guess that was a good sign. I took one final swig and held it over my head, looking through the glass to the gray ceiling, pausing to listen for something to speak to me. Silence.

"There, now that's better, isn't it? I might even give you a wash tomorrow and set you in my window with some flowers." The jar rolled out of my hand and hit the thinly-carpeted floor, popping into four shards and untold slivers. When I leaned over to pick up the pieces, I found I had trouble getting back up, so I threw a towel over the smaller pieces to vacuum up later. I chased the sourness of indigestion with half a fourth beer, belching queasily, then laid back on my bed and closed my eyes, kicking my shoes off, feeling the room spin in lurches and listening to the drone of voices on the talk radio.

"Merry Christmas, poop guys."

18

The Blue Ridge Parkway around Grandfather Mountain looked like it was closed for the winter. I heard sometimes it doesn't open again until spring. There had been a couple of good snows, but most of it from the last snowfall had already melted from the roadways. Even so, the Parkway was never salted or plowed. A brown gate blocked the road at the first steep curvy incline.

I turned my car around on the Parkway and drove back toward Blowing Rock. During the summer and fall, I always found a good day hike cleared my head, helped me sort things out. My favorite destination was the rocky outcrop of Rough Ridge, just above the Parkway and shadowed by the higher peaks of Grandfather. I wasn't going to let a little road block get in the way, so I took Highway 221 back up the mountain. It ran just below the Parkway, though much curvier.

The sky was a cold blue when I left Boone, but began to cloud and glaze softly over like it was fixing to snow again. I made sure to wear some thermal underwear. No one else would be crazy enough to go hiking this time of year, so I probably wouldn't run into anyone else. The roads were certainly deserted. Since leaving Blowing Rock, I only met one car driving back into town.

Highway 221 sank close to the mountain and hugged each rise and fold in the ridges skirting around. Bare trees overhung the road, and even in the leafless winter they seemed to cast the road in shadow in the thickest places. Where the forest broke away, I could see the high ridges above me, and I kept them in my sight. Eventually I saw what I was looking for, the Linn Cove Viaduct.

The Parkway's greatest engineering marvel, the twisting road was like a space bridge in a science fiction story, hovering in the air above delicate rock outcroppings and mountain laurel thickets. Crossing under the viaduct was a trail that I knew led up to Rough Ridge and its rocky overlooks.

There was a bend in the road where I parked off to the side, the cold air briskly shooting down the back of my coat collar as I got out. I put on a pair of cotton work gloves, a camo hunter's cap with earflaps, and a green plaid scarf. Though I had never worn scarves before, only sissies or girls wore them when I was growing up, I was sure glad to have one now. I grabbed a small backpack in which I carried a few granola bars and a Thermos of coffee for later. Up the ravine a few hundred yards was the viaduct. I made sure to lock my car doors before walking down the road a-ways and disappearing into the woods.

The cold air, the loose rocks and steep terrain, and the fact there wasn't a trail made it difficult to walk at a steady pace, but I had all the time in the world and no obligations to anyone. Springs that hid under boulders and in deep gullies continued to trickle out of the ground, then freeze solid, continuing to freeze over the top and swell until thick, layered glazes covered the ravine. The wind had scoured dry leaves from the forest floor and covered some of the ice slicks, hiding them, and a few times my feet slid out from under me as a result. My shins sure took a beating. I wondered if this was how people trained for climbing frozen waterfalls, like I had seen in *National Geographic*. If only I had a pair of crampons, I thought. After much panting and huffing, and a slight burning in my lungs from the cold air, I made it to the viaduct and the trail.

My body warmed to the exercise, and I could feel my blood pumping back the cold from my extremities. My fingers, cheeks, and ears glowed and throbbed from the surge of warmth. Only my nose refused to warm itself as I walked the trail's upward slope. The going was much easier, and I was able to dodge the patches of ice. I heard the quietness of the woods through my earflaps and the wind rattling the dry, curled leaves of the rhododendrons as it whistled around treetop branches. Normally the occasional hum of a passing car would be heard on the Parkway below, but with the road closed I felt I had the whole mountain to myself. I got to thinking about what everyone else was doing right then. It was only nine a.m., and most people I worked with at the pizza place would still be in bed. Cassie was at home right now on Christmas break, probably preparing to celebrate the New Year with her family. She has probably completely forgotten about me. Then I got to thinking about home. I wondered if my mom was alone or if my father showed back up for her to take him in again. As much as that disturbed me, the thought of my mother being alone was worse. My throat began to thicken a little, breathing the cold air into my lungs so quickly. I wasn't going home, that was for sure. I couldn't. I felt that if I did, I would somehow never be able to leave again, some force of gravity would hold me there and suck the living breath out of me. A part of me ached at the thought of my mother worrying if I was okay, though. I wished to God she didn't sound so desperate when I called her. Surely, Aunt Faith had checked in on her from time to time.

I thought about Cathy. She was probably sitting around the breakfast table right now with her parents, trying to snag the last pancake from one of her brothers. Last winter it sleeted so hard I was stuck at Cathy's house, and I ended up sleeping on her couch. Her mother fixed the biggest stack of pancakes and sausage links the next morning. I thought I would pop from eating so much. All of these thoughts erupted pangs of guilt in my chest and a buzzing current of anxiety in the back of my head, so I tried to clear my mind and focus on the trail ahead, the views of the hills below through the leafless trees, and making sure I didn't step on another patch of ice.

It took about 45 minutes, but I eventually made it to the top of Rough Ridge, a rocky outcropping above stunted thickets of Mountain Laurel and Rhododendron. In the summer and early fall the ridge is alive with rare wildflowers, not to mention the pink clusters of Rhododendron blossoms. Now, however, the landscape was in hibernation – not even the winter birds were out. The wind stiffened above the trees, and now and then it howled around me. I clamored to the highest rock and sat down, looking southeast toward the viaduct and the Blue Ridge, trailing away toward Mt. Mitchell. I opened my Thermos and poured a cup of coffee, which steamed furiously for a few seconds before the cold air made it tepid. I drank it in warm gulps as the rock's iciness seeped into the seat of my pants and through my long johns. What looked like low clouds began curling around the hoar-frosted peaks of Grandfather Mountain like an icy tongue, and little flakes of snow started to cut through the air. I took a deep breath and imagined I was in a tall bastion of a castle, safe from the arrows and rocks that the rest of the world cast at me, far away from all that lurked in the shadows, waiting to pull me down. Below, down in the valleys and flatlands, I imagined them toiling and warring with one another while I stood steadfast on my mountain.

My gaze followed the ridge down past the boardwalk, built to protect the fragile ecosystem of the area, to the lower shelves of rock. Below the deserted Parkway was 221, peeking now and then from out of the woods. Out a little-ways more, I spotted my car parked in a patch of dirt and gravel. It was a direct line of sight from my rock, and looked like a little blue Matchbox car, only smaller. It amazed me that I had hiked so far. At that moment, I watched as another car pulled into the spot and sat there for a while. Someone got out of the car and circled around mine. He wore a dark coat and what might have been a red ball cap. An alarm suddenly went off in my head, and I stood to my feet.

"Hey! Get away from my car!" I yelled at the top of my lungs, jumping and waving my arms. The winter wind caught my voice and dissolved it. He didn't see me. His arm pulled back with something in his hand, slamming it into my passenger-side window. Not even the breaking glass made a sound from where I stood.

"No!" I cried. I jumped up and down and waved my arms again. I wanted to leap off the rock and fly down to my car, but it was too late. I heard a tinkling sound of dull metal as I looked down over the cliff. I had kicked my thermos over the side.

"Please, God, don't let him steal my car." It would take 20 to 30 minutes to get down there, even if I ran all the way back to my car and didn't break my neck. He would be long gone before I made it back. All I could do was watch him. It was too far away to see exactly what he was doing now. I stayed and watched the crime like an invalid, frozen in horror. I squinted hard and shaded my eyes from the gray-clouded sky. It looked like he was rummaging, pulling things out and tossing them in his car. I saw another car approaching the scene and had a faint hope he would get caught in the act, but instead he dove into my car and shut the door until it quickly passed, then got into his own car and drove away.

I was a little relieved, but still enraged that someone had broken in, pawed over, and stolen from me. I ran back down the trail in hopes I could get back in time before he returned with a friend to hotwire it and finish the job. The cold air burned my lungs. Three times more I fell and banged my shins on a root or rock. It was beginning to flurry, and hard snow pellets were filtering through the bare limbs, tinkling against the leaves. I wished I had a cell phone. I would have called the police. But then they would have started asking a lot of questions about me, and what I was doing out there, and I might've been on one of their missing-persons lists. On the way down the steep gully, I slipped and fell on my ass, sliding about 15 feet down. It felt like I sprained my wrist trying to catch myself.

I spilled out of the woods, and ran across the road to my car to assess the damage. Glass was all over the seats from where he broke my front passenger side window. He took my tape deck right out of the dash. The molding was broken where it used to be. The glove compartment was open and my maps were scattered in the floorboard. From it he stole a lock blade Buck knife, the change from the ashtray, and every cassette tape I had in the door pockets, except for Chuck Denson's Band – Greatest Hits. I guess he wasn't a country music fan.

*　　*　　*　　*

I drove down the road, cussing out my busted window and for having to run the heat full blast to keep from freezing. I was beyond furious, thankful that I still had my car, but frustrated out of my head, wanting to scream at God.

"Why me?" It seemed I couldn't get a break, couldn't be much more out of God's favor.

I passed an old green pick-up truck on the side of the road with the hood popped open. A half-mile later an old man was walking slowly along in the same direction with no hat, his long grey hair in a ponytail and blowing wildly in the wind. I never stopped for hitchhikers, as watching reruns of *The Twilight Zone* had taught me not to, but when this guy stuck out his thumb and turned to look I had a sudden urge to stop. The man looked homely, with Pointer overalls, long white beard, mustache yellowed from smoking. I drove a little past him, and then carefully pulled over onto the shoulder still heaped with dirty snow. It crunched sharply under my tires.

The old man sauntered to my open window, observing the broken glass. "Looks like you had an accident. I had a little problem myself back down the road a stretch, and didn't have my toolbox with me. Can I get a ride into town?"

"Sure, I guess so, as long as you don't mind sitting in some broken glass," I replied. I made a half-attempt to brush the bits of glass from my passenger seat, trying not to cut my hand.

"Don't worry about that. You heading to Blowing Rock?"

I was going to take Flannery Fork Road back to Boone, but instead said, "Sure. It wouldn't be out of my way. Hop in."

"I just need to get to a service station where I can get a-hold of someone with a tow truck," he said as he opened my windowless door and climbed in. "There's one on Main Street." Reaching for the seat belt, he looked out the window. "So, how'd it get busted?"

"Someone broke into my car."

"I tell ya, there ain't many people nowadays you can trust. I used to know everyone who lived in these parts. Now there's all these pinheads from out of state building their summer homes up here. Called the police?"

"No. I was out for a hike, and only saw the guy from a distance. It's not worth reporting it."

"Hiking, in this weather? It's awful damn cold to be hiking in the woods. Of course, you don't have to worry about snakes or mosquitoes, I suppose. I've been out hunting in the winter before, but nothing's moving in this kind of cold. All the animals are bedded down tight. Where'd you go?"

"Rough Ridge, and the trail that runs along the Parkway from the viaduct."

"Whew! That's a walk. I thought I saw your car parked on the side of the road in that little pull-in area, but didn't think much of it. Listen, I just want you to know how much I appreciate you pickin' up an old man like me. The name's Joe." He stuck out his hand with the introduction.

"It's no problem. I'm glad I could help. I'm Randall – Randall Spivey." I took his hand to shake, which was as thick and calloused as a dog's foot pad.

"So what did they swipe from ya?" he asked. "Besides your car radio?"

"Well, a lock-blade knife, some money, and all my cassette tapes except for that one." I pointed to where it lay on the dash.

"I've got that on LP at home. Chuck Denson can sure fiddle a tune."

"Yeah. That's one of my favorites, too." Joe smelled like stale cigarette smoke and motor oil.

"I'd ask you if you minded me smokin', but with the wind comin' from the window, I don't think I could keep it lit. I don't guess you'd care if I took a chaw."

"I don't mind at all. I guess you can just spit out the window." I was glad he didn't light up.

"If you don't mind, I'll just use this soda bottle here in the floor as a spit cup. Otherwise, I'd just end up getting juice down the side of yer car. You didn't piss in it or anything, did ya?" He inspected the inside of the green plastic bottle with a wry smile.

"No, be my guest. It's clean enough, I guess."

"You know," he said with tilted head, inspecting the open window while he pulled a pouch of Red Man out of his back pocket, "all you would need is some clear plastic and a roll of duct tape and you could fix this here window, at least for the time bein'." He dipped out a stringy wad of tobacco from the green foil pouch and placed it gingerly in his cheek, then ran his coarse fingers along the side of his pant leg. He reached up and picked a little piece of glass stuck between the rubber seals of the window and inspected it.

"That's a good idea." That *was* a good idea, I thought. "I could stop at the hardware store on the way into town and pick up some."

We passed some little houses on the side of the road, and drove by what looked like an old motel. The air blew around the back seats and swirled cold around my face, despite having the heat cranked up. I ran out of things to say, and we drove for a minute or two in silence before he spoke again. "So, are you from around here, Randall?"

"I'm originally from Galax, Virginia."

"Ah, home of the Fiddler's Convention. I used to go there and pick a little guitar with my cousin's group. I never entered any of the contests, but sat around and played at the campsite with whoever joined in. Chased a little tail around, too, but I'm too old for that now."

I remembered how my mother never liked me going to the Fiddler's Convention by myself. She said there were too many dope-smoking hippies down there, not like it was when she was growing up. I was a little dubious about it being that much different then. Still, my friend James and I managed to ride our bikes down there a time or two and walk around the vendor's booths and campsites. I thought how I might have even heard this man play. "I always wanted to learn how to play the guitar, but couldn't afford the lessons."

"Aw, it's not that hard. I taught myself from listening to the radio. After learning a few chords, you can just about play anything. So, are you in high school? College?" He took a short spit into his bottle.

"I'm a student at the community college, just on the other side of Boone. Then I'm transferring to Watauga State. Working and paying my way as I go."

"Ah, that's good. Honest work will teach ya more than you will ever learn in those college classes. I bet you meet some cute ladies at school, don't you? I see them walking downtown in Boone during the summer. Those little short-shorts, I tell you what!"

"Yeah. I know what you mean."

"Shoot, ain't hardly enough fabric to keep those little hind ends of theirs covered."

There was something about this guy that was familiar at first, like I might have delivered a pizza to him or something. Then I remembered the "dirty old man" as Lindsey called him – the anchovy pizza guy from a few months ago. Not one person had ordered an anchovies since then, and I was glad no one had. I hadn't been able to walk in the cooler and look at those tin cans of salted fish the same since.

"Got you a steady girlfriend?" he grinned, skin stretched over the wad of tobacco stuffed low in his cheek.

"I've been out on some dates," which was a lie, "but I'm not seriously dating anyone right now. I'm too busy with work and school."

"Man, you've got to make time for such things. You don't want to pass the opportunity to get to know a pretty young thing and regret it. Pretty soon you'll be old like me."

"Yeah, I understand."

"I don't know if you do, son. I attended this boarding school in Nashville back before the war, and met this girl who was a few years older than me, pretty in the face except she was blind in one eye. She had curves, though, and knew how to move them on the dance floor. And her daddy made bootleg liquor, so she always had a little flask on her to liven up the mood. We ran around for a few months when I could get away from school. Then the war started and I went into the Navy. Got shipped to California and never saw her again. But to this day I'm fond of that memory, and have no regrets."

"Well, I met someone a couple of weeks ago. I tried calling her, but she wasn't home. I didn't want to seem desperate." We passed by the state-road turn off to the Parkway.

"Call her again. Does she live around here?"

"She goes to college here, and her family lives somewhere in the county, some place named Sugar Grove."

"Sugar Grove, ya say? That's only a five-to-ten-minute drive from the town limits of Boone. You should call her this afternoon and ask her out on a date. The worst she can say is no. Then ya just move on."

"Maybe I should, even if it's just to talk to her. She's probably already got plans for New Year's, though."

"Randall, if there's one thing I've learned, it's that you got to *make* life happen, sometimes, not just let it happen *to* you. Take a chance when you see it. Chances are opportunities. You won't seem desperate as long you play it cool. Let her know you would like to go out with her, but it wouldn't be a big deal if she said 'no.' Turn right at the light," he pointed. "I'll just use the pay phone here at this convenience store."

We came to the stop light on Main Street, and I turned on red. Blowing Rock was decorated for Christmas in green tinsel wreaths and red bows hanging from the streetlights, and people strolled the sidewalks with dogs or shopping bags. "Are you sure you don't want me to drive you further? I could take you all the way into Boone, or drop you off where you live."

"No, but that's mighty kind of you. Most young folks these days wouldn't give an old coot like me a second thought. I could've caught my death out there."

"Well, I'm glad I could be of help." It did feel good to help this guy out. I almost forgot about my own problems for a while. I pulled up to the front of the gas station.

The old man got out of my car and shut the door, then leaned in through the broken window, spit bottle still in hand. "Hey. I don't suppose you have a quarter I could borrow. I don't know if I could ever pay you back, and I already feel like I owe you one."

I looked around. "No, I wish I did. The guy that broke into my car stole all my ashtray change."

"No matter. I bet they'll let me use the phone behind the counter." Then, almost as an afterthought, he said, "You work at that Papa's Pizza Place, don't you?"

"Yeah. I do," I replied.

"Y'all have some good pizza there, a lot better than most."

"We try."

"Remember what I said, and thanks again!" He patted the roof of my car as a signal for me to go, and waved as I pulled away.

I should've stayed with the old man, Joe, to see if he got the help he needed, I thought afterwards. I said a little prayer that God would watch after him, and drove back to Boone. The cold wind swirled around me with the heat of the vents.

19 _____

I held the phone tight in my hand as I nervously dialed Cassie's number from the slip of paper I carried in the back flap of my wallet. I thought I would have to beg Dean to let me use his office phone, but when I told him I was going to try to ask this girl on a date he just smiled and said, "Okay, Rocker. Five minutes. And it better be a local call. No 1-900 sex numbers!"

"Hello? Miller residence," came a soft, but more alto voice than what I expected. It must have been her mother.

"Yes, can I speak to Cassie please?"

"May I ask who's calling?"

"Uh, this is Randall. Randall Spivey." I cringed when I realized I had the phone too close to my mouth, as the sound of my nervous breathing came through to my ear.

"Honey! Phone," her mother called, and then with the phone receiver muffled I faintly heard her say, "Some boy on the phone wants to talk to you."

"Hello?"

"Uh, hey. It's Randall. From the coffee shop." There was a short pause. "Pulled me from the black hole of self-esteem?"

"Oh! Hey Randall. I wasn't expecting you to call. It's been a couple of weeks. I thought you might have forgotten about me." Not on your life, I thought.

"I'm really sorry. I've... been kinda busy at work. How was your Christmas break?"

"It was good. Santa brought me clothes, mostly. I did get a new CD player. It has detachable speakers."

"Cool." There was a lull in the conversation where I knew it was time to go ahead and ask her. "Hey, I was wondering if you weren't busy, would you like to go out to dinner and maybe catch a movie?"

"That would be great. I think I've caught cabin fever. These past few days, my family has driven me crazy. There's only so much time you can spend with the grandparents, uncles, and cousins over the holidays before they get to you. So when would you like to go?"

"How about Saturday night, New Year's Eve?"

"I see what you're trying to do."

"What?"

"You want to keep me out so you can kiss me on the stroke of midnight, don't you?"

"Uh, no. – I'm just off that night. A couple of drivers came back from visiting their folks and Dean gave me the night off, so I...."

"I'm just teasing you. You know that movie *When Harry Met Sally* don't you?"

"Not really."

"So. Do you want to come pick me up, *or* we can meet somewhere if you like?"

"I'd be more than happy to come pick you up at your house, if you could give me some quick directions."

"Sure. You're probably good with directions, aren't you? Do you have something to write with?"

I looked around on Dean's desk for a scrap of paper and a pen, and then looked up at Dean who was standing by the ovens, staring at me with displeasure and tapping his watch. "Okay, I got something," I said as I smiled at Dean.

"From Boone, drive out King Street like you are going toward Tennessee, past the 105 bypass. When you get to where 421 and 321 split..."

"At Villas?"

"It's Vilas, 'Viy-lus,' but that's close enough. You want to turn left there and follow 321. When you see the Sugar Grove post office and a big old white house across the road, start looking for Phillips Branch Road on the right. Turn onto that road, and look for a John Deere tractor mailbox on the left. You can't see our house from the road, but it's only about a quarter mile up that driveway. Yellow house, can't miss it."

"Gotcha."

"Oh, and don't worry about the dogs. They bark a lot at everyone who comes in, but they're harmless."

"Okay. Well, I better get back to work."

Dean was holding up a pizza cutter, wiggling it in the air as a signal. "Get off the phone," he silently mouthed.

It was nice talking to you, Randall, and I'll see you tomorrow night. Oh, I guess we can decide where to eat then. Anything but pizza, right?"

"Right!" I chuckled.

"Okay, bye!"

"Sorry I took so long, Dean." I was so happy I almost danced over to the counter as I grabbed the peel from Dean and scooped a pizza off the oven's conveyor rack into a box.

"You know I can't allow people to make personal calls on the business lines. It sets a bad precedence. I told Aaron that the IRS was talking to you about unreported tips or something like that."

"I have to report my tips to the IRS?"

"Geez, nothing gets past you, does it, Nancy Drew?"

* * * *

I was a little nervous, of course. It had been a while since I'd been on a real first date, since high school, and I don't think

145

hooking up with Lindsey at that party counted. I remembered how I felt when I first met Cathy. We met at a Carroll County High School's home football game. They were playing Galax High's Maroon Tide, and James and I were on the home side because their cheerleaders were cuter than ours. During a Cavalier touchdown, Cathy, who was sitting behind me, got up to cheer and accidently spilled a drink on my head. She apologized, and asked how she could make it up to me. I don't know what gave me the courage, but I told her she could go out on a date with me. In my bravado I forgot I wouldn't have my driver's license for another seven months. After she surprisingly said yes, I found out she already had hers. She picked *me* up at my house and we went bowling. It was like I was living some wonderful dream then.

I had a strange dream about Cathy the other night. We were sitting together in our favorite grassy spot along the Blue Ridge Parkway to watch the sunset and talk, her dad's Buick parked behind us. It was so vivid, I could feel how the curls of her dark hair tickled my cheek and how the warm grass smelled in the sun. I had my arm around her waist, when she grew stiff in my arms. I pulled away, asking her what was wrong.

"You need to stop lying to everyone, you know." She cut a glance toward me, then turned away. "Especially yourself."

"What?! What do you mean?"

She looked straight out to the horizon and asked me, "Who's Cassie?" I was dumbstruck, and for a moment I really didn't know what she was talking about. But then all the events of the past year came rushing in like an ocean wave around a sandcastle. Pieces of the scene around her began to wash away. Trees twisted out of the ground, vines unraveling from them. Flowers and grass ripped themselves up by their roots and blew away. Her dad's Buick lifted into the air, and I watched as its rusty underside disappeared into the foamy void. She looked at me, distraught, and screamed, "Liar!" Then all went blurry, and I heard rushing wind mixed with the sound of breaking glass and my alarm clock. I immediately jumped up, reached for the baseball bat I kept under my bed, and checked the windows for an intruder. Nothing. Only then did I turn my alarm clock off.

Wisps of that dream still hung in my mind as I got dressed and cleared my car of empty Sun Drop bottles and delivery receipts. It was a futile attempt to air the pizza smell out, but I left my windows cracked in front of the apartment for an hour or two beforehand, every window except the passenger side covered in clear plastic and duct tape. That's not going to make a good impression with her parents, I thought. It's almost as trashy as if I drove up to her house in a big brown van with a bald eagle and snow-capped mountains airbrushed on the side.

The directions weren't hard to follow. I turned up her driveway next to the homemade John Deere tractor mailbox, complete with what looked like little Tonka truck wheels attached to the bottom of it. The road to her house was as much field rocks as gravel, especially where there were a few ruts that looked recently filled in. The sky was cloudy, but didn't look like snow, and the way the trees seemed to hang over the road reminded me of driving to my Grandmother Spivey's house out in the Buck Woods. It lifted my spirits a moment before the cream-yellow house came in to view. Then a sharp tinge of anxiety came over me just as the dogs began barking. I quickly swallowed, took a deep breath, and pulled over to the right of her house, trying to face the good side of my car toward her front porch. The house stood on a steep hill, so the front porch jutted out about ten feet from the ground.

Three dogs came to greet me, circling my car, all some sort of German Shepherd mix. One jumped up on my driver's side door and licked the window. "Jasper! Get down, now!" Cassie yelled from her front porch, leaning on the rail. I got out amidst a flurry of fur and panting tongues. "I see you didn't have any trouble finding the place," she said.

"Not at all. It was easier to follow than most directions to deliver pizzas, trust me." I tried placing a hand on one dog's head to keep it from jumping on me. "Easy boy!"

"That's Charlie B. Charlie B. Barkin. He lives up to his name, but he's harmless." She wore a cranberry-colored fleece sweater and stone wash jeans, and her shoulder-length strawberry blonde hair was tucked behind one ear. Man, she was beautiful! "Come on in and meet my folks. Just for a little while," she added

147

with reassurance, maybe in response to the wide-eyed look I had on my face. "The wind's really blowing out here!"

I walked up the twelve or so steps to her front porch. "Wow. What a view!" Woods and pastures rolled along the valley between two mountain ridges, and here and there little patches of snow could be seen in the shadows.

"Yeah. They say snow that sticks around for seven days or more signifies that another snow is coming soon. You know how it is around here. If you don't like the weather, wait 15 minutes because it will probably change. Come in." She opened the storm door and I stepped in. The air was humid inside, and I immediately caught a familiar whiff of country ham or something simmering with fatback. The radio was playing a gospel station, not the old-timey bluegrass gospel, but the more contemporary vocal-sounding. The living room wall behind the couch was crowded with family photos of varying sizes.

"I'm in the kitchen, Honey! Bring him in," said her mother from the back. Cassie led me through the darkened living room into the kitchen, which was bright and decorated in red apples – apple-patterned curtains, apple dish towels, apple cookie jar, and apple pot holders hanging behind the stove. The dining room even had an apple wallpaper border around the ceiling. Her mother washed her hands at the sink. "So, this is the boy you were talking to on the phone the other night."

"Hi, Mrs. Miller. I'm Randall Spivey. Nice to meet you." I smiled.

"Now there's no need to be that formal around here. You can call me Rita," she replied, apple dish towel in her hand. "So, you go to WSU as well?"

"Uh, yeah. I'm a sophomore there." Dang. I forgot that I hadn't told Cassie yet that I actually only attend the community college, so I had to lie to her mother. Now how was I going to tell Cassie?

"You look awful young to be in college, Randall."

"Mom."

"Yeah, well. Runs in my family," I laughed, feigning confidence. "When I turn 50 but still look 30-something it will work to my advantage."

"Remember, Mom, I told you that we had the same biology class together our Freshman year and didn't realize it?"

"Oh, yeah. Didn't you and Andrew take a couple of the same classes your Freshman year?"

"Mom!"

Who's Andrew? I thought.

"Where's Dad at right now?" Cassie asked her mom.

"Your father and brother are still out back, splitting wood. They'll be in here any time now if you want to wait. Why don't y'all sit down and I'll fix you a cup of coffee or some hot chocolate maybe."

"We really need to get going if we're to eat supper in time to see the movie," Cassie said with a little urgency in her voice.

"Thank you for offering, Rita. Maybe another time I'll take you up on that coffee."

"Awful confident of yourself, aren't you? Already planning a second date." She said over the bar with her head cocked to the side. Then she flipped the end of her dishtowel at me and my blank stare. "I'm just teasing ya. You are welcome back any time." Cassie rolled her eyes and shook her head. "Invite this boy back sometime to supper," her mother said to her.

I laughed politely and felt a little reassured, until I looked at the front of the refrigerator. It was covered in magnets, mostly in the shape of apples. Under at least four of the magnets were photos of Cassie arm-in-arm and in different poses with a blonde-headed guy in glasses. One photo looked like a prom picture.

"Mom! You are so incorrigible sometimes!" Cassie huffed.

"I was just having a little fun! And do you have to use those big college words with me, like I wouldn't know what you were talking about?"

"We're leaving."

"Have her home by 11 o'clock," her mom said to me.

"Uh, okay."

"It's New Year's Eve, and I'm not a teenager anymore."

"Okay, Cassie," said her mom, tickled to get a rise out of her. "Just don't keep her out all night. Let's say one o'clock the latest?"

Cassie grabbed a black parka from the back of the couch and pulled me by the hand out the front door. I didn't realize until now that I left my coat zipped up the entire time I was inside, and the cold wind actually felt good as it dried the perspiration from around my neck. "I'm sorry you had to be subjected to that. I didn't realize my mom was in smart-ass mode today. Pardon my French."

"No pardon necessary."

"And, yes, my mom still has pictures of my ex-boyfriend and me on the fridge. I'm sure you noticed. I took them down once and she put them back up again. She still thinks somehow we are going to get back together, but that'll never happen."

"Don't worry about it. Your family seems like the Waltons compared to mine."

As I was about to unlock the car door for Cassie, her father and brother came out from around the other side of the house. Her brother looked almost like her, but more chiseled in his features, and her father had a warm, wise look about him. "Heading out, Sweetheart? And you don't introduce me to your date?"

"I'm sorry. Daddy, this is Randall. Randall, this is Hank." Her father extended his hand. I shook it. His grip was strong.

"Oh, I see you forgot about me, Cashew!"

"And this is my annoying older brother Dennis, the Menace."

"It's a tough job, but someone's got to do it," her brother smirked. The two men's faces glowed like hot coals from working in the cold air.

Her father eyed my passenger-side window. "Looks like you had a little glass breakage recently. Your insurance cover that?"

"No, sir. I only have liability."

"Well, I know a guy works at a body shop in Boone that does good work quickly and doesn't overcharge. I'll have Cassie give you his number later."

"Thanks. I'd appreciate that."

"Take good care of her, all right," her father said.

"I will, sir."

"Yeah, see ya later, Cashew," her brother teased.

"Grrrrr. Stop calling me that!"

*   *   *   *

On the drive into town we talked nonstop. It was as if we were old friends, just catching up on what occurred since we last saw one another. She told me her brother attended N.C. State and was getting his masters in some type of agricultural science to work with cows. He was three years older than she was. I was a little envious of her for having a sibling, and told her it must be nice not to be an only child. I wanted to tell her so many other things, about me, about my family. Maybe later. I thought desperately of how to break it to her that I wasn't a student at the university. Would she be angry at my deception? Would I ruin the date?

We decided to eat at MacArthur's, since it was right next door to the dollar theater. I insisted on paying for everything, and thought about taking her somewhere nice like the steak house and then to the big theater at New Market Center, but she insisted that since I was determined to be all old-fashioned and chivalrous, she would be a cheap date. The sun broke through the clouds just in time for it to disappear over the hill on the far end of King Street, but the sky still held its warm glow a little longer. The sidewalks were alive with people, especially near the movie theater, so rather than circling around looking for a parking spot close to the restaurant I parked along West Queen Street behind the old post office. She waited until we were out of the car before she asked me.

"So, what happened to your window anyway? I don't mean to pry," she asked as we walked down the hill.

"Did the whistling bother you? I knew it. I tried to tape it up good, but it still looks trashy. All I need to do now is replace my gas cap with a wadded up rag, and then I'd really be stylin'."

She laughed. "No. It was fine. I was pretty impressed that you were actually able to stretch the plastic tarp out as well as you did, and two ply I might add." She smirked a little, and I didn't know if she was being sincere or teasing me again.

"Well, I was hiking around Grandfather Mountain the other day, and to make a long story short someone broke into my car and stole my stereo. I saw it, but was too far away to do anything about it."

"It's fine," she chuckled, then slipped her hand around the back of my elbow. "Brrrr! It's cold out here now that the sun has set." She shivered and pulled herself a little closer as we walked. She was about a head shorter than me, and I could smell the sweet fragrance of shampoo in her hair. I felt myself warming from the inside out.

As we crossed King Street, she pulled me in the direction of a short man with a wool cap standing on the sidewalk. Slightly hunched with a dark, coarse beard and matted dreadlocks, he had a hand full of pamphlets. "Have you ever met Joshua Watauga before?"

"Not personally." I remembered seeing him many times on King Street or occasionally on campus, but never approached him. He seemed like a man whose cheese had slid off his cracker. Sometimes, I crossed to the other side of the street so I wouldn't walk past him. "Who is he, a local panhandler?"

"He doesn't like taking money unless he has a poem or a crystal to sell you." Cassie walked right up to him. "Hello, Joshua."

"Hello," he replied.

"Do you have a copy of 'Pretty Pear', by any chance?"

"Not today," he says in a gentle voice." I looked into his face and was startled to see a balance of serenity and feral energy in his clear eyes. Cassie gave him two dollars.

"Here," he said, and handed me a sheet of paper with a copy of a hand-written poem.

"Thanks," I said, not knowing what else to say.

"You stay warm okay?" said Cassie.

"I will." He smiled, his eyes glinting behind his bushy eyebrows.

As we walked back in the direction of the restaurant, I read the short poem surrounded by strange hieroglyphs and curling marks:

Every month should be like
August. Suppose the idyllic warmth
would last, suppose trees would
remain green forever. Mantis', cate –
pillers, foxes, even plants all
know their purpose. That's the
object o' life; to know your purpose,
and "no man will teach another
man."

I'm not sure what the last quote was about, but I liked it. There was something wistful in it, tranquil and wild, like the pools behind his eyes, which made me want to decipher its hidden meaning. I handed the paper to Cassie as we walked to the door of the restaurant.

"No, you can keep it. I have several of them. Some people say he was a student at the university a long time ago who couldn't handle the pressure of his studies, but I've heard other stories as well. Thank you," she said as I held the door for her, and then walked in after.

We were seated fairly quickly for New Year's Eve. Over our sandwiches and chips, we continued talking. She ordered a Julius Caesar, which was really just a chicken parmesan sandwich. She requested French bread instead of the Kaiser roll it came with, which cost 50 cents extra. "I'll *try* not to be an expensive date," she kidded again. I told her this date was courtesy of Friday night's tippers. I got a Reuben sandwich. I forgot what they called it. The menu had a bunch of funny names for their sandwiches, like the Don Juan or Mae West, most of which I didn't get the connection.

"Thanks for suggesting this place. I've never actually been in here before," I said.

"Are you kidding? My friends and I eat here at least once a week."

"Well, I keep myself busy. And I guess I never had the right company to join me before." Her slender fingers lightly held her drink straw to her lips. I looked around, hiding my nervousness. "I like the old movie posters on the walls, but that gorilla hanging from the ceiling is giving me the creeps. I think he's eying me."

She laughed. "Oh, I don't know. I think he's eying *me*. Gorillas like blondes, don't you know. You've seen *King Kong*?"

Sitting across from her in the restaurant, sipping our drinks and talking, I wondered what I could've done right to deserve this. I didn't have any expectations, but I didn't want this evening to end anytime soon, either. How was I going to tell her that I hadn't been completely truthful to her about who I was? I decided I must tell her soon, before the evening progressed further, so if she dumped me afterwards at least I wouldn't have fallen for her any more than I had.

"I have a confession to make." I tried to say it without sounding grave.

"What is it?" she smiled. "You have an evil twin – or worse, you're a sideshow carney!" She chewed a bite of her sandwich, and dabbed a bit of marinara sauce from the corner of her mouth with her napkin.

"Huh? No, I mean I need to tell you something. I haven't been completely honest with you." A shadow crossed her face as she looked at me from across the table. I took a deep breath. "I told you that I'm a student at WSU. Well, the truth is I'm a student at the community college. I'm a first-year student, actually. When I talked to you in that laundromat for the first time, it was a knee-jerk reaction. I guess I wanted to impress you, or I didn't want to seem like a loser or something." She just kept looking at me with a concerned face. "When we met again by chance, I was so blown over that you took an interest in me that I didn't want to ruin the moment. I was embarrassed enough that I didn't even have a phone number to give you. So many things have gone wrong for me lately, I didn't want this to as well. I'm really sorry."

She took a few seconds to chew her food, and to process what I said, then replied, "What's wrong with community college? There's nothing to be ashamed of. My mom took the nursing program there to become an RN." She took another bite of her sandwich.

"Well, if you knew my whole story you probably wouldn't give me the time of day. I mean...." I said too much, and a wave of panic rose up and caught a bite of sandwich I just swallowed, almost making me choke. She was going to ask how old I was, I just knew it.

"It's okay," she consoled. "You don't have to be ashamed of where you're from, your car, or what college you go to. I know what it's like to grow up not having a lot of money. That's not what impresses me in a guy, anyway. Trust me. You are already heads-and-shoulders ahead of my last boyfriend."

"When you say, 'your last boyfriend,' are you saying that you have one now?"

"Well, the gorilla's quite a flirt, but he's probably all hands." She smiled as she reached across the table to press her hand into mine, giving it a gentle squeeze. Her face glowed as she looked into my eyes, her mouth full of food. I must have blushed three shades of red, for she chuckled as I curled my fingers around hers. Her hands were so slim and womanly next to my stubby, boy-like paws.

She looked at my hardly-eaten sandwich and replied, "You must think I'm a pig. I've gotten so tired of my mom's cooking over Christmas break, I was dying for something different. Is your sandwich not good?"

"No, it's great. I like a good Reuben. They didn't drown it in dressing, either."

As we finished supper, I told her about my father, how my grandfather tried setting money aside for college, his death, how my

155

father ran off and left Mom and me, my mom's drinking. I wanted to be honest with her, but avoided sharing my biggest secret. I was so elated to be with her I believed at that moment that I *was* the guy she saw before her, not a 16-year-old runaway. I felt so relieved in confessing what I did, it was as if I told her everything. My old life was no more. I was Randall Spivey, struggling community college Freshman. Those were the cards out on the table, all the ugly truths. The waitress kept coming by with dirty, sidelong looks because we were sitting there for so long.

"But look at you now," she said. "Look at all that you have accomplished. You're putting your way through college, working a steady job, and all this on your own."

"I guess you're right. It doesn't make it all any easier, though."

"Do you still keep in touch with your mom?" I remembered that call I made to her from the gas station pay phone.

"Every now and then."

"You should tell your manager, what was his name again?"

"Dean."

"You should tell him to give you some time off to go see your folks. You could afford to miss a class or two. It sounds like you need a break."

I looked down at my watch. It was almost eight. "You know, we missed the seven o'clock showing of the movie." I picked up the receipt, wet with drink condensation. "If you want, we could go for a walk on campus. The exercise will keep us warm, and then we could go see the nine o'clock."

"Sounds wonderful. I'll leave the tip."

* * * *

We walked up Locust Street between the old Delbert Library and Woodford Hall. I reached for her gloved hand as we passed the bookstore, and she entwined her fingers with mine. From the restaurant, we walked slowly and talked the whole way about growing up and high school. I didn't tell her about Cathy. Maybe later. I didn't know if she would understand right now just how much of a clean break I had to make from my old life. This moment, however, felt so familiar, like what I always wanted home to feel like. We walked all the way to the campus entrance, and heard loud music and drunken shouting coming from the Yukon Café across the road. We walked past the baseball field, and back up River Street. The sodium vapor streetlights seemed to cast everything in a bronzed glow.

We circled back to the center of campus. Cassie led me to a picnic table overlooking Sandford Mall, and we sat. It wasn't bitter cold, but now and again a gust of wind would sweep around the buildings and catch trash and debris, spinning it in circles on the sidewalk. I looked up, and though the lights from campus muted those of the night sky, I could tell it was clear by a few bright pin pricks of starlight that made its way to us. We scooted closer to one another, and Cassie took both my bare hands in hers for warmth.

"Randall, there's something I want to tell you, too, since we are being honest with each other."

"It's okay. Go for it," I said, sensing apprehension from her.

"I don't want to be too forward, but you seem like you are a really good guy. You know that, don't you?" I smiled, my insides all fluttery and my head light.

"Well, I try."

"Which is why I don't want things to go too fast." She continued to hold my hand, and I shivered a little, but not from the cold.

"I want to tell you why Andrew and I broke up." She paused for a few seconds, trying to find the words to start. "When you spend that long with someone, well, I thought for the longest time that he was 'the one.' We had been dating since our junior year of high school. Both our families were good friends with one another. Everyone thought we were the perfect couple. We had even been talking about getting married one day. So I guess you could say we were engaged without the ring. That was why we decided to attend WSU together, since we both lived so close."

"No big deal. It was just the opposite for me and a girl I used to date in high school. She talked about staying back home to go to college and I wanted to come here."

Cassie continued before I could say more. "Both of our families attended church, and we decided to save ourselves for marriage. It seemed like what God wanted us to do. We wanted our relationship to be special." She took a deep breath. "Well, when you spend that long with someone, things happen. He wanted more from me, and I gave in. I thought it would bring us closer. But he changed; he wasn't who I thought he was anymore." She paused again. I looked at her sincerely, trying to understand the gravity of what she was telling me. "He became very possessive, and jealous. Then to top it all off, I found out he was cheating on me with his lab partner for almost a year."

"I want you to know I would never do that," I said.

"Randall, you have made me feel very special tonight, and I appreciate that." She took a deep breath and continued. "I need to take things slow, though. I'm not ready for a serious relationship right away."

All of a sudden, she began to tear up in short, brief breaths, and I put my arm around her shoulders, but she held her body firm. "It was a messy break up. My mom doesn't even know what a douche bag Andrew really is! She still thinks one day we are going to get back together and have some perfect little wedding in our little mountain church, and give her blonde-haired, blue-eyed little grandchildren. But it's not going to happen, not with him!" Her whole body went into a spasm of anger. She took a deep breath. She looked at me with a feigning smile, exhausted.

That moment I felt so in love with her, I couldn't speak. She never looked more beautiful. Wisps of her strawberry-blonde hair twisted in the cold breeze, and the freckles on her cheeks were barely visible through the red flush of her embarrassment. I felt I could float away with her. I leaned closer, lightly brushing my finger under her downturned chin, and felt her warm breath on my face. I kissed her, softly but intently. I must have closed my eyes, because I didn't know until after we bumped noses that I forgot to tilt my head enough to the side. She laughed.

"It's okay," I said, my teeth chattering. "I d-don't care how you were. I know you for how you are now. You are beautiful, funny, warm and c-caring. *You* are worth waiting for. And I would be honored to have someone like you, even if just for this moment, in my life."

"I hope it will be for more than just a moment." She smiled and looked into my eyes, her own eyes twinkling.

"I promise we will take it slow."

I leaned in to kiss her again when a group of students came traipsing past us, huddled together, wearing pointed paper hats and giggling, blowing on silver party horns. Cassie turned around as they passed.

"Jonathan, I thought that was your loud mouth. I could hear you all the way from Candler Hall!" She wiped her cheeks on the back of her glove and smiled.

"Hey, Cassie! You want to come to the Wesley Foundation with us? They're having a little New Year's get together in Wendy's apartment upstairs. Spiced cider and some Chex mix, you know, the fancy stuff."

"Yeah, you can bring your friend, too!"

"What time is it now?" Cassie asked.

"It's nine-thirty," someone replied.

Cassie turned back to me and smiled, "So much for the movie in our Dinner-and-a Movie Date!"

"There wasn't anything good playing this week anyway." I took her hand, and we joined the merry-makers in their trek back to King Street.

We played Bullshit for over an hour, only everyone called it "I Doubt It" instead. One card game lasted for over 30 minutes. I didn't catch everyone's names, but everyone was friendly. I got invited to their Wednesday evening program, which included supper. I whispered to Cassie what it would be like to see Gwenofar's face, or Jennifer – whatever her name was – when I showed up with her. She laughed and said she probably wouldn't remember who I was, she was so self-absorbed. Jonathan, who ended up winning the most card games, was originally from upstate Virginia. He turned the television on to watch the ball drop in Times Square. We talked for a few minutes while Cassie and a few of the girls went back to the kitchen, giggling. He said he grew up Baptist himself, but likes the Wesley Foundation because people here weren't a bunch of "Right-Winged Nuts."

Cassie came back with two mugs of warm spiced cider and a cinnamon stick in each. Wendy carried the rest out on a tray for the others. "I have such a bad habit of collecting coffee mugs from the Foundation's kitchen," Wendy said, "that one of these days I'm going to have to take them all back. Somebody's going to think they've been stolen!"

Though these people didn't know me, I felt so welcomed, such a part of the group, that the more the evening progressed the more I lost track of time, until several people began chanting, "Ten, nine, eight, seven...." They were all crowded around the television screen. "Three, two, one!" A few people blew their party horns, while others shouted "Happy New Year!"

Cassie turned to me, smiling. "Happy 1996, Randy." She leaned in to kiss me, so effortlessly, so naturally, it felt like we had been together for ages. Her breath tasted of cinnamon and apples.

One of the guys turned to catch us in the act, and said, "Hey I don't have anyone to kiss!"

"At your service," Jonathan chirped quickly, placing his hand over the other guy's mouth, and then leaned in to kiss the back of his own hand. He made an exaggerated smooching pantomime, which seemed in imitation of Cassie and me.

"Ugh, gross!" The other guy laughed in disgust.

"Get a room, guys!" said Wendy.

"They don't call us the Wild Wesleys for nothing," Cassie shrugged her shoulders and smiled. My head swirled with names of people I was sure to forget, but I was so ecstatic to be with Cassie it didn't matter.

* * * *

I never remembered feeling this awkward at the end of a date before, even with Cathy. I was afraid that if this moment

160

ended, it would cease to exist, as if the only thing making it real was the tenuous connection to some waking dream. But this was real. I felt Cassie's hand in mine over the armrest; she pulled my arm over to her lap. I was in a euphoria of love and anxiety, driving her home, the warmth of her legs soaking into my cold hands.

We didn't talk much on the way back to her house. We didn't have to. I pulled into her driveway, past the John Deere tractor mailbox, which glowed comically in my headlights against the darkness of the road. Shadows danced behind the fieldstones of her driveway. I drove as slow as I could.

"Well, I didn't keep you out too late past your curfew, did I?" I asked.

"No, only by an hour, but what are they going to do, ground me?" She chuckled. "They still treat me like I'm 16 sometimes."

"Yeah, I know what you mean."

I pulled up in front of her house, and put my car in park. The lamp in the living room window was on, and there was a blue flicker of light from one of the bedrooms. "I bet my mom is still up waiting on me."

"Your mom didn't care much for me, did she?" I asked, a little reluctantly.

"Oh, don't worry. She'll warm up to you. Give her a little time."

"I really had a good time tonight."

"And I had a wonderful time." She leaned in to me and we kissed over the armrest. Cassie pulled on the front of my shirt to draw me closer. "Don't wait so long to call me again!" she playfully scolded.

"I promise!" I held up my hand in a mock Boy Scouts salute. She laughed. "Cassie, I...." I had a hard time saying it. "For so long I just felt alone in the world, and it's been so discouraging. You are like a breath of fresh air to me."

"Randall, I don't know exactly what it is," she paused and squeezed my hand, "but you know exactly what to say. You have such an innocence about you that I find intoxicating. Promise me you won't ever change."

"Sure. For you, anything." She looked out the windshield at her house. Condensation was forming around the edges of the driver's side window.

"Well, I better be going. If my mom looks out her window and sees the car windows all steamed up, she'll think we've been going at it hot and heavy or something."

That last remark sent a tingle down my stomach. "Well, at least let me walk you to your door. It's my duty, you know."

"You just want another kiss, don't you?"

"Can you blame me?"

I followed her up her front porch steps, and couldn't help but notice her curvy, taught thighs as she bounded up ahead of me. "Okay, I now relieve you of your duty, kind sir. I believe this is what you came for." She placed a big, silly smooch on me. I wanted to kiss her closer, just to breathe her in a little bit longer. I could have given up oxygen and lived on the apple-cider sweetness of her breath.

"One more thing," she said.

"What?"

"Get yourself a phone at your apartment, so I can call you!"

"Sure thing." I heard the venetian blinds crackle from the living room window, and exaggerated kissing sounds from behind it.

"Ughh, Dennis. Will you please stop? You are the only one who thinks you're funny." She spoke loudly through the glass.

"Bye," I said as I looked deeply into her eyes one more time.

"Call me soon," she replied. I turned and bounded down the stairs and out to my car. "Randall!" she whispered loudly.

"Yeah?"

"Get an answering machine, too!"

"Okay!" I whispered back, grinning as I stepped into my car.

20 _____

I had a wonderful, dreamless sleep. When I awoke at ten a.m., she was the first thing on my mind. For once in a long while, I didn't wake to feelings of anxiety or hopelessness. Cassie's smile, her touch, kept replaying again and again in my head. The second thought on my mind was that Winter Quarter starts tomorrow. I made it through my first session of classes, and was sure I made at least a B in every course. I thought I might have even made an A in English because I did so well on Ms. Belvin's written exam. I was supposed to get a report card in the mail, but the whole apartment complex shares one big mailbox, so sometimes other folks picked up other people's mail by mistake and then fail to return it for a few days. It took me a few minutes of stretching to realize how chilly it was in the room, so I turned up the thermostat on the baseboard heater.

I felt so good that I thought about going to church, maybe that Baptist church down the road, or slip in the back at the big Methodist church on King Street for the 11 o'clock service. I felt I had a reason to praise God. I didn't have any clean dress clothes, though. I thought about going shopping for a new phone, a cordless one with an answering machine, that afternoon.

I got up to walk to the bathroom and stood in front of the tarnished mirror, checking for beard stubble on my neck and wondering if I needed to shave today or not. The whiskers on my chin seemed to be growing in quicker, so I got out my razor. The sun filtered through the leafless trees and my filmy back window, highlighting my dark hair as I stared back at myself. I looked older, I thought. My hair was touching the tops of my ears, reminding me that I needed a haircut. I also remembered that I had to go into work this afternoon at four. I walked to the pantry, pulled out my dummy can of tomato soup, and peered inside the slit in the bottom. I fished out a couple of fives and a ten with a butter knife to buy me a phone later. Then I remembered about the answering machine, and pulled out a 20, which ripped a little on the jagged opening. I would have to call the phone company to reconnect before I would be able to use it. I should probably open up two of the four cans I used to squirrel away my tip money and deposit it in the bank, I thought. I could maybe also buy Cassie a late Christmas present, or one "just because." I couldn't wait to see her again.

After getting a shower and getting dressed, I decided to drive into town and grab some breakfast from McDonald's, biscuits and gravy perhaps. As I stepped out into the parking lot of my motel apartment, I saw the black Chevy Silverado pickup truck immediately, Virginia plates on the front with a cracked frame around it shaped like a lasso that read "Cowboy Up!"

Oh shit.

I was a fish hanging on the end of a line. For every breath I took in, I felt like I was drowning in air. He stepped out of the cab when he saw me walk to my car. For a fleeting moment, I thought about springing into my car and speeding out 421 toward Mountain City. I froze, though, like a deer caught in a hunter's spot light. He slammed his truck door brusquely. I looked down both sides of the door fronts to see if anyone was watching out their windows.

"Well, hello Son," my father said to me, like he'd just come home from work, yet a little too chipper. I looked into his face blankly, half out of shock and half out of outrage and disbelief. "Were you beginning to think I would never track you down?"

"What do you want?"

"Well, first of all, I have to say. You are good. Real good. I never would have imagined you would be able to pull this off like you did, to get by this long. I didn't think you had it in you."

"What are you talking about? What in the *hell* are you talking about?" But I knew. My hands shook in my coat pockets as

165

I stood there. My heart was racing, but I tried to hold still. I tried to stand firm.

"Second of all, how *dare* you raise your voice to me like that, after what you've done." His face grew stormy and deep, then softened slightly. He looked like he was choosing his words. "Look. It wasn't until I went back in October to get your momma to sign the divorce papers that I heard you run off. She didn't even say anything to me about you for two months. You shouldn't have done that. You shouldn't have left your momma like that."

"Why would she feel like she needed to tell you anything? *You* left her for another woman, so how is what I done worse? Who are you to tell me what I should or shouldn't do?!" I was so angry and scared, I felt like I was standing out of my body.

"Listen to yourself. You don't even know what I'm talkin' about. Not the slightest idea."

"I know how you took the $10,000 Papaw was going to give *me* for college." It made me angrier to see how cool my father was acting, like he had some winning poker hand. The storm was still brewing underneath his calm exterior, I knew.

He shook his head in frustration. "We've got some things that are gonna be straightened out right here, for sure. I ...," he hesitated a moment, softening again, "don't suppose you could invite me in. We could sit a spell, and get out of the cold. We *need* to talk."

"No. I don't think we do."

"Fine. Suit yourself. I don't suppose your momma would have told you this in the state she was in. You see, I couldn't make her happy anymore. I tried son, I really tried."

"Like hell you did."

He continued, taking a deep breath first, "And as for the money, I didn't see that your grades were strong enough for you to go to the university anyway, at least not yet – and that when you graduated high school – going to the community college would be a good start. I took the money and paid for the rest of what is now your momma's car, for which I was still making payments on at the time. She needed to keep her car to get her to work, and I had a few debts to pay off myself."

I didn't even hear exactly what he said at first, I just stood there, three steps away from him, furious. "That wasn't your money! And what do you know about college? Since when did you care anything about *me*?" I yelled; my head rang. My hands came out of my pockets and balled themselves into fists.

"You feel like throwing a punch? You want to have it out with your old man?" He held his arms out from his sides in defiant invitation. I saw someone's curtains move as someone peeked out, and I hoped they weren't calling the cops. At that moment, though, I wanted more than anything to smash his face in, to knock that chew of tobacco right out of his mouth, to watch it spin in the cold wind.

"No," I feebly replied. I felt buried under, my body weighted by invisible shovels of dirt. I broke down into a snot-dripping snuffle that shuddered my shoulders.

"Are you sure you don't want to go inside, son," his voice changing, eerily different. "We can talk more about it inside." He slowly and awkwardly approached me, placing his unfamiliar hand on my arm.

"No!" I yelled, and drew back a step. "I don't want you to do anything but leave me alone. I've got my own life now, and you aren't going to control it anymore!"

"Now, see, that's where you are wrong. Don't you want to know how I found you, how I figured out your scheme? Your momma didn't know anything about your elaborate plan, and in her state she might have been afraid to report you missing, or even know you were missing. I had a hunch, so I paid a little visit to your Great Aunt Faith. The senile old biddy. Forgot about the little agreement between your grandpa and her. But lo and behold, what should I see in her pile of mail on her coffee table but a letter from Lenoir Community College, addressed to you! It wasn't too hard to find out where you lived and where you worked. Since then, I've been doing a little checking up on you. I called the school up, told them I was your father, and found out you were in the Associates program at the satellite campus up here. I told them

167

that was kind of odd, seeing you were only 16 years old and still had a year of high school to finish. And until you turn 18, I am certain, you are still in your mom and I's custody. You are living a lie, son. And as great as you think things are going for you right now, it's all for nothing."

It started to unravel around me. Everything I worked so hard to build, my father was blowing it down like a straw house. I should have known this day would come. Somewhere in the back of my mind, I should have known. I didn't have a backup plan for this.

"I'll go to the court and get emancipated, then! And I'm not just 16. I'll turn 17 in four months!"

"So what? And I'm not so sure how that goes, but I'm sure when the judge sees how you ran away from home, forged your high-school transcript, and left your sick mother I seriously doubt they'd grant it, especially seeing how what you've done is a serious misdemeanor, which could even lead to jail time."

"What do you mean she's sick?" I asked quickly. Anger turned instantly to fear at the words.

"Have you not been listening to me? Dammit." He took a deep breath, turned, and shook his head. After a few seconds he started talking again. "God knows there are things I might have done differently when it came to your mom and I's divorce. But it's too late to do anything now except help her through it," he said solemnly, looking down at the ground.

"Through what?!"

"She's been diagnosed with clinical depression. I think she might have even tried to kill herself." I stared blankly; it wasn't registering in my brain. He looked off in the distance like he was trying to find the words written on the hilltops.

"What? What do you mean?"

"I called to check on her about a month ago, after she got a call from you. When she wouldn't answer the phone, I feared the worst and called the police to go investigate. They found her unconscious on the floor, next to an empty fifth of bourbon. The hospital said it was a combination of that and Oxycontin that almost killed her." I couldn't take a breath, and clutched at my throat.

He continued, a little more delicately, "Now, first of all I want you to know it's not your fault. I guess I don't half blame you for running away from home under the circumstances. I... haven't been a great father. I *know* that. But I am still your father, and right now your place is at home. Your mother needs you. She won't hardly have a thing to do with me. She's now over at Marion under watch, until they can do an evaluation on her. I'm just saying... it would do her good to know her son was home and safe."

Suddenly, everything I had done to make a new life for myself, college, my job, Cassie, went from being completely destroyed to completely irrelevant. I set my jaw tight, though, and tried to force resolution through my teeth.

"I might have left abruptly last summer, okay, but I can't just pick up and go right now. I need some time to tie up loose ends."

"You have a week, no more. I'll even come back with a moving van. I *am* keeping an eye on you, though."

"Did you tell the cops or the place I work at about...?"

"Running away from home? Lying about your age? No. Not yet. I almost put out a missing persons on you, before I visited your Aunt Faith. Anyway, the community college probably won't take you back after I talked with them, I don't know. They might revoke your credits once they call your high school, so you really have no choice but to come home."

If Mom needs me, I'd do it for *her*. But not for you, not because you told me to. The words didn't make it out of my mouth. I wiped some snot from my nose on my back sleeve and just stared at him.

"Listen," and here he sighed heavily, "if high school was so bad, you can get your equivalency at the community college in Wytheville or Surry. You can do that while you're at home, for now. What's one more year? Then we'll see about college or something like that. We're not getting back together, your mom and I, but believe it or not we *do* care about you. Hell, you're my only son. Here's my cell phone number," and he handed me a slip of paper, his hands shaking, "but don't get any ideas of running again, because I can easily put out an APB on you."

Since when did my dad get a cell phone? I wondered. He gave me an up-and-down, quizzical look not entirely agreeable, like I had just sprouted an extra head or grew a third arm. He walked back to his truck, shaking his head, and opened the door with a creak. Only son – so what?

"Remember what I said," he said finally, and then climbed into his cab and drove off, not looking at me again. The diesel motor purred away into the distance, mingling with the silence of Sunday morning.

21 _____

I thought about James and me swinging on that grape vine
down by the river, when the air hung sticky and full of expectation.
I have never found out where he went for sure. It seemed so long
ago, but hardly more than a year and a half has passed. I wonder
where he is right now, if he is faring better than me. I feel forsaken.
I am at the end of my rope, and there is nothing for me to swing
out and grab next. Maybe I didn't reach far enough, think big
enough. But no. It isn't that at all. I still carry the mistakes and
baggage of my parents with me, I guess. I wish I could have
travelled lighter.

This is where the story ends, I guess. Yes, it is all a lie. I'm
coming to grips with that now, but the truth seemed too hopeless
to accept. I don't expect anyone to understand. When I just
floated through life, letting things happen to me, not doing anything
about it, failure was easier to take. Then I decided to strike out, like
the pioneers, and take control, to eke out a living in a new place. I
expected hardships, sure, but I thought I could anticipate and adapt.
But so much effort now for nothing. I don't know what to do. I
can't stay here anymore, thanks to my dad, and of course I want to
be there for my mom, but how? Why did she do it? Why did it
have to happen this way? It isn't fair. Aren't adults supposed to
have it all together, or at least enough so their kids don't have to
suffer because of their own shitty, grown-up mistakes?

I hoped God would see what I had done, how I had toiled
to make something good of myself from nothing, and find favor in
me. Like starting a garden, breaking into the rocky soil, turning it
under, pulling the weeds, planting the seeds. But the rains didn't

come. I worked and waited, the desire for rain so close I could smell it, but nothing came of all my efforts but choking dust. Some poet said April is the cruelest month. Hell, I didn't even make it to February.

*   *   *   *

I nurse a warm soda someone left unopened on the break room table and take a few bites from a cold slice of pepperoni pizza, before my shift starts. I didn't go to classes today. I mean, what is the point now? It's probably too late to get a tuition refund as well. Chalk that up to one more example of waste in my waste of a life. And if I don't tell Dean I'm quitting tonight, he's going to fire me when my dad calls him and tells him the truth about things. Dean is a good guy; he should have gotten a two-week notice.

God has truly forsaken me, and though I don't know how, I suppose I deserve it. This is my punishment for being selfish and thinking only of me. At this point, I just don't care anymore. Aaron walked by when I first came in and asked who pissed in my cornflakes. I told him to fuck off. That shut him up, but it didn't make me feel any better. I even snarled at Sam n'Eric when I came in because they were goofing around. They just gave me a funny look and whimpered something to each other out of earshot. I was supposed to have started ten minutes ago, hoping someone would say something critical of me, just so I could go off on them.

"Randy! Are you ready to go, man? We've got delivery orders waiting to ship out," Dean comes in the room, full of pep. Then he sees me. I don't even have my shirt tail tucked in. "Dude. Are you alright? No offense, Marcie, but you look rough."

"Thanks. It's my new 'I don't give a donkey's dick' look."

"Hey, hey, Andrew Dice Clay. I'm sorry you're having a bad one, but you're needed out there. Ollie and Aaron are the only ones besides you delivering, and I have a feeling it's going to be a busy night. Our new guy quit on us."

I blow out a deep breath. "Dean?"

"Yeah?"

"I need to talk to you about something after closing."

172

"Okay, sure thing. But for now, get back to work," he says, an awkward concern in his voice.

* * * *

"Hey, Rocker! You want to take the next delivery?" It is an hour and a half before closing, and Ollie is looking at the green screen, his back turned to me.

"Why the hell not. It's been a slow night tonight, anyway. Where's it going to?"

"Out Meat Camp Road."

"We go out that far to deliver? Farthest I've ever been that way was Howards Creek."

"It's actually off Meat Camp on Snake Mountain Road. Walt's family lives out 194, so our delivery range gerrymanders that way. Someone must have seen the delivery sign going out there this week. But, hey, you need to get out and make a few more deliveries. You've been moping around here all evening letting Aaron and I get all the big orders." Ollie points with a pencil to a thin red line on the topo map hanging on the wall. "Right up that way," he says.

"Why is it called Meat Camp Road?" I ask Ollie. "Sounds kinda lascivious."

"Sounds kinda what? Don't use that college with me. Back when Daniel Boone travelled this area there was a cabin or smokehouse built up there. Hunters used to cure and dry meat for travel, and store hides, or at least that's what I've been told."

"Fine, I'll go." I box the two large pepperoni pizzas, slicing them quickly and throwing in the pepperoncinis and garlic sauce cups.

"Got you a couple of warming sleeves ready to go." Ollie already had them in his hand, and set them out for me.

"Uh, thanks."

"You never know. They might tip big."

"Yeah, and monkeys might fly out of my ass!" I give Ollie a half-hearted grin as Aaron comes in to the room from the back.

173

"If the tip's big enough, I want a cut of it, since I'm giving you the run."

"What? Fine, Ollie, whatever."

"Hey, it's my turn to make a delivery!" Aaron asks.

"Shut up, Aaron." Ollie snaps back.

*　　*　　*　　*

I've been out this way before, but only on joyrides that took me out to places like Jefferson or Trade, Tennessee. There wasn't a state road sign for Snake Mountain Road, but I remember it was the first left after passing a fork in the road where an abandoned gas station stood. It is a clear night, but also moonless. Not many houses are around, from what I remember in daylight, and those that are must stand well off the road, too far back in the woods and thickets even to see the lights from their windows. It feels kind of lonely and desolate out here.

I make a left onto a gravelly dirt road and start driving up. It's a little steep, but looks well-maintained, like someone just graded it not long ago. Maybe there is a radio repeater tower at the top or something. I keep waiting for a driveway to appear to the left or right of me, or the warm glow of a framed window, but it is all wooded and dark as the road hugs the slope of the mountain. The trees become shorter and more scraggly the further along I drive, until up ahead in my high beams I spot an open gate. I am so relieved to see some form of civilization that I don't even care that I had driven more than a mile since I left the pavement. I get to the top, and the woods open up to a clearing. It looks like a huge summer home is being built, complete with a fish pond, with crusts of ice along the edge. Huge mounds of dirt were piled right next to a concrete foundation and a Caterpillar dozer.

My heart sinks as I realize that I'm probably not in the right place, that maybe there was a second driveway I missed back on the main road. Just as I am about to turn around and leave, I notice a small Airstream on the other end of the clearing and someone's silhouette darkening the illuminated backdrop of an open door. There is no road at this point, so I just cut across the clearing, hitting ruts, stunted patches of briar bushes, and the occasional stump. I realize I must look silly on this mountaintop with my lighted pizza sign out in the middle of nowhere. I forgot to unhook it. No driver wants to deliver this far – it wastes time – and a glowing sign is too much of an advertisement that we do. The man continues to stand just to the inside of his doorway, leaning against the frame.

I get out of my car with pizzas in hand. The inside of the warming sleeves is wet with condensation. "Good evening! Whew! What a drive up here! Did you guys order two pepperoni pizzas and two orders of bread sticks?"

The inside of his Airstream is so bright behind him I couldn't see his face from the shadows. "Bring them here," he says.

"Well, they probably aren't piping hot, but I got here as quick as I could." I take a few steps closer. The man's head was shaved, and I can tell he has a neatly trimmed beard and mustache.

"Let me see the pizzas." His voice is guttural and sharp. I begin to pull the pizzas from the sleeve. "Leave them in the sleeves, if you will."

I start to get a panicky gnawing in my gut, but try to shove it down. "Sure, sir," I reply, and hand him the pizzas, "but we really need the warming sleeves back for other deliveries." He pops a lock blade knife open with his left hand and cuts into the back padding of the top sleeve. "Whoa! What are you doing?"

He pulls out a long, thin wafer of something wrapped in cellophane, pokes the tip of his blade in it, and puts it to his tongue. "This is it!" he yells, a little too loud to be speaking to me. I feel a sharp blow to the back of my head and see stars, as I fall to my knees, rolling to the side. Someone puts a burlap bag over my head with a drawstring, and uses cord ties to cinch my wrists behind my back. I'm not out completely, but my eyes flash with rushing pin-pricks of light, and it is hard to think. I lie to my side on the uneven ground, and I hear voices, at least three, someone speaking in Spanish, and someone going back and forth between broken Spanish and English. Harsh voices, distorted voices, like the incantations of a nightmare. I don't know how bad I had been hit. My whole head hurts. I am dragged by my shoulders into the camper trailer by two men.

"Siéntate! Sit up!" one of them growls at me, then punches me in the stomach. I lose my breath, and double over in a dry heave. I try opening my eyes, but the rough fabric presses against them. I feel light headed and woozy, and hear metal clacking against metal, like two horseshoes being held together. Someone pulls me up by my head and slaps me in the face a few times. I taste a sharp metallic tang on my lips, and realize I'm bleeding. A heavy brace snaps around my neck, followed by four clicks. A larger, heavier piece sticks out from my throat. It was cold and heavy, and smelled oily like an old machine shop.

"Are you awake? Can you understand me?" one man standing overhead calmly asks.

"Yes," I feebly reply. "Why are you doing this to me?"

"Shut up! Listen good. We run a pretty big business, and we don't mind locals doing a little here or there. But you have stepped on one too many toes, Ollie," a thick, guttural accent hisses.

"Please, sir. My name's not Ollie. I work with him at the pizza place. I c-can assure you that I haven't delivered any moonshine, or marijuana even. I d-d-didn't know those warming sleeves had anything in them, I promise!" My whole body shakes.

"Shut up, pendejo!" My left eye explodes in pain, as I am struck down by a brutal punch from someone in a standing position. The burlap is abrasive, and cuts into my eyebrow and cheek like rough-grained sandpaper. My head reels.

"Whiskey? Pot?" I realize it is the bald man with the guttural accent speaking, the one who stood in the door of the Airstream when I pulled up. He must be the one running the show. "No, you are in much deeper. Though I have to say that this little package you delivered here is poorly cut and not to my taste or standards. You see, it's like a local produce stand. You have your market around here for local goods, like white liquor, pot, or meth. What I have a problem with are local yokels like yourself trying to horn in on my import trade. So, I want *you* to do a little business for me now, and I've got some insurance that will see to it that you keep your end of the deal, and perhaps keep your life. Consider it a little game. You feel this?" With that he jerks on the large metal piece clamped to the front of my neck. It pinches my skin from the weight of it, and sticks out almost as far as my chin.

"This is what I call a collar bomb. It is set to detonate in two hours," he pauses. "Correction, in one hour and 56 minutes, unless you do what we tell you."

My heart almost stops, and then skips a beat or two at hearing that. I have trouble taking a breath. My throat begins to swell with mucus. "Please," I plead, clearing my throat. "I'm not Ollie. I'm just a delivery boy," I sniffle.

Another blow to my face comes unexpectedly from the darkness. "I don't care who the hell you are. If you *ever* sell coke again, if you even so much as pass off a crack rock to someone, I will come after your family, your friends, your friends' friends, *then* I'll be coming for you." The bald man hisses slowly through his teeth.

I lie crumpled in the floor, shaking, the smells of soured dirt and vomit in my nose. Someone grabs me by the collar and shakes me as if trying to keep me conscious. "W-what do you want me to do?" The collar scrapes my Adam's apple as I try to swallow.

"Now, that's what we like to hear, right boys?" The other two men chuckle. He directs his words back to me. "It's very simple. I want you to rob your manager of his night drop, then follow a set of instructions we will give you in which you will then drop off the money at a secure location, and if you are good, you get the keys to take this collar off. But I'll tell you right now. There's a switch in this collar. If it is in any way tampered with, or if someone attempts to saw the collar or unlock the three different locks before it's time – boom! If it so much as seems that you don't intend to follow through with this – boom! You get my drift?"

"Y-yes sir."

"All right, let's get him ready to go!"

The door to the Airstream opens. I can feel the cold wind rushing around me. They pull me up and cut my hands free. With the bag still over my head, I am ushered back to my car. My legs feel weak.

"The door's locked!" One of them said.

"Here." With their hands under my arms, I reach into my pocket for my extra key. "F-force of habit. I sometimes leave the c-car running, but lock the door." I blindly feel for the key opening.

I bump my head on the door's frame as they push me down into my seat, rattling the tumblers in the heavy piece sticking out above my collar. I hold my breath and wonder how much rattling it could stand before it went off. I didn't want to find out. As I sit down, one man loosens the bag around my head while someone else opens the passenger side door and throws something heavy in my front seat with a thump.

"Hey, look at the redneck repair job here," one of them comments and thumps the plastic and duck tape of my passenger window.

"What do I do now?" I ask.

"Shut up, and listen good. Do not take this bag off until you hear our car horn. We will be following you from a distance. We know where you will need to go, anyway, so don't bother trying to lose us. In the seat next to you is a snub-nosed pistol and a set of detailed instructions. Open and read as soon as you get on the road, *before* you get to town. Do not deviate from these instructions. We can also remotely detonate this bomb if we think you are not following orders – boom! Do you understand?"

"Yes, sir."

"Okay, then." With that he slams my car door shut. I sit with my hands on the wheel, feeling every bone pressing into my grip as if they are going to pop out of my fingers. For the first time, in the silence of my car, I hear a faint ticking, like that of an old wind-up alarm clock or a kitchen timer. Each tick sounds louder than the next, each half second like a sledge hammer striking time with the throbbing in my head. A car horn blares from somewhere in the distance. I pull the bag off my head, and my hands go to my neck. I feel wires bundled around what feels like a giant handcuff attached to cold, sharp edges and corners of a heavy metal box, about the size of a can of soda. The metal feels thick, too, and the edges were welded and cut a little uneven in places. My heart sinks into my stomach. This is for real. I immediately reach down and put the car in gear, flip the headlights on and spin my car around to head back down the gravel mountain road.

After I get back to the hardtop, I turn the interior light on to look at what they left for me in the front passenger seat. It is a small pistol, all right. They also left a couple of sheets of yellow legal pad paper, folded together. I take a deep breath and try swallowing a growing lump in my throat. I can't stop shaking, and I can't keep the lump in my throat down. And then a thought occurs to me. I'm probably not going to get out of this. Of all the things I think I could do, drive to the city police office, try to get caught speeding in town, or just leave town, all ended in one scenario: death. I don't even know if it would be a quick death. I might die even if I do everything they want me to.

So that's how it is going to be, then?

I feel an eerie sense of calm with this new concept, although it is just as likely I am going out of my mind. How many times I have felt like wanting to end my loneliness by taking my own life. No use crawling into a hole and sucking my thumb now, huh? If this is how I'm going, I might as well go out with a bang. I laugh strangely at my own joke. There is still one thing that galls me, though.

"I suppose *this* was your plan all along?" I shout out loud. "I know I've screwed some things up in my life. I know it's my fault, God. I know that. I realize that! I accept it, okay? But why this?! Can you share at least a little of the bigger picture as to why I'm driving in my car with a damn bomb strapped around my neck to go mug someone for a bunch of damn drug dealers?" Silence. Of course.

But that *can't* be it. That's not the way I want go about it. I don't want to curse God and die. What's that Psalm, I can't remember, something about when I need help the most? But I don't know how to ask. I'm certainly not in God's favor, with all that I have done. Do I even deserve help? I left my mother who then became suicidally depressed after her father's death, when *she* needed me the most. I abruptly broke up with Cathy. She didn't deserve that. She was one of my best friends. If she were here right now, *she* would give me some hopeful words. She knew me better than I did sometimes. To top it all off, I've been living a lie for the past seven months, deceiving everyone, including myself. Who am I to pray to God?

"I just wanted to make something of myself, Lord! I felt trapped. I wanted more than to just survive in a town with no prospects. I wanted to live. I've seen them. Kids ahead of me in school. They looked *so* confident their senior year. And six months after graduation they were still bagging groceries, hanging out at Felts Park downtown, sitting on the swings and in the picnic shelters smoking cigarettes, going nowhere. They looked like dogs on the end of a short chain, choking on their collars. Is it wrong for me to want more?" I hear the slow ticking of the timer around my neck, and silence.

"Okay, Lord. Your will be done, whatever *that* is," I say with more than a tinge of resentment in my voice.

I look at the top sheet of legal paper. It read in large letters: **Don't go back to the pizza store....**

* * * *

The parking lot of Boone Federal is deserted. A couple of the lights looked busted out, so at least it's dark where they told me to park, against the retaining wall. In front of me are the drive-through lanes and the night drop box. The ATM machine is on the other side of the building, so there isn't any traffic in the back. I check the scarf I wrapped around my neck to make sure it covers the metal collar I'm wearing. That was one of their instructions: **Conceal the bomb from everyone and do not let anyone know you are wearing it – or we will remote detonate it.** Every other instruction came with the warning of remote detonation.

Any time now Dean would be driving down the hill, pulling into the parking lot on my left. I wonder where those three guys are watching from, if they are watching. I don't want to take a chance. All of a sudden, a harsh realization comes to me. Dean always has someone follow him to the night drop on his way out, as a second party witness. I don't know how I am going to hold up Dean when someone is right behind him in another car. **Do not deviate from our plan,** the note said.

Dean's Subaru Outback pulls slowly into the lane closest to the bank. Behind him is Ollie in his Mustang. Shit. I grab the gun that the men gave me. It feels cold in my sweaty hands. I quickly look into the revolver chambers to notice that it's empty. Great. They didn't even give me a loaded gun. I step out of my car and walk past Ollie's car to Dean's, who is just stepping out of his vehicle. Their headlights give their faces strange glows.

"Randy? Where have you been? We've been wondering where you got to. I thought you had car trouble or something, or that you just got tired and went home. What are you...?" He stops in mid-sentence as I lift the gun and point it toward him. I feel like my body is being held up by strings, my arm heavy with the weight of death.

"Give me the money or I'll shoot you! I mean it." I say.

Ollie steps out of his car and walks toward me, yelling. "Rocker, what are you doing?" He sees my gun, and my cut and swollen face, and his expression changes, his jaw drops. He knows something. I keep the gun pointed at Dean.

"The money, now!" I yell. "Throw it over!" Dean looks me over again like he doesn't know me anymore, then tosses over the blue canvas zipper bag. It scoots on the pavement and then turns over a few times, the metal lock clinking. Grabbing the bag, I take a few steps back and point the gun at Ollie now, motioning for him to stand next to Dean.

"Move!" I choke. My heart is beating so fast I think my head is going to explode before the bomb. Ollie puts his hands in the air and walks down to Dean, who is also standing with his hands up. "Dean, I need your keys. Throw them over to me." Dean reaches slowly into his open door with one hand, pulls the keys out, and tosses them to me. I lose them in the darkness, until I hear them jingle a step behind me. The instructions were also detailed enough to say: **Take the manager's keys so he can't follow you.** I guess they knew I couldn't shoot out their tires.

"Ollie, you too!" He reaches into his pocket slowly and throws his at me as well. They land at my feet. I back up and squat down to get both of them, stuffing them in my pocket, still pointing the gun.

"Man, I don't know why you are doing this, but you won't get away with it," Dean warns.

"I don't care. Just don't try following me, though. I have a... I'm a dead man if you do." Ollie looks at me with stern concentration. "Guys, I got to have your word that you won't try to follow me or to call the police, at least for an hour. After that I don't care."

"Okay, Rocker. We won't follow you," Dean says. "Just quit pointing that gun at me."

"One more thing, guys. I'm sorry."

"Yeah," Ollie replies. "I know."

* * * *

The last page of my instructions told me to drive behind Winn-Dixie, off Blowing Rock Road: **Behind the dumpster is a red brick. Underneath that brick is your next set of instructions.** Next set of instructions? I drive right past the Boone Police Department, wishing they knew somehow what was going on without me tipping off my perpetrators. I make a left onto Boone Heights Drive, and pull around the pot-holed parking lot to the back of the store. It is dark in the back, but my headlights land on a couple of brown and green dumpsters. I step out of the car with a pocket flashlight I always keep under my car seat, and begin searching for the brick.

I can feel the collar soaking up the cold from the outside air, despite the scarf I wrapped around my neck to conceal it. A rank, soured smell of cabbage and cheese wafts from the oily pavement. There it is, the brick, and under it the same yellow legal paper, this time folded up in plastic wrap. It is sticky from dumpster sludge. Not wasting any time, I jump back into my car and peel the sticky film from the paper to read the next set of instructions by the interior light: **You are to drive to The Bagelry on King Street. Behind the handicap parking sign is a sticker. Underneath the sticker is a slip of paper with your next set of instructions.** I can't believe it. They're toying with me. It's like a damn scavenger hunt. All I want to do is give them this stupid money and get this bomb collar off from around my neck, and they are playing a game. My thoughts of possibly getting out of this alive dwindle even more. What can I do any differently, though? I put my car in gear and head out State Farm Road. After making a right onto the 105 Extension, I look into the windows of Papa's Pizza. The store is dark, save for the security lights. How I wish I could be back in there, spreading sauce, popping some dough bubbles in the oven, listening to Sam n'Eric talk about their Sony Playstations, or, hell, even listening to Aaron bad mouth his ex-wife.

A left on King Street, and I am almost there. I look in my rearview mirror to see a dark car also making the same left turn. The car passes out of the glow of the corner street light before I can get a good look at it. Could it be the drug dealers? I try to act natural, as if I didn't notice them following me. I hope they are going to tell me soon where I am to leave this money and how to get this collar off. The blue moneybag lies like a dead animal in the passenger floorboard. I can even smell the stink of the money every now and then over the sharp metallic tang of the collar.

A stoplight catches me. I look at my watch, but cannot remember when I first had the collar put on me. I know I don't have more than 45 minutes. My heart races. While I wait at the light, nervously tapping my fingers on the steering wheel, I look behind me. The dark car had pulled off into a church parking lot, turned around, and is waiting to pull back out, I'm sure, as soon as the light turns green. They don't want me to see their faces. The shape and placement of the headlights look familiar, but I can't put my finger on it. Most everything is closed on King Street, so pulling into The Bagelry's parking lot is not a problem. I just hope some passerby doesn't see me.

It isn't as dark here as it was behind Winn-Dixie, so I don't need my flashlight. Behind the handicap parking sign were several stickers, but the largest one, a close up of a square face with dark eyes and the word **Obey**, has a lump beneath it. I pull out my pocketknife and slice around it, and a small, folded-up piece of paper comes loose. I look up and around to see if anyone noticed what I did as I walk back to my car. I see the dark car driving down King Street towards me. It is Ollie. How could I be so stupid?! He must have thrown me his spare set of keys, the ones he made after Tyler and those frat boys hid them from him that one time. Ollie drives to the stop light and makes a left on red, down Appalachian

Street, but I know that he knows I saw him. Oh God, I hope he doesn't blow my cover. No telling what he is going to do. I am already on edge as a swell of anger washes over me. Why did I apologize to him earlier? It should be him in this damn bomb collar, not me. If I was really nihilistic, I would chase *him* down and blow his ass up along with mine. Whatever he's up to, I've got to go along with my captors' plans regardless. It's the only known avenue where I've got a sliver of hope to live, where no one can say I didn't at least try – in the end.

My breath quickens as I unfold the instructions. This time they are written on thin tracing paper. The writing is small, but looks the same as the other notes, penned in a thick, blocky print: **Drive to the park at the top of Howard's Knob. If gate is closed, park and walk to the picnic shelter. Drop the money in the trash can lined with an orange plastic bag. Do not deviate from these instructions. We are watching you. Your next instructions will be waiting under the lid. They will include where to find the keys to unlock and disarm the bomb. If anyone follows you we will remote detonate it. Hurry. You don't have much time.**

"Ha! As if you need to tell me to hurry!" I say out loud. I laugh at the understatement.

I turn up East Junaluska with a little renewed fervor, and make my way up the steep switch-back climb to the top. My 4-cylinder whines as I floor it. I tighten my grip on the wheel and pull back on it, wishing it could go faster. I hug the inside of every curve. A set of headlights appear from behind and below me, on the lower switchback. At first I think they are just driveway lights of a house I passed, but they come up on me quick. My heart drops a gear when I realize it's Ollie. He drives up behind me fast and bumps my rear fender. Why is he doing this? Somewhere I know the drug dealers are waiting, watching. If they see him, I'm as good as dead.

My little engine can't compete against his big block. I take the inside curve again and he throttles his Mustang. With a deep growling rumble, he tries to pass me on the outside. "Oh God, he's going to cut me off!" He honks his horn, but I dare not look over for fear I would lose control. To the left I see the green reflective sign for Junaluska Road up ahead. As Ollie pulls ahead of me, I brake and cut left onto the road. It's gravel, and I begin to fishtail some, which spikes an adrenaline rush to my body. I let off the gas a little and straighten it out, and for a few seconds it's dark behind me. I think I lost him, though I don't know of another way to get to the top of Howards Knob without turning around and going back up the road I just turned off. The hill is so steep here that the houses only sit on the uphill side of the road, and every curve turns downhill. I then hear the rumble of exhaust, even before I see his headlights.

I can't go much faster. I feel the gravel roll under me as my car lunges right, scraping against a grassy bank. One quick jerk of the steering wheel would send me flying off the road and into an upstairs room of the houses below me, so I try to ease it back out of the ditch, but not before I take out a mailbox with my right fender, cracking my windshield. The debris rolls over the roof of my car as Ollie catches up with me. He swerves to avoid the dismembered mailbox and bumps my fender again while honking his horn.

"Shut up!" I scream.

The road turns back into pavement, and I know where I'm at, back to King Street. With a left turn, I run a red light and start to panic anew. What the hell is he trying to do? Collect the money for himself? Try to help me? I can't take the chance. I try to make my way back to Grand Boulevard or even Eastbrook again to get me back on Junaluska, but the mental map in my mind is scrambled and I can't remember which road comes first or where it is. Maybe I could catch him in some traffic at a stoplight or pass a slow-moving car. That could buy me a minute. That's all I would need. But he's right behind me, though, driving a little more cautiously now as we are back in the middle of town.

My car falters, shudders. I look down at my dashboard and notice that my fuel indicator light has been on. Stupid! I was planning on filling up on my way home after closing. I lose acceleration again, and another wave of panic pours over me. I'm not going to make it. At all. In a split-second decision, I turn right onto the 105 Extension and pass the pizza store again. The last vapor fumes of gas in my tank are sucked dry, as my engine shivers

185

to a halt. I quickly put it in neutral and coast. The steering wheel is stiff without power, but I do not brake for fear I won't make it to the pump at the gas station at the bottom of the hill. My mind feebly and desperately races as to what to do. I don't care about Ollie or those damned drug dealers, but I am going to put some gas in this car, drive my ass back up that hill, and get this collar out from around my neck! I clench my teeth and reach for the gun I forgot I had in the passenger seat in case Ollie wants to stop me from filling up, and then toss it in the floorboard. It's not loaded anyway. Looking into my rear-view mirror, I see him. He's still following me, a few car lengths behind.

I wrestle with the steering wheel, putting all my strength into trying to keep it in the road, but I cross over the yellow line, making a VW Beetle swerve to miss me. I saw it out of the corner of my eye then, a town police car was pulling out of a side street. The panic clings to me like motor oil and molasses, filling every pore of my body, ears ringing, my nose and throat tightening, making it harder to breath over the weight of the metal collar.

What am I thinking? It *is* all over. Any second now I know I'm going to hear that last tick followed by explosive silence. The siren blares loudly behind me in accompaniment with flashing blue lights. I drive through the intersection at the bottom of the hill, running a red light, past the gas station, bottoming out on the curb and barely missing a telephone pole, finally coming to a stop in the deserted parking lot of First Union. I hit my head on the steering wheel and see stars.

The police officer gets out of his cruiser and shouts from his loudspeaker. "Get out of the car with your hands where I can see them!" I pull the scarf off from around my neck. No use hiding it now. I open my car door and step out, hands extended.

"Officer, sir, you've gotta help me. I've got a bomb locked around my neck that could go off any minute!"

Out of his vehicle, now with gun drawn, the officer takes his other hand and says something urgently into the radio receiver clipped to his shoulder. At the same time another police car pulls in from the other side of the parking lot, headlights on high beam. "Get on the ground, now!" an officer yells. I take a few steps away from my car and sit on my knees. No one approaches me. "All the way down!"

"Please, officers! I don't have much time. Call a bomb squad or something. I'm not lying. I'm going to die soon." My last words to them barely makes a sound. The flashing lights, the pulsating blues, and now reds, melds with the headlights of patrol cars and passing traffic of the intersection. My head swims as sparkles appear, and I begin to lose sight. Everything swirls together, the lights, the popping crackles of police radio, and my own voice pleading again in no more than a whisper. "Please help me, please help me God."

I hang my head, and saliva and snot pour from my nose and mouth. I am crying, though I do not hear my cries. I'm not even aware of my own breathing; my head feels so full of congestion. Everything darkens. The gravelly pavement tilts under me like I am going to fall off the edge of it all.

I am spinning, with no frame of reference for my eyes, until a figure appears out of the colored fog. The spinning stops. I see the silhouette of my grandfather outlined by bright lights. He is carrying a briefcase, no, his toolbox, and walking stoop-shouldered like he always did after a hard-day's work.

"Papaw, I didn't expect to see you so soon." He gets closer, and I realize as my eyes clear that it is not him, but an old man with a yellowed beard and overalls. My current surroundings rush back to me somewhat, the cold asphalt, the police officers, the sharp flashing lights, the tumult of conversation 20 feet away from me.

"Let go," he says. It's Joe. I recognize his voice, urgent but calm.

"What?"

"Let go of the collar, son!" he repeats, "so I can get a better look at it." I realize my hands were clutching the cold metal. He rattles around in his toolbox. "What it took me to get them to let me through. Now let me see, this should do it." He pulls out a cordless rotary tool with a circular disk.

"Hold still. I'm going to cut the top bolt off." He pulls the Papa's Pizza hat off my head.

"Wait, wait!" I remember. "The bomb is set to detonate if tampered with. See the wires?"

"What, all these wires twisting around here?" He pokes around the collar with his thick fingers. "Those are dummy wires, dressed up to make this thing look worse than it actually is. The only detonator is the timer." He leans in close to my face with his ear, and I can smell the stale cigarette smoke in his hair. "Yep, still ticking."

He turns the rotary tool on and puts his warm hand to my chest, large and calloused as a bear's paw. "Breath, but hold still." He then grabs the bottom of the hinge. Sparks began flying from behind my neck all around me like shooting stars as I fade in and out. They burn a little as they jump down the back of my collared shirt.

The whirring stops as quickly as it began. He drops the tool and picks up a hammer and a punch awl, and begins deftly tapping the bolt out of its hinge. "I used to work in the machine shop on the USS Iowa during the Korean War. We made all kinds of clamps and parts like this. Now hold still again."

Joe gingerly gives one more tap to the bolt, sending it clinking to the asphalt. With both hands he pries the clamp apart; it slides right off my neck. I am crying again, as if from a release of great pressures, and manage only to say "thank you" under my breath. I begin to regain consciousness.

"It's alright. Now you just wait here," he smiles as he stands up and slowly walks away. His back seems as broad as the horizon. I hear additional shouting, and see men wearing thick padded suits rushing out to Joe with arms extended.

A sound like a loud pop, the sound of a car backfiring, sends pin pricks through my body. The parking lot begins to spin again, sending Joe in a sideways pitch to the ground. I try to stand up and go to him, but the tilt of gravity pulls me back. The flashing lights fade to darkness as I sink to the pavement, my face pressed with gravel.

22 _____

I had a terrible thirst, and I couldn't wet my mouth. I walked down the faintly-worn cow path to Grandma Spivey's springhouse. Everything was cool and damp – with a slight mist hanging in the trees – as in the early morning before sunrise. The sky was still dark enough, though, for the stars to cluster in the west. Out of the corner of my eye I saw a brighter star flicker with intensity, but it disappeared when I tried looking straight at it. It took me a while to make my way down the darker path, through the cow pasture, after looking at the brightening sky. My eyes wouldn't readjust to the dark; there were streaks of ghost lights in front of me. My feet were sluggish as I feebly hopped the fence, like I had lead weights around my ankles. I got my pants caught on the barbed wire, then tripped to the leaning door, which opened when I pulled the rope through the hole that lifted the latch inside. I knelt on the pebbly ledge with the tin dipper in my hand. I felt the cool darkness of its air, its own little atmosphere stirring on my face. I pulled the dipper to me, could almost feel the water on my lips and taste the cold, but my hands were suddenly empty. I tried cupping them together and drawing water to my mouth, but my hands were dry.

Coming back into consciousness was like climbing out of a deep hole, and the sides crumbled with each foot and handhold. I eventually saw a dim light through my eyelids. I felt the I.V. tug in my arm, heard a pulse in my ear. I knew where I was by the muffled voices in the hallway and the occasional beep of a monitor beside me. The creak of a chair or someone scooting around on a vinyl cushion came from the other side of the room. I didn't want to wake up. Part of me just wanted to sink into the hospital bed and hide. I slowly opened my eyes, but they were blurry and matted. Blinking a few times and rolling my eyes around, I managed to get rid of the film. My cheekbones were still tender and puffy from being beaten, and there were tinges of pain from the stitches around my left eye and temples when I tried squinting. It was dim in the room, so I wasn't sure who it was at first until I heard her voice.

"Hey Randall. You're finally up." It was Cathy.

"Hi." My heart jumped, then sank back down.

"The doctors said I could stay in here for a bit, while you rested, if that's okay."

"Where am I at? How long have I been here?"

"You don't remember? You're at Winkler Memorial Hospital. You have been in and out of it for three days. The doctors said you had a nasty concussion. You are going to be okay, though. They said that the best thing for the time being is for you to get some rest."

Suddenly, everything that occurred leading up to this point came rushing back to me. My head and chest suddenly burned with embarrassment. I tried to get up. "Am I in trouble?"

"Shhh. Lay back down. Everything's fine. The police have investigated the events around your last pizza delivery," she paused, collecting her thoughts. "I'm sure the cops will eventually want to ask you a few questions. They came by yesterday to check on you, but nothing to worry about." She paused. "Randall, now don't flip out, but your story's made the local paper, and even the *Charlotte Observer!* So you are kinda famous."

"Oh, Hell."

"Randall Aron Spivey, you really shouldn't cuss like that," she clicked her tongue.

"What have they been... does everybody know?"

"I think the newspaper articles have been pretty thorough about you, I suppose. They talked for a while with your dad."

Getting up from her seat, she pulled a rolling chair next to my bed. Her hand was cold as she lightly clasped my fingers. "I wanted to tell you something before everyone else comes in and crowds around you. I'm sorry. I'm sorry I couldn't be there for you like you needed me to. I thought maybe you just needed a little space to sort things out."

"You shouldn't be the one who's sorry. I'm... the one that left you. I'm the one that wouldn't return your calls. Don't apologize." There was an awkward pause in our conversation. I didn't know what to say next.

"You know, I never did tell your father where you went. He came by my house a few times, and called my parents on numerous occasions asking if they heard anything from you. I feel like now maybe I should have said something."

"Thank you. I know I caused you a lot of trouble. And there's something else, too." I stumbled with what to say. "I've... I've been seeing someone else."

"I know. I met her. She came by yesterday to see how you were doing. She seemed nice. But...."

"But what?"

"Well, she asked me a lot of questions about you. You must have kept some things from her." There was a silence in the room for a few moments. I tried thinking of something to say to Cathy, to explain, tried thinking of what I wish I could say to Cassie to explain myself. To break the awkwardness, she added, "She thought it was funny that she and I had similar-sounding names."

"What else did she say?" My face flushed.

"Well, she stepped out to the front desk at one point, then came back with a sealed envelope, said she wanted me to give it to you. It's in the night stand drawer next to your bed."

I wanted to read it immediately, yet felt guilty for my gushing concern for Cassie's feelings right in front of Cathy. I felt like such a heel. "Listen, Cathy. I know I don't deserve to even have you in the same room with me, but thank you for being here."

"Randall, I've never stopped believing in you. I still do. You have always been too hard on yourself. I still care for you, and part of me always will." She paused, choosing her words. "But there are some things you need to take care of, some things I'm

191

sure you need to get straightened out in your life." I wondered how much she really understood about what I needed to do in my life, but tried to shrug it off. Another awkward silence brooded in the room, and I think Cathy sensed it, too. "Did you know your mother…?"

"My mother's here?!"

"Your mother has been by your side since she's gotten here, praying over you. She stepped out with your father for a bite to eat an hour ago, but they should be back by now."

"How does she look? Is she feeling well? Is she upset at me?" My father's here too, I thought anxiously, but didn't say it out loud. The thought of my parents eating a meal together made me feel funny inside. I didn't know whether to feel happy about that or not.

"She's doing fine. She was frantic for a time when she called me with the news of what happened to you. The police found your father's cell phone number on a slip of paper in your pocket, or we still wouldn't have known about what happened to you. We drove down from Carroll County together to come see you as fast as we could. Would you like for me to go see if they are back?"

"No. Not just yet." I knew that as soon as Cathy revealed I was awake, people would come in asking me questions.

"Why don't you talk to your parents for a while? They've been waiting for over two days to see you awake, to talk to you. I'm going to see if they are back in the waiting room. I'll be right back, I promise." I wanted one more moment with Cathy, to try to talk to her about all that had happened to me, but it seemed the moment had passed.

After a few minutes, I heard my father's booming voice outside my door. He was talking to some police officers, it seemed. "My son's been through a lot," he said, "so I hope you don't mind if his mother and I see him first before you start bombardin' him with questions." More muffled voices. "Okay, if you don't mind sitting and waiting." My dad came in the door almost eagerly, followed by a full-uniformed police officer.

"Hey, son! Glad to see you are up and alert."

"Hey."

"This here's Officer Monroe, he's going to ask you some questions later, and is just sitting in here right now so nobody'll think you were 'coerced' into giving any other story but the truth. I'd like to hear the whole story myself, but maybe later."

A look of fear must have come over my face, for the officer assured, "You aren't under arrest – because you were considered a hostage; don't worry, you're just under observation."

"Your mother's going to come in here and see you in a little bit, but first...."

"How's she doing?"

"She's doing fine. She got out the day after we last talked. She's agreed to see a shrink over in Blacksburg a couple of times a month. I thought this thing, this incident, was going to send her into a fit, but it's amazed me how she's held up. Listen, I wanted to run something by you." He paused, eagerly choosing his words. "First of all, I want you to know that your momma and I aren't getting back together, but we are going to take a closer interest in your future and well-bein'." I wanted to scoff, but refrained.

"I wanted to tell you about some plans I have for the old Spivey farm. I was planning to wait and tell you later, when you got back home and stopped bein' so pissed off at me. I need your help. I've decided I'm going to start raising beef cattle, organic beef. It's a new trend. The market's predicting that in the future people are going to be willing to pay a little more money for produce and meat that's certified organic, that isn't farmed with chemicals or hormones. It's pretty amazin' the profit they say you can make! I've been reading about it at the library, on the internet. Your Grandma Spivey deeded the farm over to me, and I'm going to get an agricultural loan through the farm bureau." I could tell he was trying to contain his excitement as he explained his plans to me. "The barns are still in good condition, and we could convert the dairy parlor into feed storage or something. I ain't messing with cow teats like my dad did, that's for sure." He laughed, then stifled his enthusiasm a little self-consciously when he remembered the officer was in the room with us.

"I've got the hay and grazing pastures, and your grandma sold a little piece of land my dad bought when they started talking about building Interstate 77. It's right out there on Exit 19 just above Five Forks. A guy is going to pay her ten times what my daddy paid for it, think he's going to build a convenience store out there or something. I told him it would be a great idea. The Buck Woods community's been without a gas station since Reid's General Store burnt down back in '84."

It was strange. I had never seen my father so passionate about something before, especially a job. I wondered where he was going with it, though. "That's sounds great, Dad. It sounds like you've got a good plan."

He pursed his lips, then turned to the officer. "Excuse me, could we get a little privacy here for just a moment? I'm trying to have a talk with my son."

"Sure. Take all the time you need. I'll be outside the door." The officer turned and walked out, pulling the door shut behind him.

"What was I saying? Oh, yeah. Some of the money from that land is going toward initial operating costs, but the rest I am setting aside for you to go to college. For you. In the meantime, Son, I would like you to come live with me and help me out, be a business associate, so to speak. While you are doing that, your mother and I can enroll you in Wytheville Community College and you can get your diploma. I know how much you hated high school, anyway." He paused, waiting for my reply. When I didn't, he continued.

"Ultimately, I am leaving it up to you. You can come home and live with me or your mother, but you can't stay here. I think your momma will be okay, now that she knows where you are. But – you must start being 'yourself.' No more lying about your age. I mean, I want you to be yourself, who you really are."

He grew quiet for a moment, his eyes misting over. "You can talk it over with your mother if you like. I can't promise that we won't have our disagreements, but I promise you I am here to help you from here on out. We need to stick together. I mean, there just doesn't seem to be any more good ol' boys left in the world. Everyone's living too fast and getting above their raisin'." Here, my dad bowed his head a little, his shoulders hunched. "I just want you to grow up right." I didn't know what to say. Who I really am? Grow up right? "Listen. It'll just be you and me and Grandma Spivey."

"What about the woman you are seeing?"

"Don't worry about it. She and I aren't seeing each other anymore."

My stomach turned queasy. My mind rebelled at the thought. I wanted to say no, hell no, fuck no. I had too many friends here. I had a life here. But I really didn't. It all belonged to a 21-year-old college student – recently revealed in the news to be a 16-year-old fraud. I had nothing. He was right; I couldn't keep it up any longer. So many things were going through my mind, I hardly knew what expletive I was going to say exactly until the shock of it came out my mouth. "Okay, I mean, I'll think about it."

He exhaled, like he had been holding his breath. "I appreciate it. Sure, think it over." He remained calm, but I knew this made him very happy.

"What if I needed time to do my homework after classes?"

"Absolutely, we can work out a schedule. It would be like a part-time job. I'll even pay you a wage once we get to earning some profit.

"Would I be able to go places when I wanted to, not have to ask for permission all the time?" I was grasping at petty conditions, hoping he would get frustrated at me, and his usual demeanor shine through instead. There were so many things I wanted different, I couldn't think of them all.

He pursed his lips, then nodded his head. "Okay. I understand. Shake on it?" His eyes were still watery, but his jaw set in a rigid smile.

I took his calloused hand and gripped it firmly, the I.V. tugging at my wrist. I felt queasy, but I couldn't think of any alternative. Dad got up quickly and went to the door.

"Let me get your mother now. She would want to talk with you for a little bit before the cops do." He stepped out the door for a minute, and came back in with her.

My mom stood between the officer and my father, looking a little uncomfortable but smiling at me nonetheless. "Sweetheart, I'm so glad to see you up." She seemed to want to rush to my bedside, but hesitated. "There are some police men that want to ask you a few questions about some things."

"Carla, the cops already said they ain't in a hurry. No need to rush."

"Take all the time you need," said Officer Monroe.

Two nurses came in while Dad and the second officer stepped out. "Is my son better enough yet that he doesn't need to be hooked up to the tubes and wires?" my mom asked the nurses as she sat down next to me. She looked considerably older than the last time I saw her.

"The doctors will be finished with their observations by the end of the day. In the meantime, would you like for us to get you something bland, like a Sprite and some saltines?" one of them asked me.

"Sure, that would be great." Although I wasn't hungry, I realized my mouth was still dry and pasty from when I first woke up.

I sat with her for what seemed like forever, though only a minute passed, not knowing what to say or how to say it. She sat as if patiently waiting on me. I thought she was going to speak at one point, but she just drew her breath in through her mouth. I looked out the window. "Mom?" I turned to my mother finally and tried to say something to her, tried to explain things. Before I could, she leaned in to hug me. "Mom," I whispered. "I'm so sorry for what I put you through. I hope you'll forgive me." I tried to hold it together, but my eyes began welling up with tears.

"Son, it's okay. It's okay."

"I think I'm going to come home," I said. Mom shuddered with a half-sob, but instead of saying anything else she just held me tighter. "Dad wants me to come live with him, to help him fix up the old farm."

"Yes, of course that's fine." I looked into her eyes, caught a tinge of disappointment.

"I'll come and see you every week. You could help me with my homework some, like you used to do."

She laughed, and tried changing the conversation. "Did you know your Papaw in his will requested that my older sister Carol Ann's casket be moved to him and your Granny's plot at the top of the hill? Had it already paid for, headstone and all. Left your Uncle Blake at the bottom of the hill by hisself. The Shumaker family still hadn't put a headstone up for him yet. Your grandfather could sure carry a grudge, even from beyond the grave."

I laughed, feeling the stitches in my forehead tighten. "I guess that's where I get my stubbornness from."

She laughed nervously. "Go ahead and talk to the cops now, so they can quit bothering us. Then maybe we can leave," she said, wiping her face dry.

When she opened the door, there were not only police officers, but what looked like reporters as well. One man held a video camera on his shoulder. Dad was just outside, pushing the reporters away at the door, only letting the officer in.

"Back away you damn papa-ratsy." My dad waved his arms like one would shoo away crows from a garden, as my mother turned to leave.

The door shut, and the three officers spent little time with introductions. "I'm Officer Burnette and you have already met Officer Monroe here. Alright, let's start from the top. Tell us about Oliver Starnes."

I told them everything I knew, about what other drivers said about him, the mountaintop drug delivery to the three men, the notes of instructions, the money I stole at gunpoint, and Ollie chasing me around town. "I just don't understand why Ollie would trick me into doing this. He seemed like a nice guy."

"We've run the instruction notes through an analysis, and checked out the delivery site, but the Airstream seems to have

197

disappeared. Do you know how much money was in that deposit bag, by the way?" The officer asked me. "About four grand. Small change for a drug dealer. We believe they were never after the money in the first place, but to send a message to Ollie and his cohorts."

"That makes sense, I guess." I said. "I heard you caught someone?"

"We have a suspect in custody. We believe he is one of the men that sent you on that fool's errand. We'll have you try to identify him in a police lineup later today if they discharge you. Unfortunately, there has been a rise in drug-related gang activity in the mountains lately."

"I didn't see any of their faces, just heard their voices. They made sure I didn't. I don't know how much I can help you there. Where's Ollie, by the way? Have you caught *him*?" I wanted to hear what he had to say, about the mess he got me into, and why he insisted on chasing me in his Mustang all over God's creation.

The officer with the clipboard looked at the other officer for confirmation of some sort before turning back to me. "We were hoping you could help us find him. We had been watching him for a while, and when your manager Dean mentioned Ollie's name in his account of your robbery, we went to his apartment with a warrant to investigate. It looked like he had moved out that same night."

They asked me some other questions about Ollie, and mentioned the ATF might be interested in asking me about his family's alleged moonshining operation in Wilkes County. "Though the family is claiming no ties to his actions or whereabouts, of course," one of the officers said. Despite the resentment, despite all the things Ollie did to set me up for this mess, I couldn't help but feel a little sorry for him, now *he* was on the run. I'm just glad it's not me. I am through with running.

"Are there any other questions you guys might have?" I asked. I couldn't think of anything else to say to them.

"Not for now, but we'll let you know if we need you."

"Go ahead and let everyone else out there come in if you want to," I winced.

My room was a weird carnival of people, coming in and out, going out and in. I had some cousins and an aunt show up that I hadn't seen in years. In fact, I couldn't remember their names until they introduced themselves. Craig and Paul came by with a pepperoni pizza, which was missing a slice and on its way to being cold. Walt Groves, the owner of Papa Pizza's Place, came by with his grandsons Sam n'Eric. Though they were only a year younger than me, they looked much smaller in the room of adults. Walt took a photo opportunity with me for the news reporters. The reporters also asked me some questions, but I didn't go into much detail. I just kept saying, "I'm just lucky to be alive and here with my family."

"Do you think you will ever be a pizza delivery driver again?" one annoying reporter asked.

"Well, they don't have a pizza parlor in the Buck Woods community where I'm from, but they are going to have a gas station pretty soon, and if enough traffic comes off the interstate we may even get a real stop light. Then we'll be moving up in the world, I tell ya what," I said, while laying on my best Southwest-Virginia accent. They just smiled and left soon after, much to my relief. How's that for a sound-bite, I thought.

Dean came by to see me, and talked to my parents a few minutes. I told him I was leaving and returning home to Virginia. He was sorry to see me go, told my parents what a good worker I was, and said I had a job if ever I came back. "You can use me as a reference any time, too," said Dean. Before he left, and while my parents had stepped aside, Dean leaned toward me in a confidential manner and said, "These are the years the rest of your life is built on, so make the most of it. Rock on, Rocker."

"Thanks, man," I replied. Dean grabbed my hand in a brotherly handshake, patted me on the shoulder, and swaggered toward the door.

At one point I looked around the room as people were leaving, still in my hospital bed and attached to an I.V., and saw Cathy standing at the far end of the room, talking to my mother and nodding her head. And then, like a lantern flame smokes, then

199

flickers, then turns steady and blinding-white with that even release of pressure, a thought burned hot in my head. I motioned Cathy over without drawing the attention of the others.

"The old man. Joe. The guy who removed the bomb collar from me. Is he okay?"

Cathy turned her head for a moment in thought, and then frowned as if she remembered. "Do you know him?"

"In a way, yes."

"I heard the bomb detonated in his hands. He was hit by several pieces of shrapnel, including one that lodged in his chest. They don't think he's going to make it."

"I want to go see him. Can you take me to him?"

"Well, I don't know. He's probably in ICU."

"Help me get rid of this I.V.," I said. Cathy hesitated. I quickly sat up, which made me dizzy for a second or two, and proceeded to peel back the tape from around the needle, yanking it out in one painful pull. "Turn off that machine right there next to me. That button, I think." Cathy flipped a switch that turned off my vitals monitor. I found the cords that ran to my chest and proceeded to pull them out as well. I had forgotten that I was just wearing a hospital gown, and of course it was open in the back. "Are there any clothes I can put on?"

"I think there is something on the table next to you in the paper bag your parents brought from home, but I really don't think you need to be...."

I found a pair of underwear, blue jeans, and a shirt. Cathy reddened and turned away as I bent over to put on my boxers.

"Where are you going, Randall?" My dad asked as I yanked my pants up and pulled a t-shirt over my head.

"I'm going to use the bathroom down the hall. Stretch my legs."

I turned back to Cathy in a hushed voice. "Now, where's the ICU?"

"Second floor, I think."

"You can stay here if you want. Just give me a few minutes before you tell anyone where I went."

"No. I'm coming with you, Mr. Stubborn Pants. You haven't been on your feet in days."

The floor was cold and clammy on my bare feet. Outside my door was a chair with a folded newspaper where someone sat – maybe one of the officers perhaps – but there was no one in the hallway now. I couldn't believe no one even mentioned Joe's name to me. It made me a little angry, the one person who should be getting all the credit and attention and nobody had even mentioned his name. We quickly made our way to the elevators. My heart rate jumped a little as we waited for it, like someone was going to come along any second now and ask me why I was out of my room. The doors opened. No one was in it. We got in and I mashed the second-floor button as firmly as I could, and then kept pressing it when the doors wouldn't shut fast enough. When they opened again, there was a desk with a woman in magenta scrubs.

"Hi. I wanted to check on a friend of mine admitted three days ago. I don't remember his last name, but his first name's Joe. An old man, long beard?"

"Let me ask a nurse. Judy!" A woman with a tight blonde perm in aqua blue scrubs passed by the desk, holding a clipboard. "Have you seen Judy?" The woman shrugged her shoulders. "Anyway, anyone over 50 with a beard named Joe come in the past couple of days?"

"Oh, yeah. Joe. Carpenter. He's a few doors down this hallway. I'll take you there." She motioned for us to follow her. "I just started my shift actually, so I haven't had time to check on him today yet. He had a few reporters that wanted to visit him, but he's not been conscious since he was admitted." She spoke over her shoulder as we walked.

I was suddenly filled with yearning to see him sitting up in his bed, bright-eyed and flirting with a nurse. There was so much I wanted to tell him, thank him for, more than I could begin to think about at the moment. The nurse stuck her head in the door first, which was already opened wide. There was no one there. The room was empty.

"I'm sorry, uh...."

"Randall," I said.

"Oh! So you are the boy he saved from that weird bomb collar contraption? Well, I'm sorry, Randall. I suppose he passed away in the night. I regret to be the one to break the news to you. I can't imagine how you must feel." She looked at the now empty bed and noticed the sheets had been stripped from the mattress. They were folded at the foot of it. "Well, that's weird. Normally the sheets are taken down to the laundry room already."

My eyes began to water as I looked at his blood-stained sheets. The fluorescent lights gave the room a white, empty glow. Cathy put her arm around my shoulder to comfort me as I clenched my teeth to keep from crying. It was the way the sheets were neatly folded, like napkins at a dinner table, like someone would do when they got up in the morning and made the bed.

"I'm sorry, Randall." Cathy said.

The nurse put on latex gloves and quickly grabbed the folded, soiled sheets. "Sorry you had to see this. I don't know why the orderlies left them." Annoyed, she took them out the door and down the hallway, and came back in the room. "Would you like for me to check about any funeral arrangements being made, or what relatives might have come to get his belongings. I don't see them sitting around anywhere here."

"No. Thank you," I told the nurse, in between stifled sobs. "That won't be necessary." I was in tears, but inside I welled with joy. I felt like I had just walked across a newly built bridge, the oak boards so sturdy not even my wide gait sent a shudder through them. I had a new chance at things because of him.

"Randall, let's go back," Cathy asked. "Before people wonder where we are."

* * * *

After most of the people left, a doctor came by and gave me the green light to leave. He told me my blood pressure was too high for my age, and that I needed to take it easy for a while and learn to manage my stress better. The usual stuff. Dad was going on about needing to rent a moving van, but I told him all my furniture was salvaged from dumpsters or came with the apartment, anyway. He cringed at that. I told him he should be glad that everything I wanted to keep would fit in the trunk and back seat of my car.

I collected the get-well cards, and the work clothes I was wearing at the time of the accident. I wanted to read the letter Cassie left me, but I was afraid to read it in front of somebody. I waited until there was a moment when my parents stepped out, and sat on the edge of the bed with my belongings and Cassie's envelope in my hand. Looking up one more time to see if anyone was around, I tore the end off, blew it open, and pulled out the note. It was short, written in flowing, graceful penmanship on a prescription drug notepad advertising Paxil. I read it quickly.

Dear Randall,

I'll be honest with you. I was pretty upset. Here I thought I finally met someone who likes me for who I am, who respects me, and then he almost gets killed. The thought of losing you after finding you scared me. When I go to see you in the hospital, though, I find out you're a 16-year-old runaway? You were dishonest with me. It angers me at the same time as it disappoints me. Then I saw you lying there in the bed unconscious, helpless. After talking for a little while with Cathy (friend, ex-girlfriend? she didn't say) I realize maybe you are a good guy after all, a little misdirected maybe. We're just not at the same place in life right now.

I want you to know I forgive you, Randall. Maybe things did go a little too fast with us. Regardless, you picked me up when I was feeling low. You made me feel like I was worthy of being loved for who I was, not what you wanted me to be. I truly feel you were honest in your feelings, and that you were being genuine in that respect. I appreciate that. I hope you realize that I am too old for you, though. I will be finishing college soon. You will just be getting started. We can never have a relationship like the one we both might have wanted. I will say this, though. You made me realize that there are still guys out there with good hearts. One of these days you will make the right girl very happy.

Your Friend Always,

Cassandra Miller

I waited for the lump in my throat, the tightness in my chest, but nothing came. Her words rang true, and I tried to be okay with that. I did feel the weight of remorse on my heart, and knew it would stay with me for a while to come. But it was a dull ache. I took a deep breath, and put Cassie's letter in my back pocket.

There was one more thing I wanted to do before leaving. I wanted one more time to say thanks to Cathy for coming to see me, maybe apologize again. I had probably hurt her more than I realized. I wanted some sort of recognition that maybe we could still be friends. That moment didn't come, though. As I stepped to the door and looked out, past a few nurses, I saw Cathy at the end of the hallway. She was talking with her father, and saw me. She hesitantly waved with a curl of her fingers, and then turned away quickly. Her father didn't look at me, but put his arm around her and led her around the corner out of sight.

23 _____

Dear Cassie:

Hey! I hope you don't mind that I'm writing you. I've been thinking lately about how you are doing, and hope the last few weeks of your semester are going well.

The cold of winter has finally passed to spring here in Virginia, and as the sap rose in the trees so has my spirits. I'm living with my father and my grandmother now, and started going with Grandma Spivey on Sundays to Staunton Branch Church of the Brethren. She doesn't get around as much as she used to, with her arthritis like it is. She still walks the quarter mile to her mailbox and back every day, though.

I worked on my Grand Am. Got the windows replaced and bought a new stereo with some of the tip money I saved, this time with a CD player. Now I just need to buy some CDs (Ha!). I even gave my car a good wash and a couple coats of wax the first warm spring day we had. The salt from the roads this past winter had started some rust spots bubbling under the paint, and thanks to the many potholes (you know how Boone is) I hit while making deliveries, I will be needing new shocks and struts soon.

I stay with my mother a couple of nights a week when she isn't working the late shift at the new auto parts factory in Wytheville. Sometimes she will cook supper, and sometimes I take her out to eat at the Chinese restaurant downtown or make a run out to Kenny's to get a bucket of chicken and fried biscuits to go. She seems happier now, and she hardly drinks anymore (between you and me, I check her liquor cabinet regularly).

I decided to start classes at Wytheville Community College this coming summer, and found out that several of the elective classes I took at the community college in Boone were valid and transferable, despite me taking them under false pretenses. I am still going on to get a four-year degree when I finish the community college, maybe Watauga State or somewhere further away. I may even have a summer job set up for me. Grandma Spivey's pastor told me their church has a summer camp in the NC mountains, somewhere near Hendersonville, and that anytime I am interested they are looking for camp counselors with a love of the outdoors. Can you imagine, getting paid to go camping and hiking?

Despite my father's protests, I know now what I want to major in: English. I don't know exactly what I'm going to do with it yet, but I do know that the only way to truly understand the world and how it shapes us is to study the human condition, human nature. And what better way to understand past our own experiences than through other people's stories. Art imitates life, isn't that what they say? Part of me still thinks my dad isn't confident that I can cut it in the real world, without faking it. Maybe he thinks I'm just filling my head with stories. If that's the case, at least he isn't letting on.

I hate to admit it, but I feel closer now for having been away from these hills and hollows, the familiar people and the way we talked, as warm as a plate of pintos and cornbread (maybe I'm just hungry right now). Their voices rise like steam from bean broth as I sit in church with Grandma Spivey.

I don't think I'm going to stay home, not forever. The wilderness may be gone, but I still have an urge to set my feet straight and blaze a new trail. I wonder what Daniel Boone felt when he left the warm hearth and roof over his head to scout the Wilderness Road? Did he secretly feel a hesitance, that gnawing in your gut when there is no barrier between you and the unknown? Sorry, I seem to be rambling some.

Dad keeps me busy, but I welcome the work. It isn't the same as hustling to make pizza deliveries, that's for sure. I have been cleaning barns out and building a new catch pen for the livestock we'll be getting soon from auction, among other chores. The first couple of weeks my muscles ached in my shoulders something fierce, but the work feels good, and it felt strangely good to work with my dad – up until he hurt his back. We still don't see everything eye to eye, but at least he's home now.

I've been working on my own lately, but I know what needs to be done around here and it gives me time to think – about what has happened in the past year, about my plans for the future, where I came from, where I am going. One day I was in the process of repairing a stretch of fence. Most of the posts stood the same as they did when Grandpa Spivey set them in the ground 30 years ago, sometime before his death. They were locust posts, weathered and covered in lichen crust, but still standing. I was to yank any posts that were loose and replace them with new ones, and to check the wire for weak spots. It was humbling in a way to stand on this spot of land, knowing the sweat my grandparents poured into it, the drops of blood shed from paring knives and saw blades, the same blood that courses through me, and now my father and I are picking up where they left off. Now I stand on that same ground feeling how firm my grandfather set each post. They are a reminder that I have come a long way by the grace of sweat and blood.

Do you ever wonder about God's plan for our life? I've questioned it a lot in the past. I often wonder if life is written as we go, or if God has our lives already written out. If He is all-powerful and all-knowing like they say He is, then He would already know my story no matter how many times it might change by my own actions. I think about that a lot. I've come across a verse, Psalm 139 I think, that says something about that. I think I would be okay with Him knowing, it being all there, written down like the choose-your-own-adventure books I used to read when I was younger, in which, when given a choice, I could flip to the corresponding page based on my decision. I think my recent mistake was that I tried to skip several chapters ahead instead of taking the time to read, living my life for today. I think I am back to the correct page now, I hope! One can only hope, and there is something comforting in that hope, I think.

I read your letter, of course. I wanted to immediately call you and explain myself and my actions, but I didn't want to make excuses. You were right about everything. I am sorry for deceiving you. I should have apologized sooner in my letter. I regret a lot of things I did, but I don't regret meeting you. I want to thank you for giving me confidence in myself when I had none.

There are times, though, that I am still haunted by insecurities, feelings of not being in control, waking dreams and dark memories from that night (I'm sure you read about it in the papers). I was up on the roof of the big barn just last week replacing a couple sheets of tin and admiring the wispy ending of a sunset when I heard a Mustang come roaring across Mill Hill, only to look up and see nothing. My throat thickened. I felt the cold metal clamp around my neck. I didn't have anyone else with me to tell me if it was real or all in my head, you know. I thought Ollie was after me again. I had to fix my eye on a faint star in the eastern sky to stop my head from spinning.

Did you know they never found Ollie, the guy who set me up? They never caught any of the drug dealers, either, at least not that I have heard of. The one they had in custody at first was just an illegal immigrant. I felt sorry for him. I swear, though, I sometimes hear the bald man's inflection in others voices, when I am in a crowd of people at the hardware store, or in line at the Old Town Market. I get an irrational feeling that I'm being followed. But after the first few panic attacks, I learned to close my eyes for a moment, breathe, and remember that some things are out of my control, and that was okay.

I know it is cliché, but the Lord does work in mysterious ways, how people are put in your life for a reason, how coincidence seems not so much so. I must be meant for something more, something important, to still be alive when by all accounts I should not be. I have a life to live; I can't keep looking over my shoulder, right?

I know it's over for us, but I hope we can still keep in touch. If I do go back to Watauga State (for real this time), I could sure use some good pointers on which professors to take and which to avoid. Maybe in a year or two the newspapers will be finished with my story and nobody will remember me or what happened.

I miss you. I can't help but admit that. You say we shouldn't see each other anymore, and I understand why, but if I'm ever up in Boone again, would you like to go get some coffee or something, just to talk, as friends? I'll bring you a can of my grandma's homemade blackberry jam or a fresh loaf of her sourdough bread.

Write me back when you get a chance. It would be good to hear from you, if nothing else than to know you are doing well and moving on with your life. Thanks for everything.

Take care,

Randall Spivey

I sat at Grandma Spivey's kitchen table, still a little dusted with flour from her biscuit making early this morning. I could see her outside through the window, reaching up with a clothespin to hang laundry on the line. A pot of pinto beans simmered on the stove. After finishing the letter, I reread it twice, then lifted the lid of the cook stove and dropped the pages onto the hot embers. I watched as the paper smoked, flamed, and then curled into brittle ashes. My handwriting was still visible on the charred pieces as I rattled the lid back down. From the living room, the sound of gunfire and Indian war whoops blared from Dad's television as he sat in his recliner. I grabbed my work gloves off the table before walking past him and out the front door. I did not look back.

David Wayne Hampton grew up in the mountains of Carroll County, Virginia, where much of his family still resides. He lived in Boone, North Carolina, for eight years and attended Appalachian State University, while working the gamut of various jobs from dishwasher to pizza delivery to editorial assistant of the *Appalachian Journal*. He graduated from ASU in 1998. Since then he has taught high school English and currently lives in the foothills of Morganton, North Carolina, with his wife and two children. He is a member of the loosely-knit band of varlets known as the Southern Appalachian Writers Cooperative (SAWC). His first book, a collection of poetry entitled *What Makes It Taste Better*, was published in 2010.